SAIGON
RED

OTHER TITLES BY
GREGORY C. RANDALL

NONFICTION

America's Original GI Town: Park Forest, Illinois

FICTION

THE ALEX POLONIA THRILLERS

Venice Black

THE SHARON O'MARA CHRONICLES

Land Swap For Death
Containers For Death
Toulouse For Death
12th Man For Death
Diamonds For Death

THE TONY ALFANO THRILLERS

Chicago Swing
Chicago Jazz

SAIGON
RED

AN ALEX POLONIA THRILLER

GREGORY C. RANDALL

THOMAS & MERCER

Published by Thomas & Mercer, Seattle

www.apub.com

Amazon, the Amazon logo, and Thomas & Mercer are trademarks of Amazon.com, Inc., or its affiliates.

ISBN-13: 9781503904439
ISBN-10: 1503904431

Cover design by Jae Song

Printed in the United States of America

War is hell, but family relations can be worse.

—*Anonymous*

CHAPTER 1

Ho Chi Minh City, Vietnam, Present Day

In the predawn fog that drifted off the Saigon River, Detective Tran Phan leaned against the door of his white Toyota police cruiser and inhaled deeply. The stench of rotting vegetation, oily smoke, and burnt wood filled his nose. He'd hoped that the smoke from his cigarette would mask the smells. He looked at the gray-black clouds lit by the buildings of Ho Chi Minh City, then checked his watch: sunrise would be in less than an hour. Walking through the narrow gap between the warehouses, he reached the skeletal remains of a burnt-out Humvee. Firemen were pulling hoses down across the cracked asphalt.

"Where's the body?" he asked, looking down at the debris strewn about the alley.

"Just past the burnt vehicle, Detective," answered the fire captain.

"Thanks."

The call about a vehicle and structure fire had come in an hour earlier. All routine. It'd been the follow-up call about the body found at the scene that made him turn the Toyota around and head across the Saigon River to District 7, Ho Chi Minh City's main port. On his way there, he'd received the second report of yet another body found. There at the port, the decaying remains of old warehouses still stood, many built during the war, when the Americans had made this the largest and most active port in Southeast Asia.

The alley vibrated with the idling noise of the fire truck parked next to the blistered and charred Humvee. In the gloom, the truck's flashing overhead lights filled the space with a silent yet bizarre light show.

Phan washed his flashlight over the remains. The body was male, possibly Anglo. One of the legs was missing. Phan moved the flashlight beam around the perimeter and spotted the severed leg a few meters away, at the base of the warehouse wall. He flashed the light down the alley and looked at the exterior walls of the warehouse: clean. No graffiti, even—surprising for this part of the city.

The far corner of the building was twisted and collapsed. Another fire engine continued to stream water on the burnt ruin. Steam rose, mixed with the heavy air, and transformed into a yellow haze that mixed with the fog drifting in from the river.

"The other body, it's inside the warehouse?" Phan asked, turning to one of the policemen watching the firemen.

"Yes, Detective Phan. The door was open when we arrived. After discovering the body in the alley, we searched the building. That's where we found the second. Then we were stopped and told to leave the building. Something about diplomatic sovereignty."

"Who told you that?"

"Him, the *tây*. Said he didn't arrive till afterward." The policeman pointed to a man in a brash Hawaiian shirt and khaki slacks standing in front of the door under a wall-mounted light. He had a vague Asian look about him, as well as a bald head and a short beard that strapped his dark face from ear to ear. He was talking on a cell phone.

Phan walked over to the man. "I'm Detective Tran Phan," he said in English, holding his badge up. "I'm going inside to see the body."

"Can't, sir. This is United States embassy property and, as such, is diplomatic property." The man kept his phone to his ear.

"Bullshit. No such thing—and you know that. Who are you?"

"One second, Chris," the man said into the phone, then pulled it away. "Harry Karns, chief of security for the owner, Como Motors. My company, Teton Security and Defense, is based in the United States. We're under contract to Como."

"So, Mr. Karns, are you going to let me pass, or am I going to have my men arrest you for obstructing my investigation? A few days in jail might change your mind about which country you're in."

Karns ended his call, slipped the phone into his pocket, and raised his hands in surrender.

Phan pushed his way past the man and walked into the warehouse. High above, a dozen ceiling lights illuminated the concrete floor, which was filled with long tables. On each were computers and monitors. He had never seen a technology center, but he guessed this is what one might look like. Small office cubicles, also full of technology, lined the back of the space. The farthest corner was walled in with no windows. Over a door that was twisted and hanging on its lowest hinge, a sign read "UFFICIO." He guessed it was the office.

The acrid smell of explosives and burnt wood hung in the air, along with thick dust and smoke that floated motionless, like speckled fog. Three meters in front of the door lay a body. Phan crossed the facility to the bloody remains. It was ripped apart, half its upper body shredded. Next to the body lay a large-caliber pistol; it looked like a Colt. He heard footsteps behind him.

"You know this man?" Phan asked.

"Yes, an associate," Karns said. "When I find that bastard that killed him, I'll gut him from his balls to his chin."

"You know who did this?"

"No, but we should have him on our security cameras."

"I want them," Phan said. He looked past the body to the office with the twisted door.

"I'm not sure I can allow you access to the security tapes. I need to make a call, Detective."

"I don't care. Call whoever you need, but I want those tapes or digital records—and I want them today. Is there coverage outside?"

"Yes, but he avoided those cameras."

"He? How do you know it was a he?" Not waiting for an answer, Phan walked through the shattered doorway and into the office, and Karns followed. The detective scanned the dark room, then stopped, his flashlight beam on the safe. "They weren't able to get into the safe? Is it still locked?"

Karns hesitated. "As far as I know, they were not able to get in. It was closed and secure when I arrived."

"And when was that?"

"Twenty minutes after the alarms were tripped. I was across town. My man texted me."

"Which man, the one in the alley, or the one in here?"

"The man in the alley; he sent a message."

"Show me your phone, Mr. Karns."

"I'm not sure I can," Karns answered.

"Either show it to me, or I will take it from you." Phan motioned to one of his officers and said something in Vietnamese.

"Okay, I get it," Karns said.

"You understand Vietnamese, Mr. Karns?" Phan said. "Excellent; it will make my questions easier for my men to understand. The phone, please. Open it and show me the message."

Karns punched in his password, scrolled through the messages, stopped, and held the screen up to the detective.

Alarm at Como Tech Center—Duke and I are going to see what's up—will follow up.

"Did you reply?" Phan asked.

"Yes. I told them I would be there in twenty minutes."

"Your guys are security. Why weren't they here?"

"I gave them the night off," Karns said. "They'd just come in from Tokyo. They spent the afternoon here, and I gave them the lay of the land. Then I told them to report tomorrow—I mean today. They weren't supposed to be here. The facility's personnel left at six. We were here until seven o'clock."

Phan wandered around the office, studying everything on the tables and desks. "Did these men work directly for you?"

"They're on my team. We all work for Teton on contract to Como Motors."

Using it like a spotlight, Phan panned the flashlight across the room, and a vase of flowers caught his eye. When he studied them, he saw they were plastic. A thin mist drifted among the fake petals. He stuck his nose into the arrangement and sniffed loudly. He gingerly grasped the flowers and removed them from the vase. The lowest stems were stringy and wiry, and they appeared fused and melted. With his flashlight, he peered inside.

"Well, well," he uttered. He pulled a pair of green vinyl gloves from his pocket, slipped them on, and reached into the urn. A moment later he held up a device that looked like an old BlackBerry cell phone with an antenna-like apparatus attached to one end. "I assume this is *not* one of your security devices, Mr. Karns?"

"I have no idea what that is."

"It's evidence now." Phan removed a large Ziploc bag from his pocket and dropped the device into it. "Still warm. So, it was purposely destroyed, or my guess, there was some type of self-destruct process involved. This room is unharmed—the gadget obviously did not start the fire in the corner of the structure. My people will see if we can figure it out. I suggest you inspect the safe, Mr. Karns. It may have been tampered with."

Phan walked out of the office into the facility, lit another cigarette, and waited a moment for Karns to catch up. "Teton what?"

"Teton Security and Defense," Karns said. "American."

"Obviously." Phan looked again at the body. He'd never seen such physical destruction. The arm looked like it had been explosively

5

amputated—whatever did this was a vicious weapon. He turned to Karns. "You look military; maybe you have experience with explosives? Any idea what happened to him?"

"Duke was a good man. They were both good men. I've known them a long time. And no, I don't. Whatever hit him packed an incredible explosive punch but was also localized. I've heard rumors about exploding bullets. Never seen one. If this is what it was, it's powerful."

"Mr. Karns, my people will go over everything. I expect your cooperation."

"I have to get clearance from my boss and the owners of the facility."

"What are you guarding here, Mr. Karns? I see computers, servers, locked cabinets, and a lot of other high-tech stuff. Whoever did this was after something. My guess is that you have an idea as to what that is. So, enlighten me."

Karns said nothing.

Phan waited a few beats, then turned and walked across the warehouse. Halfway to the door to the alley, he noticed spots of what looked like blood on the floor.

Phan walked outside and removed a notebook from his pocket. He casually noted the blood trail and a few more details. His eyes followed the red dots to the base of the wall of the warehouse across the alley. There the blood had collected into a pool about the size of his hand. Additional splatter surrounded it. He looked up the wall to the parapet and with his flashlight spotted additional traces along the parapet's edge. He made more notes, then proceeded down the alley toward his car.

Karns followed him. "Sorry, Detective, I have my orders. When my boss says I can, I'll come and talk to you. Until then—"

"Mr. Karns, do not piss me off any more than you already have. Who really owns this place, and what was taken?"

"Like I said, Como Motors owns the place. But, Detective Phan, I honestly don't know what happened here."

"Mr. Karns, I will see you at three o'clock at my office. Here's my card. The address is on it. Don't make me look for you."

Phan walked past the still-steaming Humvee. Four of his people, in white paper jumpsuits, were walking up the alley toward him.

"Good morning, Mr. Tan," Phan said to the lead forensic man. "Rip this place apart and tell me what happened. Have the bodies checked for explosive residue and shrapnel. There are spots of blood on the floor—I want samples. There's also a blood pool opposite the door, next to that building, and what looks like a trace at the building's eave directly above. Maybe they're from a victim, but I don't think so. Sample them. I also saw a pistol—look for shell casings. There's a lot of damage in there. Find out all you can. I want the works—DNA, everything."

"Yes, Detective Phan."

Phan turned to Karns and said, "You will provide ownership information, phone numbers, and the names and passport numbers of the dead men. Got it?"

Karns looked at Phan. "I'll see what I can do." He squinted and looked Phan up and down. "I didn't realize they had Americans in the Saigon police."

"Ho Chi Minh City, HCMC for short. Not Saigon. This isn't 1975. And my father was American. I am Vietnamese. And from your looks, there's also some Vietnamese in your family, am I right?" Phan, not waiting for an answer, turned to the policeman he'd talked to when he first walked onto the scene. "Don't let them take anything from the facility or this property. I'm holding you and your men responsible if there are any fuckups."

"Yes, sir."

Leaving Karns in the alley, Phan walked back to the street and climbed into the white Toyota police cruiser, turned the air-conditioning to high, and punched in the number of his chief on his mobile phone. After updating his boss about the bodies, the destruction, and the blood trail, he was told to put it all in his report. When he started to tell him about the fire, the chief cut him off and reminded him it was too damn early to discuss such unpleasantness. He would see him later. Phan hung up. "Pompous asshole," he mumbled as he lit another cigarette.

Phan picked up his radio. "Central, get me air control."

"Yes, sir."

A few seconds passed. "Air control."

"Air control, this is Detective Phan. Do you have a helicopter up?"

"We have one. Over District 1, doing traffic and surveillance."

"Can you send it to my location in District 7?"

"Location?"

Phan told the woman the address.

"Yes, Detective. Four minutes."

Leaving the engine and air-conditioning running, he exited the car and walked back to Karns, who was still standing next to the burnt-out Humvee.

"Now what?" Karns said.

Phan pointed upward. "It seems that our criminal may have climbed to the roof up there. One of our helicopters will be over the warehouse in a few minutes. I want them to take a look."

"For what?"

"Your employee may have gotten lucky and wounded the suspect. Maybe he's still on the roof. I intend to find out."

From the parapet of the neighboring building's roof, a high-pitched whirring—a sound Phan couldn't quite make out—cut through the thick air.

CHAPTER 2

Con Ma, hidden in the shadows, peered over the parapet and watched the police detective walk the length of the narrow alley. The lights from the fire truck intermittently exposed the detective's face. Con Ma adjusted his night vision visor, softly said, "Magnify three times," and studied the man.

Detective Tran Phan. Of course. Who else would it be?

Con Ma hated the detective and everything he stood for—honor, family, duty. It was all he could do not to shoot the man where he stood. However, at that moment, he had only a few minutes to escape. Shooting the detective, while satisfying, would alert the other policemen. He leaned back out of sight and removed a syringe from the small case on his belt. He placed the tip against his leg, an inch above the bullet wound, and for the second time, injected the anesthetic. Instantly, the pain began to ease. He'd already packed the coagulant against the wound, stopping the blood flow from the finger-sized hole in his leg. He sucked on the stimulant tablet to reduce the chance of shock. The whole operation was now seriously fucked up.

Earlier, the flight on the prototype cycle-drone from his base on the far side of the river had been uneventful. The landing had gone unnoticed. As he'd walked across the roof, he asked in Chinese, "Time?" The headphones inside the helmet replied, in an unhurried female voice, "Four thirty. Local." He had fifteen minutes to complete the operation.

He secured the thick rope to a vent brace and dropped it over the parapet, and in seconds he was on the pavement of the alley. From his belt, he removed a black box, placed it over the electronic lock of the door, and stepped back. A slight buzz filled the air, then a pop, and smoke rose from the lock. He turned the handle and pulled the door open.

The room glowed green through the night vision visor. It was as he expected. The large space was set up similarly to technology facilities he'd visited in the United States. Computers, large tables, and cabinets filled the room. In the corner, past the cubicles, was a door with an overhead sign: "UFFICIO." He tested the door—locked. He retrieved a second small box secured to his belt that had a key-like extension on one end and pushed it into the lock. In two seconds a green light flashed once. He turned the handle and opened the door, closing and locking it behind him.

The office's layout was typical: desks, chairs, a copy machine, computers on two of the tabletops, stacks of paper covering most surfaces. A large safe—taller than him by at least a head—sat at the rear. He placed a third device adjacent to the safe's lock and began to spin the combination dial, first to the left, then slowly to the right, then left again. A series of numbers glowed on his device's small screen. He spun the dial to the designated numbers and tried the handle. It opened with a soft click.

Inside were stacks of money in various currencies, papers, a pistol, and, on the top shelf, a small computer server with lights that blinked green and orange. Taking the same device he used to unlock the office door, he removed a plastic cap and inserted the device into one of the server's USB ports. A green light on the device flashed.

"Countdown: one minute," his artificial-intelligence-enabled helmet said. Then added, "You are running late. There are men in the alley."

He heard the audible tick in his helmet as the countdown began. He needed one minute to download the data onto the device and upload a corrupting virus onto the server. The device's internal processors would transmit the information via satellite to a Chinese facility.

"Con Ma, someone is approaching the office door," his helmet said.

This was unexpected. He went to one knee, pulled his weapon, turned to the door, and waited. His helmet's visor displayed the halo of light around the closed door as someone turned on the lights in the facility.

The door shook violently.

"We know you're in there. Come out now, and no one will be hurt." English. A male voice and, based on the accent, from the southern United States.

Con Ma frowned. The warehouse was supposed to be empty. He looked at the device in the server. The light was now solid green, no flashing. He removed it and scanned the room. A vase full of plastic flowers sat on a desk's corner. As he crossed the room, the door rattled again.

"Out, you son of a bitch. Now."

He removed the flowers from the porcelain urn, clicked two switches on the device, and placed it inside. He then replaced the flowers. After the device finished transmitting the files, it would self-destruct, destroying the files. His job was done. He was now on his own to save his own ass.

"Out, Goddammit! Now!"

Con Ma raised the large pistol-like weapon and issued specific instructions to his helmet: "Doorframe." He pulled the trigger, and the augmented bullet exploded on contact with the frame. The door twisted away and smashed into the wall behind it. Con Ma ran out the door and turned toward the entry. A man stood in the middle of the aisle, his pistol pointed at Con Ma. The man fired; Con Ma felt a searing pain in his leg.

Con Ma raised his weapon and fired, but the enhanced bullet missed its target and exploded against the wall of the facility. Instantly fire and debris filled the corner. The guard fired again. Con Ma felt the bullet nick the side of his helmet; he again fired his weapon. The guard's right shoulder and arm exploded, and the man was tossed across the floor. His pistol flew into the air and skidded on the concrete floor. The man lay broken and still.

Con Ma reached the door and stopped. He removed his helmet to check the damage from the bullet, pleased that it was just grazed, then replaced it. He took a quick look up the alley. A Humvee sat idling. A man with an automatic rifle stood next to it and, upon spotting Con Ma, started firing.

"Vehicle, maximum effect," Con Ma said as he raised his weapon and aimed it at the Humvee's grille. The impact was like a grenade's. The shock wave ripped the man apart and threw him across the narrow alley, slamming him against the building.

"Time left?"

"None; you are out of time."

He limped to the rope and climbed. Reaching the parapet, he gritted his teeth from the pain of his bullet wound and fell to the roof. He found the anesthetic syringe, jammed it against his leg, and fainted. When he regained consciousness, he asked again, "Time?"

"Five fifty-two, local."

Damn, he was seriously behind schedule. He'd been out for almost an hour. Not good. Dawn was breaking.

Now, looking again over the edge of the roof, he saw a man talking to the detective. He had been told that the facility would be clear, that the operation would be clean, in and out. No problems. Well, now there were problems—big problems. At least, he hoped, the transmitter had sent the data out before it self-destructed. So, that part was done. He had fulfilled his contract. His leg burned like a thousand fires. He hadn't counted on being shot in the thigh and passing out once he'd reached the roof. Rope sat coiled next to the parapet. He didn't remember pulling it up. *Luck,* he thought.

He scanned the roof across the alley. A stream of water rose above the parapet as the fire department doused the charred corner of the adjacent building. He staggered across the tarred roof toward the cycle-drone, which looked like a motorcycle that could fly. He left the rope behind. He climbed aboard, secured himself with the seat belt, and tightened the strap to his helmet. With his right hand against the iPad-sized glass of the control panel, the drone lit up, all its avionics activated. He looked across the river and spotted the flashing lights of a helicopter headed toward him.

"There's an approaching aircraft," he told his helmet. "Data, please."

"Aircraft's transponder says HC120," his helmet responded. "Registered to the Ho Chi Minh City Police Department."

"Activate police scanner."

Con Ma started the drone's four electrically driven double rotors. Their whirring increased until the vehicle began to gradually rise.

"Con Ma, are you injured?" his helmet asked. "Your vital signs show stress due to injury."

"Yes," he answered. "I've taken necessary precautions. Right thigh wound."

"Do you wish me to take control?"

"Stand by to assist. I'm okay."

"Standing by. Returning to scanner intercepts."

"Detective Phan, on your location in ten seconds," the helicopter pilot said. "I see the lights from the fire trucks."

Con Ma twisted the handles, and the drone rose three meters off the roof. He leaned to the right, and the machine rotated away from the fire trucks and the lights.

"Detective, I see something on the roof next to the address you gave," the helicopter pilot said on the scanner. "I don't know what it is."

"Describe it, Eagle One."

"Looks like a drone. But a design and size I've never seen before . . . and there's someone on it."

"Say again," Phan said.

"It's a motorcycle built into a drone. That's all I can say. Oddest damn thing."

"What's it doing?"

"Flying, sir. It's flying and leaving the scene."

"Where's it headed?"

"Toward the river. Should I follow?"

"Yes, Eagle One—follow the fucking thing."

Con Ma smiled. Now to find out what this contraption the Chairwoman had given him could do. He twisted the controls, and the drone shot away from the warehouse district, as if an enormous hummingbird had been kicked in its ass. He skimmed the rooftops; the control panel read 104 kph. He hunched under the windscreen and sharply banked the machine toward the river. The sun was just breaking the horizon. The river's surface was like glass. He dropped to six meters above the water and headed north and away from the port. He knew he couldn't outrun the Chinese-made helicopter. His top speed was at best 140 kph, the helicopter's almost double that. His advantages were size and maneuverability.

He looked at the radar display as one ping flashed. "Display, identify, and confirm ping on the radar."

"Confirmed," his helmet replied. "Ho Chi Minh City police helicopter, Eagle One."

"Distance and heading, please."

"Two-point-three kilometers. At current speeds, it will intercept in one minute, fourteen seconds."

A shot of pain racked his leg. He gritted his teeth.

"I sense that the trauma is impacting your control of the aircraft. Would you like assistance?"

"Stand by to assist."

"Yes, Con Ma. Standing by."

The scanner squawked in his ear. "Detective, the craft is attempting to escape. Should I fire?"

"See if you can force it down," Phan said. "Wait to shoot until it's clear of residential areas."

"Roger that."

Con Ma rotated the drone toward the opposite side of the river. Ahead was the Sai Gon Bridge. He lowered his altitude above the river to three meters. A tug pushing two barges raced past him on his left. A small fishing boat flew by on the right, its captain waving at Con Ma. The cycle-drone barely cleared the bridge's arched supports.

"ETA on Eagle One?" Con Ma asked.

"Distance now one thousand sixty meters and closing. Do you need assistance?"

"No. But thank you."

"You are welcome."

After clearing the bridge, he aimed the drone up the river. A thousand meters farther, he veered left into the Kinh Thanh Da canal.

"They are shooting from the helicopter," his helmet said. "Autonomous evasive countermeasures under way."

The drone violently rotated right and almost touched the river. Con Ma, holding tight, watched a series of small waterspouts appear immediately to his left and below. They popped along the surface of the river in a ragged line.

"Automatic weapons. AK-47."

"Too much information."

"Understood. Eagle One is now one hundred meters to rear, ninety meters above."

The drone buzzed under the cross-canal bridge and back over the central part of the Saigon River. Con Ma's goal was simple: reach the Binh Loi Bridge complex.

"On my mark, take control and spin out to starboard, and take a tactical position behind the helicopter."

"Yes, Con Ma. Waiting."

He turned and looked at the helicopter. The rising sun brightly illuminated its blue-and-white markings as if a spotlight had hit it.

He cinched the seat belt tighter. "Mark."

The drone banked and rolled, the g-forces nearly throwing Con Ma from his seat. It spun out and came to an abrupt stop. The helicopter, thirty meters over him, roared past. He could feel the downdraft of the main rotor blades. The drone adjusted to the shift in air pressure. The helicopter then began its own adjustment, banking wide to the right.

"Activate weapon," Con Ma commanded.

On a small sponson mounted to the front cowling, a weapon—similar to the handheld one he'd used in the warehouse—angled up sharply and rotated left to right.

"Target helicopter's tail rotor."

"Target set."

Con Ma watched the helicopter complete its bank. Just inside the open side door, a man crouched with a rifle.

"Detective, should we fire again?" the pilot said over the scanner. "He didn't respond to the first burst of fire."

"Yes, fire," Phan said.

"Fire weapon," Con Ma said.

"Weapon fired."

The bullet invisibly traveled the distance from the drone to the helicopter. The hub of the tail rotor assembly exploded, shearing off the last meter of the helicopter's tail boom. The aircraft immediately began to uncontrollably gyrate under its rotor.

"I'm hit; tail rotor gone," the pilot said over the scanner.

"Damn it," answered Phan.

The pilot pushed the helicopter to the left and headed toward the open fields of an abandoned boatyard along the north bank. Untethered, the rifleman lost his grip and tumbled thirty meters to the river. The spinning helicopter, barely clearing the trees, crashed and skidded across an open patch of concrete.

"Detective, I'm down near the Binh Trieu Bridge. My copilot's in the river. The drone was last heading toward the Binh Loi Bridge."

"Shit," Phan said.

How many times had Con Ma heard that voice? God, he hated that voice and the man that came with it.

"Detective, I don't know what that thing was or who was driving it, but they disappeared like a ghost."

CHAPTER 3

For Cleveland Police detective Alexandra Polonia, it had been a busy twelve months. First her husband, Detective Ralph Cierzinski, was arrested for running both a murder-for-hire ring and a meth lab that sold crank and other drugs to kids, and she'd spent the last year, and nearly all her money, proving that she knew nothing about any of his illegal activities. She'd had him sign the divorce papers the day he climbed, in chains, onto the bus to prison. Then—strangest of all—was her uncanny resemblance to a Croatian journalist, a resemblance that ended in terror and death in Venice, Italy. Then there was her husband's escape from prison that left at least two people dead. And last, and certainly not the least, was her falling head over heels for CIA agent Javier Castillo from Waco, Texas.

Things went even further south when Alex's police captain ordered her home from her Venice vacation. Back in Cleveland, she ran smack into the teeth of a political witch hunt looking to collect heads. The higher-ups had been relentless during the months that followed her husband's arrest—she was guilty, no proof required. But now, after Ralph's murderous escape from prison, their reasons for wanting her sacked grew dramatically. They wanted a head on a stick, and Alex's would do nicely.

After the "unofficial" commission's ambush and her insolent responses, her captain had no option but to place her on administrative leave. The official reason was for not cooperating with an informal and unofficial investigation. She understood where this was heading. Her union representative said they would handle it, which gave her no great sense of confidence.

After enduring the kangaroo court review, she spent the next few days going through every remaining financial resource she had. Her kitchen table looked like the week before tax day. Paper was strewn messily across the Formica tabletop. Not only was she on administrative leave, but she was broke too.

Now, a week after her return from Venice, she was at her parents' place for Sunday dinner. She had come to two conclusions: she had enough money to survive on for three months, assuming that she ate only ramen noodles, and there was no chance she was going to stay with the Cleveland Police Department. It was every woman for her damn self.

"Honey, are you okay?" her mother asked at the table. "You seem out of sorts."

"She's okay," her father said. "Just been a couple of tough months."

Alex smiled at her father, and he returned it. "It's Ralph," she said. "All the stuff from last year keeps coming back. They've put me on administrative leave—indefinitely."

"That's such bull," her brother John said. "They're leaving you out there to twist in the wind. They need a scapegoat, and it's you."

"I know you, sis. You'll never be anyone's stooge," Rick, her youngest brother, added. "Why didn't they do something before you went on vacation? Mom says you went somewhere nice."

"Venice," Alex said. "It *was* going to be nice, and then it became the reason for my suspension."

"Why?" her father asked.

Through the rest of dinner, Alex told them the whole story: the Croatian journalist who had a terrorist for a son and who looked enough like her to be her twin; the war criminal running for president of Croatia; the CIA agent from Texas (she left out *all* the intimate details); and the email from her husband that led to a trap he'd set up to facilitate his escape, a trap that led to the death of the special response team state trooper.

"I never liked Ralph," her mother said. "But he was your choice."

"Mom," Alex said. "We've talked about this. Yes, I was a fool to marry that man. But that's done. I'm moving on—I have to."

"That woman in Venice . . . As a mother, I understand what she did. It's so sad. I'm sorry for you, honey, so sorry."

"You said she looked like you?" John asked.

"Like looking in a mirror," Alex said. "That was the strangest part. I thought we had trouble in Cleveland, but for people in that part of the world, when you combine the Bosnian War and seven hundred years of hate, our difficulties seem trivial."

"What the city is doing stinks," Rick's wife, Julie, said. Julie had been married to Rick for almost fifteen years. Alex thought of her more as a sister than an in-law.

"Thanks. I'm just trying to let the dust settle. The department doesn't know what to do with me. They believe I'll sue, but most of all they want me gone. I think I'll oblige them."

"Quit?" John asked. "You'll let them get their way?"

"At least I'd be in control. If I wait for them to make up their minds, it might be summer before I can return to my desk. If I resign, they'll have nowhere to go. Maybe then it will all be dropped."

"And Ralph?"

"I'll play that game when I have to."

"And Mr. CIA?" Julie asked.

"Don't go there," Alex said with a smile. "Javier's a nice guy. But he's in Italy; I'm in Cleveland. The two worlds could not be farther apart."

"Just wondering. Texas, you say? Like, a cowboy?"

"Julie, you stay out of this," Rick said. "Don't cause any trouble now."

"Me? Never."

"Thanks, Julie," Alex said. "Yes, Texas. And he is cute. More handsome than most men I know, especially these two." She pointed at her brothers and smiled.

"I knew it—go for it."

"Julie!" Rick said. "This is my sister you're talking about."

"She deserves a better life than all the crap she's been handed the last year," Julie said. "And besides, Sunday dinners would be so much more interesting than they've been for the last year. Conversations that didn't have the name Ralph inserted in every other sentence. Personally, I say the son of a bitch can go straight to hell."

"I appreciate that," Alex said. Her phone started to vibrate. The caller ID read *007*.

"You aren't going to answer that?" Julie said, looking at the screen. "007? Is that Mr. CIA?"

"Julie—" Rick said.

"No way I'm staying out of this. Someone has to look out for her."

Alex patted the back of Julie's hand. "Thanks, but I'm a big girl. I think I can handle this. If you'll excuse me, I have to return a call."

A glass of chardonnay in hand, Alex wandered through the house toward her old room, a refuge more than once during the last year. Sitting on her bed, she took a deep breath and called Javier Castillo, the man she'd fallen head over heels for in Venice in less than two days.

Now, why the hell are my hands shaking?

"How's Cleveland?" a voice rich with the sound of Texas asked.

"Cold, snowing, and just plain miserable. But I'm staying warm at my folks' and having a delightful Sunday dinner of roasted chicken and potatoes, a fine chardonnay, and the promise of a Cavaliers win against Chicago. I miss you. Where are you?"

"I'm still in Milan, where it's also cold, raining, and miserable. How are you?"

"Jave, it's all gone to hell. They're trying to put me in the center of the fiasco here with Ralph and all the crap he's left in his wake. I'm the target, and they suspended me."

"They had no right to."

"When did rights ever enter situations like this? You work for the Central Intelligence Agency—you know how it goes. All bureaucracies are the same."

"Can't argue with that."

"On another note, my sister-in-law is pestering me about some Texan I know."

"Is this guy cute?"

"Shut up. You think I would like a guy who isn't?"

She waited. She could almost hear him smile over the phone.

"You like me? You really like me?"

"Shut up. I said cute. Let's leave it there. I have a few weeks to make a decision."

"What's that decision?"

"Whether my days as a Cleveland cop are over. Every nearby jurisdiction is looking for experience—I have that. Maybe a spot on a smaller force would be something I could do. The change would be good."

"You'd be bored—you like the jazz."

Alex was silent for a long moment.

"Alex?"

"I'm here. Just a lot to think about. Enough about me. How are you doing?"

"The proverbial shit-meet-fan stupidity. It seems that our little Venice adventure solved a whole bunch of political problems. Some in the State Department are breathing easier, but they are bureaucrats. Everything fits neatly in the box for them. My boss understands, but he has to cover his butt as well. After all, they were the ones that said they wouldn't defend the journalist's assertions about that Croatian thug—an embarrassment there. Such is politics. I've been called back to Washington, DC, for a sit-down with the State Department, the CIA chief for Europe, and a few others who have some interest in what's happening with Bosnian terrorism. Seems that Ehsan and the other two Bosnian terrorists left an odd trail behind them in the weeks before they died. The current opinion is that they were lone wolves, and that the attack was directed at the Croatian presidential candidate, Kozak, for his part in the Balkan genocide twenty years ago. But Saudi Islamists, most likely Wahhabi fanatics, used the three Bosnians for their own ends. Such is vengeance and retribution when mixed with terror."

"For those poor people on the ferry, they didn't deserve to die," Alex said. "I still can't believe what happened."

"I agree."

"You're going to Washington?" she asked.

"Yes, Wednesday. I called wondering if you might like to have dinner with me. I know a place."

"You always know a place. In Washington?"

"Of course. So, you interested?" he asked.

"I have all the time in the world. But let me see about tickets, hotel, and—"

"I'll cover the hotel," Javier said. "That is, if you don't mind?"

"Presumptuous, aren't we?"

"I'm sorry. I'll make separate reservations. But we can—"

"Discuss the details later. I'll email you. Besides, it's a short flight. You'll be the one with jet lag."

"I'll manage. See you Wednesday night."

Alex clicked off her phone and stared at the old Metallica poster still hung on her bedroom wall.

"You okay?" Julie said from the doorway. "The man didn't just break your heart?"

She smiled. "No. On the contrary, he's asked me out to dinner."

"That's nice."

"In Washington, DC. Seems he'll be in town."

"You said yes, right?"

"Of course. A girl should never pass up a free dinner with a cute international spy from Texas in Washington, DC."

"And who uses the caller ID 007."

CHAPTER 4

Washington, DC

Alex gazed out the window of the Metro train car and into the blackness of the tunnel. The crowded car clattered and screeched as she traveled into downtown Washington, DC, from Reagan National Airport. Sitting among the press of the late-afternoon commuters, she felt alone, really alone, for the first time in almost a year. The din from the train and the anonymity of a crowd allowed her to lose herself in the noise. It was impossible to believe that two weeks earlier she'd been standing on a dock in Venice starting the vacation of her dreams. The past fourteen days were now nothing but their own train of coincidences, confusion, terror, and the arrival of an enigmatic Texan.

The two-block walk from the Metro station invigorated her. Javier had booked their rooms at the Fairmont hotel, a few blocks from George Washington University and Pennsylvania Avenue. Surprisingly for the first day of March, the day was crisp and bright, a welcome change from the dreary weather she left in Cleveland.

She'd been to Washington once to meet with the FBI over a joint task force. It'd come to nothing, but that trip had been memorable because she'd toured the usual sights and lingered at the Vietnam Veterans Memorial. In the late 1960s and early 1970s, her father had been in the army. He'd had one tour in Vietnam, but talked little about his deployment. The memorial's wall of black granite was larger than she had imagined, and afterward she felt a new bond with her father. That night, standing in the rain and running her fingers over the wall, had forever changed her understanding of her father's part in the Vietnam War. If his name were on that wall, she would never have existed.

After a shower, makeup, and donning a little black dress with a short, glossy leather jacket, she now felt ready to take on the CIA spook from Waco, Texas. Javier, perched on a stool at the hotel bar, was staring at a half glass of dark beer. She leaned in and kissed his cheek. He spun on the barstool and returned the kiss, this time on her lips.

"Now, that is a proper Texas welcome," Alex said, and slid onto a stool. She smiled at the bartender. "Belvedere on the rocks."

"You look both absolutely scrumptious and utterly sinister," Javier said.

"A girl should dress to impress. And you, in an Italian suit and a very classy tie. I do not take you for a polka-dot guy. Maybe bold military stripes, but dots?"

"From a small shop in Milan. The suit's from there as well. The second time I've worn it. My neck feels raw from the shirt. Just not used to this style of living. You, on the other hand, were made to wear that getup."

She kissed his cheek again. "All right then. Are we all done with the gushiness? Me? I'm thrilled to be here. Thank you for the dinner date." She tapped her tumbler against his glass.

"You are most welcome."

They took a table, ordered Italian, and updated each other on their trials and tribulations since leaving each other in Venice.

"How long are you in Washington?" Alex asked.

"At least three more days. I'm at Langley tomorrow for follow-ups. I might be reassigned. Milan again, but connected to something with NATO. That's all I know and can say. Never a dull moment in the spy business. So, maybe another dinner or two—maybe even breakfast?"

"Or two? Well, Mr. Castillo, this all must be negotiated. I want no assumptions on either of our parts."

"If I remember, your parts are very negotiable."

She dipped her finger in the water glass and flicked a few drops at him. "It takes two to negotiate."

After dinner, the waiter brought them glasses of brandy.

"So, you're not sure what you want to do," Javier said.

"I'm still as up in the air as I was when I walked out of the station house. Maybe I'll go with the flow and see what pops up in the Cleveland area. Experienced cops are in demand on every police force in the county, so there's that. I'm basically broke. I'll be working until I'm dead. At least Ralph could have paid off the mortgage or the joint credit cards before he was arrested. Damn, that's the first time I've even thought about that asshole, since maybe . . . yesterday."

"My therapy is working," Javier said.

"And what therapy is that, cowboy?"

"Texas charm and an Italian suit—always a winner."

"Doesn't change my situation."

"Have you thought about the FBI or the CIA? I know people."

"I'm forty-two years old—ancient in this young man's game. And my degree in public safety management may not make their cut. Plus, no army or military experience—just chasing bad guys in Cleveland's barrios."

"Don't sell yourself short. Fifteen years a cop is worth a lot."

"Sometimes I wonder what it's worth. The CIA and FBI could use a woman's touch, though. After what I've seen recently, it's a little too testosterone heavy."

"Perhaps." Javier waved to the waiter, held up two fingers, and pointed to the glasses.

"I'm good," Alex said. "Vodka, wine, and brandy—I've reached my limit."

Javier waved off the order. "I have an idea, if you're interested. I know a guy who has a private security firm that works for us sometimes—Christopher Campbell. His firm is called Teton Security and Defense. Can I drop your name?"

"I'm not rent-a-cop material."

"TSD is the real thing. He doesn't do warehouse security—unless it's full of high-grade military equipment or other valuable stuff. His clients are governments, international businesses, and very rich individuals. He's ex-CIA and employs only the best. It's a growing field, especially these days. Check out their website, the promotion video especially."

"Teton Security and Defense?"

"Yes. I'll tell Chris about you. However, right now—sadly, my love—I've hit the wall. Can I dial back the charm and try not to seduce you tonight? Will you be disappointed? Better this than falling asleep in your arms like I did in Venice."

"I enjoyed that, actually, but I do prefer the more wide-awake version. You owe me, though."

"My greatest wish."

The two walked through the hotel lobby to the elevator bank. Alex kissed Javier, and they lingered there a moment. She teased him with a whisper; he put both hands up and almost surrendered. The door opened and he backed in. She followed. He punched three and looked at her.

"Five, sir."

He pushed the button. Seconds later he kissed her cheek and walked out onto his floor, the door closing behind him.

She retrieved her phone from her bag. Other than Javier's earlier text about meeting in the bar, there was nothing. Maybe all the crap in Cleveland hadn't followed her to Washington. She hoped that this was true.

CHAPTER 5

Alex's phone vibrated, and *007* glowed on the screen. The time was nine o'clock.

"Good morning, sleepyhead," Javier said.

"How the hell did I sleep so late?" Alex asked as she walked across the room and dropped a pod into the coffee maker. "What was in that last drink?"

"A peaceful and quiet mind will help you. Last night I could tell you needed a good night's rest. Sorry again about ducking out. Can I make it up to you tonight?"

"Definitely. Do you have a full day?"

"My first meeting was over two hours ago. I've been a busy boy. I've set up a lunch date for you with Chris Campbell. He'd like to meet you. He's heard about you and Venice."

"Why would Venice mean anything to him? We just got in the way of some terrorists."

"It was our coolness under fire."

"Your coolness—I was looking for a place to hide."

"That's not the way I remember it. I'll text you his info. He's not far from the Fairmont. You decide. If nothing else, it's a free lunch, and his chef is great. Besides, in this town, it's who you know as much as what you know."

"Let me wake up, and I'll think about it. Dinner tonight?"

"There's an osteria like the one in Venice. I'll meet you in the lobby at seven. Think about Chris. Text me when you make up your mind." He clicked off before she could answer.

As she drank her coffee, Javier, Venice, Cleveland, and that ultimate asshole—her ex, Ralph—tumbled around in her head. All she wanted to do was push the bad stuff away and hold tight to the good. After her shower, she toweled off and dried her hair. Standing in front of the mirror, she looked damn good for a broad her age, she thought. Javier liked her in that dress last night. She liked herself in that dress too. Her age and heritage presented a constant battle, but she watched what she ate and hadn't yet taken up drinking alone—or not that often, at least.

Her phone rang: *Caller Unknown.* Now what?

"Alex Polonia," she said.

"Ms. Polonia, I'm Chris Campbell. Javier suggested I give you a call. He may have mentioned lunch. I'm calling to confirm. I was impressed by what I heard about Venice, as well as by how you've handled the difficulties in Cleveland."

"Thanks, I guess. You've already checked me out? Once a spook, always a spook. Impressive—though intimidating." She moved her iPad to one side, the Teton Security and Defense website on its screen.

"Touché. It is in my blood, and that's what our clients expect. Do you have dietary restrictions?"

"Excuse me?"

"For lunch—my chef would like to make sure there are no problems. Shellfish, peanuts, that kind of stuff."

Alex paused and thought about what was happening. "No problems, I guess. What time?"

"One o'clock? I'll send a car."

She looked out the window. It looked chilly but sunny. "I'll walk. Javier said your office wasn't far away and gave me your address. I need the exercise anyway."

"See you at one. I look forward to meeting you," Campbell said, and clicked off.

In the land of strange phone calls, Alex listed this one near the top. She dressed in gray wool slacks, a white silk shirt, a wine-red pullover sweater, and comfortable yet stylish walking shoes. She had a few hours before the meeting and was starving. The café in the lobby made her a plate of scrambled eggs and toast, which cut the edge. The coffee helped too. She idled away an hour reading the newspaper and watched the business of Washington pass back and forth through the lobby.

She slipped on her leather jacket and began the comfortable stroll east down M Street. She crossed New Hampshire Avenue and continued to Connecticut Avenue, then up Rhode Island Avenue. At Scott Circle, with its General Winfield Scott statue, she looked down Sixteenth Street, the roof of the White House visible through the bare winter trees. Teton Security and Defense had a modern glass facade, as unremarkable as the other buildings on Rhode Island. A simple bronze sign read "Teton Security and Defense, Ltd." The lobby was open, clean, and bright. The three outsize, sports-coated guards, the two uniformed women at the front desk, and the NFL-tackle-sized man near the bank of elevators made it clear the building was well defended.

Alex stopped at the desk. A woman with a headset in her ear looked up.

"I have an appointment with Mr. Campbell."

"Of course. May I say who is visiting?"

"Alexandra Polonia." She almost said *Cleveland police* and *detective*. Breaking old habits was tough.

"One moment, please." The woman typed on a keyboard, waited a moment, and looked back at Alex. "Mr. Campbell will be right down. Would you care to have a seat?" The woman nodded toward a bank of modern-looking chairs in chrome and black leather, lining a red shag carpet.

"Thank you, I'll stand."

The midday traffic filled Rhode Island Avenue. People hurried by, all seemingly intent on some aspect of the government's business. She tried to believe it was all for good, but her cynical heart told her that most were here for themselves.

"Ms. Polonia, I'm Chris Campbell."

She turned and was pleasantly surprised. Campbell was about her height, athletically built, tan, dark-brown eyes. His thick, prematurely white hair was cut in a look that suited a man of about fifty. The dark-gray suit looked English, the tie and shoes conservatively expensive. No beard or mustache. When he extended his hand to shake, she noticed the knotted string friendship bracelet that a child might secure to the wrist of a parent. She smiled.

"My daughter made it. She's a doll, if not a bit protective. It's a pleasure to meet you, Ms. Polonia."

"Please, call me Alex. And a pleasure to meet you."

"This way."

They headed toward the elevators, where the NFL tackle stood holding one open for the two.

"Thank you, Demetrius."

"You have the whole building?" Alex asked as the elevator started.

"Yes. We have offices in twenty-three countries and training facilities here in the States, the Middle East, and the Philippines."

The elevator opened. Alex preceded Campbell into the foyer as he said, "To the left, please."

Alex had been in hundreds of office buildings, and this one was just as unexceptional. Lining the walls were dozens of photos showing groups of men and women. Most were in military-style uniforms, clustered together. No names or identifications.

"These are some of my teams," Campbell said. "I like to have my people see these photos so they know they're part of a big, supportive team. Very seldom do we have operations that require a single operative, but everyone's training makes them think as one. Many have a military background, but some come from police departments around the world."

He ushered her into an office that overlooked the street. Near the window, a tablecloth covered a table set with china and silverware. Campbell's desk sat to one side, facing the door. Shelves filled with books, ancient artifacts, and sculptures lined the wall behind the desk. There was a surprising lack of the usual trophy photos of Campbell with one politician or another. A reproduction of a painting of Teddy Roosevelt hung on one wall, one of Abraham Lincoln on another. On the far wall opposite the desk was a world map studded with pins.

Campbell noticed Alex's attention to the map. "Current operations and deployments. We update it every morning. I like to know exactly what's happening and where."

"Impressive. Reminds me of a war-room map from the movies."

"Please have a seat. Something to drink?"

"Ice water would be just fine."

Campbell filled a glass from a pitcher, handed it to her, and took a seat.

"Mr. Campbell, why am I here?"

He poured himself a glass. "Javier thinks you're good—in fact, very good."

"How would he know? Every time there was a problem in Venice, I just threw punches or shot at someone—not much self-restraint."

"Croatian thugs, two in the canal. A pair of questionable DEA agents, who, if you haven't heard, have been fired and are facing serious criminal charges in Italy. All that while dealing with a woman and her deranged terrorist son. I see great self-restraint."

"I was just pissed. They were messing up my vacation."

Campbell laughed. "I like people who are disciplined. People who think on their feet and, to be trite, out of the box when necessary. In my line of work, the bad guys are very bad, and the good guys are not always saints."

Campbell rose, crossed the room, and looked out the window. "I'm looking for a woman, one with your skills, discipline, and experience. The position, after training, will be—"

Three explosions in the hallway just outside the office shattered the building's silence. Campbell looked at Alex, ran back to his desk, yanked open the left-hand drawer, and put two automatic pistols on the desktop. He pushed one of them across the top toward her. She instinctively grabbed it and charged the weapon. From the open door came the sound of gunfire, near and far. It echoed through Campbell's office. As she stood and went to Campbell's side, a man in a black sweater and ski mask burst into the room and fired at them. Campbell spun to his left, his shoulder instantly bloody. She raised the pistol and fired at the man. He dropped after two slugs smashed into his chest. With her left arm, she caught Campbell before he fell to the carpet.

"We've got to get out of here, now!" she yelled, her ears still ringing from the weapon's discharges. More gunfire filled the hallway. She slipped her shoulder under Campbell's good right arm. They staggered to the door. She did a quick look both ways. The image of two men on the floor in the corridor etched itself into her mind. Another flash-bang discharged to the left. She and Campbell went right. They stumbled toward the elevators. She saw the exit sign over the door to the stairs.

"Can you make it up the stairs?" she yelled.

"Up? We need to get out."

"I don't know what's down, but I hope there's less going up. We can find a secure location and then wait for help. Down? Hell, there could be a dozen bad guys just waiting." More gunfire echoed through the building.

Another explosion sent a shock wave down the hall, validating her decision. She put her shoulder into the door and pulled Campbell into the empty stairwell with her.

"How many floors to the roof?"

"Three," Campbell said through clenched teeth.

"Then get your ass moving. Best guess, they're less than a minute behind us. Go, go."

Campbell led the way, staggering at each landing. "I need to stop, rest," he said when they reached the last floor. Alex heard a door below burst open and bang against the concrete wall of the stairwell. The words yelled from below sounded like Arabic or something similar.

"No time for that! Move, Mr. Campbell. Now." She shoved the man up the last flights of stairs. "ROOF" was stenciled on a door at the top of the last flight.

"Hold," she ordered. "Quick look." She pushed the door open a few inches, expecting a volley of bullets. When none came, she looked around—the roof was empty. She gathered up Campbell under her arm.

"Are you ready?" she said. "Either we make a stand here, or we're dead."

Heavy footsteps, as loud as drums, echoed upward on the stairwell's steel treads. She pushed the door wide open, her weapon up. Campbell grunted as she pulled him after her.

The sun was brilliant, and she squinted, her eyes trying to adjust. All she saw was a half-dozen shapes materializing in the intense glare. "Crap."

"Lower the weapon, Ms. Polonia," one of the shapes said. "No one here will hurt you."

Stunned, she looked at Campbell, who gently moved her arm from under his and stood straight. He took the pistol from her and offered it to one of the men on the roof. Her eyesight now fully adjusted, she saw Mr. NFL and four other men in combat fatigues. The sixth man was the one she'd encountered in Campbell's office. The center of his black sweater looked wet where she had shot him. A few seconds later, three men pushed past her from the stairwell.

She turned to Campbell. "You bastard. What the fuck was this all about?" She slugged him in the mouth.

CHAPTER 6

"And then you punched him?" Javier asked, a huge grin on his face.

"I was pissed," Alex said. "I do not like job interviews where I have to kill someone."

"They were blanks."

"Did you know about all this?"

"No, but I have heard rumors about Chris's unorthodox interview methods. He once conducted one during a skydive."

"If I find out that you knew this was going to happen, well, I might just punch you as well. It pisses me off."

"You said that," Javier countered.

"This time I really mean it."

"Did he offer you a job?"

"I stormed down the stairs before he could ask," Alex said.

"He called. Said your reactions to the extreme situation were better than ninety percent of the applicants he's . . . interviewed. He also said you were the first to punch him. His jaw? Good for you."

"Good for me? My hand still hurts. I wonder what they do to the failures. Disappear them into the Potomac?"

Javier stirred the glass of bourbon with his finger. He motioned to the bartender and pointed to Alex's empty glass. The bartender nodded.

"It's a tough world," Javier said. "Chris just wanted to see how you would react. His people need more than physical skills. They need the ability to respond to extreme conditions. Their reactions may save the client's life and their own."

"I get it, but it still pisses me off. Thanks," she said as her drink was replaced. "And Campbell still owes me lunch."

She glanced into the mirror behind the bar and stiffened; Christopher Campbell was walking toward them. He was alone and wore a different suit than the one that was trashed by the blood pack under his shoulder. She shot a look at Javier. "Did you know he was going to be here?"

Javier looked in the mirror, then spun on his stool. "No."

"You're lucky—that punch would have been right now." She refused to leave the stool when Campbell stopped behind her. "Have you come to apologize?" She glared at him.

"No. I never apologize. What I did was necessary. My people are the best—they understand that. That's why I pay them what I do and give them the respect due them. All I ask is that my people perform their jobs and are loyal in return, nothing more. Are you interested in working for me, Ms. Polonia? I don't need to know now. No stipulations, no time limits. You have potential."

"Potential?"

"Yes, potential. Our training facilities are the best. Afterward, you'll be able to handle most anything that a SEAL or an Army Ranger could. The Cleveland Police Academy will feel like Boy Scout camp when you're through. Ask Javier—a lot of my people are from the CIA and the FBI. Many are ex-military, some from government operations elsewhere. Ms. Polonia, please call me soon. I like you. Javier, good to see you, and thanks." Campbell shook Javier's hand, then strolled out of the bar.

"Wow, what the hell have you gotten me into?" Alex said as she watched Campbell disappear.

"Nothing that you wouldn't be good at. I'm famished, and the restaurant has a chilled bottle of the same chardonnay we had in Venice. It's a ten-minute cab ride, and I have much to atone for."

"You most certainly do, sir, and I intend to make you pay."

The next morning, Alex slipped the bedsheet around her shoulders and walked to the window. The sun was breaking above the capital's skyline, creating a glow as rosy as the one she'd felt a few weeks earlier on a Venice rooftop. It felt good to be in the arms of a strong man. She turned to the sleeping Javier. After the night they'd had, she was surprised she had the energy to even get out of bed. Her head still rang from the chaos of Campbell's creative interview, no matter how hard she tried to push it out. She would like nothing better than to go home with the CIA agent from Waco, Texas, and eat his mother's cooking. She hadn't felt this way about a man since, maybe, ever. The mental baggage from the last year—Ralph, the kangaroo court, all the rest—felt much lighter. She'd be satisfied to pitch it out with the trash.

"Don't move," Javier said. "Just stand there for a few moments and let me revel in my dream."

"If you call me an angel, I'll—"

"Hardly. After last night, most of the angels I know fled the scene of the crime."

She turned to the man and dropped the sheet, padded across the room, and climbed back into his arms. Somewhere an angel had to have blushed.

After Javier returned to his room, she showered, dressed, and walked to the Starbucks two blocks away. She ate a yogurt-and-fruit concoction and left a message with Chris Campbell's office. He texted ten minutes later and they set up a time to meet. He promised no funny business.

Before Campbell, though, she had another appointment, a more important one. The walk was due south and barely more than a mile. A gray overcast had drifted in. She stood in front of the black granite wall of the Vietnam memorial, thinking about her father and all that he'd been through since the war. Alex was born four years after he had returned from Vietnam.

She knew little about his part in the war. He never talked about it. When she was about seven or eight, she'd awaken to a yell or a scream. She would peek out of her room, down the hall toward her parents' bedroom. Her father would be standing near the door, her mother holding him tight. Later, when she was a teenager, the popular talk about veterans was about PTSD, post-traumatic stress disorder, brought on by the war's lingering effects. But her dad never talked about it. As a cop, she saw it in the faces of some of her fellow officers after a particularly bad situation. The blank stare, the denials of help, the required sessions with the department shrinks—it was all there. Her father seemed to weather it, and in time the night screams went away. When she'd asked her mother about what happened, she said, "In time, all his wounds will heal."

Alex was not so sure. Some of the cops she knew took disability. They couldn't face the street again.

She touched the cold black wall again, allowing her fingers to trace an incised name she did not know. She thought about the loss. What did they leave behind? What had they missed? What child never knew their father?

Now, nearly fifty years later, her father often talked about the war, but in generalities. Nevertheless, there always was a shadow over the conversation. He spoke about the friends he made, even those he lost, whose names were on this wall. He mentioned Vietnam and Okinawa, places he'd been to, places he swore he would never go back to. She was a detective; she listened for the things not said. Often, the unanswered question was more important than the ramblings of the perpetrator or the victim. She'd sensed there was always something her father left out of his story.

Campbell was waiting for her at the National Air and Space Museum. He was sitting in front of the original Wright brothers' aircraft.

"Thanks for meeting me," Campbell said.

"Good afternoon," Alex responded, wondering if this were the correct answer from the fly to the spider. "Your text was vague."

"Sorry, easier to tell than write, and besides I leave for Marseille tonight. I have a client meeting tomorrow. So, Ms. Polonia, do you want to work for me?"

"How much downtime is there? I don't sit around well. I need something to do."

"My people normally work thirty days on, thirty days off. This schedule changes depending on the situation and the client. The time is intense. The downtime, as you call it, is balanced with the job. It includes access to the best medical care anywhere in the world. If it's not there, I'll fly you to it. There are no vacations or paid days off. You get paid a monthly rate, work or no work. The amount is adjusted depending on the location. It can change if the assignment is in an active war zone."

"Change?"

"Your pay is doubled for the duration of the job if there is a hot war going on around you. You are entitled to turn down one assignment per year. Your reasons are your own—I will not ask why."

"Assignments?"

"They are as broad and varied as the clients. We provide personal bodyguards, active on-site and off-site security, sometimes surveillance, and even babysitting, as the staff calls it."

"Babysitting?"

"Some of our clients' kids and families need to be guarded. Sometimes the children are less responsible than their parents. So, babysitting."

"Sounds thrilling."

"I have my greatest number of turndowns over babysitting. I understand. Managing a sixteen-year-old spoiled brat of a young woman who is in love can be thankless, challenging work."

"You mentioned training."

"Yes, once you are on board, three things will happen. One, a complete physical and medical workup. If you fail, you're out. Two, an in-depth psychological analysis and assessment. If you fail, you're out. And three, physical training. I give some leeway here."

"Where will this training be?"

"Until you pass the first two steps and are certified for employment, the locations for the training facilities are secret. Texas, though—I can tell you that. The medical tests and evaluations will be in Dallas. From there, you will relocate to our field center for initial training. Afterward we may send you to another facility, maybe one that's out of the country. Where depends on the proficiencies you showed or gained in Texas, as well as your assignment. So, are you ready to join us?"

She looked back at the fragile aircraft of canvas and wood and smiled. "Mr. Campbell, there comes a time when we all have to learn to fly."

"Excellent. Now you can call me *boss*."

CHAPTER 7

That evening, Alex met Javier for dinner in the hotel's dining room. She was excited and hopeful. *As they say, the world is my oyster.*

Javier sipped his wine and took her hand. "Me first. I have to go back to Milan tomorrow morning. NATO stuff. They want me there. I have no idea when I'll see you again or even talk to you. But my heart is being stretched like two bulls are trying to pull it apart."

Alex rolled his hand over and touched his fingers. "I love your corny cowboy metaphors. The same thought has been tugging at me. We're good for each other. Strange world—Cleveland, Venice, Washington, all tumbled into one. And Agent Castillo, I'll miss you. A lot." Her smile indicated more, but it was left unsaid.

Javier smiled back. "When are you leaving?"

"How presumptuous. You think I took the job?"

"Educated guess. You look content. It's nice to see."

"Chris has given me a week to sort Cleveland out. I'll also have the time to talk with my family. It will shock them. Especially my father—he's very protective."

"Fathers can be like that. Then what?"

"I have a one-way ticket to Dallas. One suitcase, no more. I was told to wear comfortable shoes. They'll pick me up at the airport. Then, as they say in the movies, 'your ass is mine.'"

"It's such a nice ass, and don't let anyone tell you different."

"You can be so romantic when you want to be."

They talked about Cleveland's hard winters and Texas's mild ones and discovered their mutual fondness for baseball—Javier was not a big fan of the Indians. He gave her the nickel tour of his family's history, going back to before Sam Houston. She told him about her family and its origins in hill country near Kraków, Poland. Two families from two very different parts of the troubled world.

The night and bedsheets tumbled into the morning, and she kissed him goodbye at her hotel room door. Alex watched the man from Waco walk the hall to the elevator. She closed her door after he disappeared and looked out the window and across the rooftops of Washington.

She sighed. "What the devil have I gotten myself into?"

"My resignation," Alex said the first morning back in Cleveland. She handed her captain an envelope. "There's no way to sugarcoat this, or even try to fight it. I'm a distraction. There are forces at work now that neither of us wants to deal with, and it is unfair to the men and women of the department. It's effective immediately."

"You can fight it," he said. "I'll work you through this."

"I've dealt with this bullshit from Ralph for the past year. Now it's worse. Someone wants to throw me out. I refuse to give them the satisfaction. You have been great, and most of the department as well. But I'm at the end of this road. If I stay, this will dog me for the rest of my career."

"I understand. Don't like it, but I understand. What are you going to do?"

"I have an opportunity. Not sure how it will turn out, but it's worth a shot." Campbell's nondisclosure agreement kept her from telling him much more than that.

"Polonia, you are smart and tough. But be safe."

"I'm just going to slip out of here. Bob and I will have lunch, but that's it—no going-away party, Captain." She pulled her shield and placed it and the department-issued firearm on his desk. "I'm sure there's other gear in my locker. I'll clear it and give it to Bob. He'll make sure you get it. The last thing I want is someone chasing me over a misplaced set of handcuffs."

He gave Alex a hug and wished her well.

After confirming dinner at her parents' that evening, she met her former partner, Bob Simmons, at Moriarty's Pub on Sixth Street.

"You going to be okay?" Simmons asked.

"Definitely. I feel better than I have in years. Venice changed everything."

"That CIA agent? The guy from Waco?"

"It's more than him. I was complacent, going with the flow, and Ralph unintentionally flipped a switch. Bob, it's a big world out there, bigger than I imagined. During the past month, my world has been turned on its ass. All I can tell you is that this girl was offered a chance to take a big step, and she's taking it."

"Be careful."

She smiled and placed her fingers on the back of Simmons's hand. "Bob, that's been my problem—being careful. I'm changing that."

After dinner, Alex's dad walked along the sidewalk with his only daughter. A warm front had moved in. The melting snow, piled along the narrow strip between the walk and the curb, left streamlets in the gutter. Their evening walks were a tradition since she'd been a teenager.

"Are you sure this is what you want?" he asked.

"More than anything."

"Is it safe?"

"A lot safer than taking down meth heads on the east side."

"How's the pay?"

She smiled. Her father always made sure his children knew what they were getting into and were being paid for their work. "Twice more than Cleveland PD. And the benefits are better."

"That means greater risks. Is it in the United States?"

"Can't say and honestly don't know. But Javier recommended them. He's known the company's owner for many years."

"And what about this Javier fellow? Your mother is concerned."

Alex knew that both her mother and father were shocked about what had happened in Venice. They had been right about Ralph, though they'd never bugged her about him until everything went wrong. She was well aware of their dislike for the man. She'd married him on an emotional fling and the fear of getting old. She didn't remember too much about love. After the last year, she learned two things about her ex-husband: one, he was a certifiable asshole and psychotic, and two, if he was still alive, she would shoot the son of a bitch if she had the chance.

"I like Javier . . . a lot. It's complicated—he's in Milan, probably for the next year. I'll be going through training for this new job, and we won't see each other. The future? I just don't know."

"Alex, you're from a family of cops. You take after your grandfather and your uncle: you see wrong, and you want to make it right. This new job had better give you that satisfaction, or I'll bet you ten to one you will be right back here. Now tell me more about this guy from Texas."

"He's good for my heart and soul."

"Do you love him? I know the difference between affection and love. Your mother and I can't stand to be apart. When I was young, there were women. I know the ways of the heart, at least a little."

Her father had never talked about his life before he married. Alex knew about the Parma, Ohio, high school he attended, his year at Kent State, his being drafted, and Vietnam. Nonetheless, Roger Polonia kept to himself a lot about the years before marrying Alice. The kids never asked; he never volunteered. She remembered the screams at night and her mother's comforting words.

"You were in love before Mom?"

"Now why would you ask that?"

"I'm a detective. I'm paid to read between the lines."

"And a good one," he said. "Yes, there was someone—I was young, scared, and I fell for her. But it ended. I almost died and then was sent home. I never saw her again."

"This was in Vietnam?"

"In Saigon, yes, but I don't want to talk about it. There's still a sharp sting to it."

"I'm sure you weren't the only one, Dad."

"Yeah, all of us were young and alone. Too much time on our hands, and death was everywhere. When I got home, I was on the edge of falling apart, and there was a big hole right here." He pointed to his chest. "Then I met your mother. She understood, and she softened all the sharp edges."

They walked a few more blocks, each in their thoughts—she mused about his past and wondered about her future.

CHAPTER 8

Lake Simcoe, Ontario, Canada

At the same time that Alex strolled the street with her father, Ralph Cierzinski lounged comfortably in the living room of his home overlooking Lake Simcoe, his computer on his lap. The lake was a frozen expanse of ice and snow. Any warmth of a Canadian spring was more than two months away. A cup of coffee steamed on the small wooden stand next to the recliner, a cigarette smoldered in a nearby ashtray, and a fire crackled and spit in the fireplace.

His real identity and location were entirely unknown to anyone. His neighbors, such as they were, knew him as Alfred Kandinsky. His mailbox read "Kandinsky," with the number 10231 hand painted under it. Alfred Kandinsky was on his driver's license, the deed to this house, and his Canadian passport. A bank in the Cayman Islands wired a set sum of money every month to a bank in Beaverton. He paid for everything with Canadian dollars or wrote a check. When asked, he would tell his neighbors that he lived in Toronto most of the year.

His nearest neighbors were retirees who spent their winters in Mexico and Costa Rica, and none had returned yet this year. Over the years he had met a few of them, often in passing at the grocery store or as he mowed his lawn. The neighborhood's sole permanent resident was an elderly woman who lived next door and never left her house.

Her children took care of her and dutifully came almost every weekend. They lived in Toronto, more than thirty miles south. At night, he could see her television flicker through the picture window that faced the lake. It appeared that she just watched hockey and game shows.

After his meticulously planned escape from prison and the brutal trick he'd played on the Ohio troopers and the special response team at his aunt's now-burnt-down house in Geneva-on-the-Lake, he was content with the week of confusion he'd thrown in their path. The border crossing went as he'd hoped. The car with its registered Canadian plates, his passport and identifications, and the bags from the Buffalo Walmart in the back seat passed through without question. If American and Canadian customs coordinated the cross-checks of the border crossing, all they would find would be a vehicle owned by Edward Wallace from Brampton, Canada. When Ralph arrived at the Lake Simcoe house, he switched out the dash's vehicle identification number and plates. His immediate goal was simple: stay off the streets for as long as possible. He shopped early, was friendly, made eye contact. The last thing he wanted was to be the questionable character living in the last house on the narrow lane facing the lake.

He'd owned the Lake Simcoe house for fifteen years, since long before he'd married Alexandra. It was where he went fishing when he told Alex he was getting away. He'd tell her he was going to Sandusky, Ohio, to a cabin shared by friends from the CPD. She had never been there. She didn't know about the Canadian house; she hated fishing. Like his aunt's house in Geneva-on-the-Lake, he had prepared it for his eventual, if necessary, escape from prison. He was fatalistic and knew that someday he might get caught. A good drug dealer always needed an escape strategy. The Canadian house was his best backup option.

The email he'd sent Alex when she was in Venice did its job. She'd acted like he expected a cop to act. It'd given him a few days of cover after his escape from prison. He was sure they had by now discovered the corpse in the cellar of the Geneva-on-the-Lake house. The house that he'd intentionally exploded and burned—with the corpse that was not him. The death of the special response team trooper had been unfortunate; the man should not have been standing at the door when he remotely activated the AR15 rifle.

C'est la guerre.

He and Alex had been married for almost nine years when he was arrested. He knew that what he'd put her through was unfair. He told himself that she was tough and obviously knew how to handle herself. Now he was trying to understand what she was up to.

He lit another cigarette and on his laptop looked at the remote recorded feed from his old house in Cleveland. There was movement. He had hardwired the three matchbox-sized Bluetooth cameras into the power of the smoke alarms a year before his arrest, as an added level of security. If someone busted into his house, he wanted to know who to hunt down. Now, two years later, they still sent their data to a compact server he'd mounted behind the fuse box in the garage. It still transmitted the data through the phone lines. And it still provided him with a window on what his ex-wife was up to. Being a voyeur had its advantages. He wished he'd put one in the bedroom, where he might be able to watch one of the hottest women he'd ever known. Unfortunately for him, the closest camera he could hide was in the smoke alarm in the hallway. The other two were in the garage and the kitchen.

A few days after his escape, he had watched Alex return to the house, back from her Venice trip. Once he reached Lake Simcoe, he reviewed the video feed again: she had been at the house for several days, then vanished for almost a week before returning.

Where have you been, baby? Back and forth, here and there. You have been a busy, busy girl.

Cierzinski fought his desire to email her to find out what was going on in her life. A life that, he had to admit, he'd royally fucked over. And the Cleveland newspaper, the *Plain Dealer*, hadn't written kindly about her either.

I'd have set them straight if they'd asked me.

He was sorry for what he'd done to her, about her probably losing her job and all, but he had to stick to his plan.

Through the video feed now, he watched Alex cross the kitchen and put a stack of mail on the counter. A minute later, she set two grocery bags on the opposite counter. For the next few minutes, she separated the letters, junk catalogs, advertisements, and general crap into separate piles. She had sorted the mail in the same spot for more than five years; that's why he'd set the camera to the angle it was. Its high-definition image, even for a camera the size of a matchbox, was excellent. He could enlarge almost anything that the lens saw. Letter after letter was placed into one stack: some with a bank's logo on the corner, bills, a hand-written letter—*Who writes letters?*—and the final envelope, which read "TSD, Ltd." in the upper-left corner. He made a note on a pad of paper.

She filled the Keurig's reservoir with water and clicked the coffee maker on, and as she waited for the water to heat, she began to open the envelopes. She moved the TSD letter off to the side and processed the rest until only a few envelopes and magazines remained. She dropped a coffee pod into the machine. Then bringing the coffee, she took the TSD envelope and the rest of the letter stack and walked out of the frame of the camera.

He crushed out his cigarette and immediately lit another. He opened a search window and typed in *TSD, Ltd.* A firearms distributor popped up, then an engineering firm and a builder. It was the fourth URL that caught his eye: Teton Security and Defense. Maybe this was it? He checked out the other sites and decided against them. They were too small or not in Alex's range of expertise. Teton's website, now this was different: international security, surveillance, and defense consulting. And the font of TSD's website matched the letterhead on the envelope.

Is my Alex spreading her wings?

She walked back into the camera's view and set the envelope back on the counter. He took a snapshot with the software. She walked away. He followed her down the hallway, and she disappeared into the back of the house.

What on earth are you up to, baby?

CHAPTER 9

Beijing, China

Con Ma sat uneasily in the back seat of the Mercedes as it passed along the congested streets that circled the Forbidden City and Tiananmen Square. An emergency ambulance's siren could be faintly heard through the bulletproof glass. It quickly passed on the road's shoulder. The dark, thick, polluted air formed a gray fog that hung above the ancient city. No, *gray* wasn't the right description. More like the color of bile and dead frogs—gray green with a touch of burnt sand. How anyone lived here was beyond him. Even surviving day to day was questionable.

He tapped his fingers on the leather armrest and wondered why his employer had summoned him. They never asked him to come to Beijing, and he preferred it that way. A text message was all he needed. In this city of twenty-one million, the chance of being seen, or exposed, or assassinated left him uncomfortable.

You will meet with the directors in Beijing next Wednesday at 10:00 a.m., the text message summoning him had read. *It is imperative that you not be late. There is much riding on this next operation. I will meet with you before the meeting in my office. Be fully prepared.*

Cryptic to be sure. More questions than answers—typical of Mr. Zheng and the Chairwoman. In eight years and four dozen operations, he had never questioned his orders. His accounts were well satisfied, and if he were to walk away, he would be a wealthy man. He could retreat to the home he'd made on an island in Hangzhou Bay, where, in the distance, the lights of Shanghai would provide a theatrical backdrop to his simple life. He could breathe clean air and smell the ocean for the rest of his days. And with his security devices, he could detect anyone approaching for more than two kilometers.

Con Ma was certain, however, that if he attempted to retire, he would be hunted. The Chairwoman and the organization would try to seize the money they had paid him. His accounts were well secured in Zurich and Grand Cayman. The Chairwoman had reminded him that management was not happy with these arrangements, but they had relaxed for him the requirement that the money be kept in China. He knew too much, and to force him to do something he did not want to do was to invite serious complications.

Looking back, other than the wound to his leg, he felt Saigon had gone well. Better than he had hoped, in fact. It was not his place to know what the data was that he sent via the transmitter. As far as he knew, it performed as expected. He remembered the unit growing warm as he'd placed it in the urn. The two dead men were collateral damage. The price you pay when you're hired guns working for a corrupt Western business. The Chairwoman said that they didn't play by the rules established and agreed to. Con Ma did not care for rules, whosoever they were.

The Mercedes stopped at a heavily secured gate at the base of a high-rise office tower that overlooked the Forbidden City and the ornamental lakes that skirted the ancient city's western boundary and the Palace Museum. The iron gate slid open, and the Mercedes proceeded down a ramp into the underground garage. At the designated parking stall, the driver stopped, left the car, and opened the back seat's door. Con Ma thanked the driver and proceeded to the glass-enclosed lobby with its three elevator doors.

At the lobby door, he placed his right hand on a glass panel and lowered his head toward a device that looked like a glass eye in a black circular socket. It briefly flashed, and a few seconds later the door clicked and opened without a touch. Con Ma made his way inside the elevator and pressed its one button. After a few moments, he felt his ears pop from the change in air pressure. He closed his eyes, controlled his breathing, and relaxed. His heart slowed, and calm returned—a warrior's preparation.

The elevator door opened upon two men in business suits. They both bowed and turned to their left, and Con Ma followed. If it weren't for the smog, the windows would have offered magnificent views for kilometers in every direction.

Reaching an elegant lobby filled with displays of ancient armor, weapons, and antique furniture, his chaperones stopped, stood silently, and waited. He stood behind them. His educated eyes caught at least three treasures from early Chinese dynasties. As a Vietnamese, he saw these items as the remnants of a failed culture that had tried, more than once, to dominate his home country. But he wasn't angry—the Chinese paid well.

A door opened at the end of the lobby, and a man approached and bowed. "Con Ma, welcome. It is good to see you again. It has been too long."

Con Ma smiled. "And good morning to you, Mr. Zheng," he answered. "Yes, too long. I believe it was in Brussels, early last year, during the international trade show. Such good pickings."

Mr. Zheng nodded. "Yes, and profitable as well. Please join me in my office. There is much to discuss." Zheng turned and walked down the hallway, and Con Ma followed. The two chaperones remained behind.

"The Chairwoman is running late," Zheng said. "She knows you're here. We have had a busy morning. Tea?"

Con Ma nodded, and Zheng poured tea into exquisite porcelain cups—Fifteenth Dynasty, surely.

"It's been a few years since I was here last," Con Ma said. "Beijing is becoming too big."

Zheng handed him the teacup. "I can't disagree, but we are here because this is where the center of the world is. And I believe that the air is getting better. The government is doing everything it can to make Beijing inhabitable."

"Ship twenty million citizens to the communes," Con Ma said after taking a sip. "That would help."

"Maybe. Please sit. I must bring you up-to-date. There are troubling developments."

Con Ma walked from the window and sat across from Zheng.

"It seems that we were misinformed about the data in the Saigon technology facility," Zheng began. "After you sent us the plans for the drone, we were told about the management and operating software. That was why you were sent back to Saigon: to acquire that software. We were told that it would be the complete data files. It was not."

"Are you implying that I failed, Mr. Zheng?"

"No. We are certain that what you transmitted was all that was in the server. But our technicians now believe that there are five parts, plug-ins if you will, required to complete the file. It's worthless otherwise. We were, as I said, misinformed."

"Or misled."

"Possibly. I understand that the first Como employee you dealt with had an unfortunate accident."

"Yes. After the man provided the plans for the drone, he slipped and fell into a canal. If he hadn't demanded more money, I could have probably saved his life."

Zheng looked at Con Ma over the top of his teacup. "Yes, I'm sure you would have. Our contact inside Como Motors says that he will acquire the remaining parts of the file. They cannot be combined until they are all together at the same time. Our techs say that if we try to piece them together separately, they will destroy each other."

"I understand. If I may be so impertinent as to ask, what is this software? What does it do?"

"We have been led to believe that the software was initially developed to help motorbikes avoid each other."

"Motorbikes?"

"Yes," Zheng said, "but the Chairwoman, in her wisdom, believes that its real purpose is to manage defenses against swarm attacks of weaponized drones and smart munitions. That makes the software critical to our artificial-intelligence program. Have you seen those videos of starlings flying in massive formations like black clouds twisting and folding in on each other? The mathematics are similar to those in this software."

"Yes, I think I understand. I can imagine a thousand small and lethal weapons, manned and unmanned, all converging on a location. Obviously, some type of management or defense system is required. But the software is in Saigon because . . ."

"We don't know. One of our people believes that because of the density of high-speed motorbikes on Saigon's streets, they may be testing the software and its related hardware under the guise of their new motorbike assembly plant."

Con Ma thought for a moment. "Five parts, you say?"

"Yes, you transmitted one of them from the tech facility," Zheng said. "We don't know which one it was. The next piece will be delivered in Dubai. You will be informed when we know where." A soft burr came from the cell phone on the desk, and Zheng looked at its screen. "The Chairwoman needs you now. I have been asked to give you this. Please read it now."

Con Ma took the envelope, opened it, and read the enclosed note. He looked up and met Zheng's eyes before returning the paper back inside the envelope and setting it on the desk.

"Do you understand?" Zheng asked.

"Are you insulting me?" Con Ma replied.

Zheng smiled. "Shall we?"

Together they left Zheng's office and crossed through a complex of smaller cubicles. They stopped at a door that Zheng opened, and he allowed Con Ma to enter before him.

Along each side of the conference room's long central table sat five men, ten total. At the head was an elegantly dressed woman. When she saw Con Ma, she immediately stood and walked past the men and took him by the arm. Zheng walked around the table and took a seat. Three attendants stood at attention to one side of the entry.

"Come, my friend," the Chairwoman said. "Sit next to me." She led Con Ma to a seat near her. "Please, here." She waved her long, elegant fingers to the tall, black-leather chair. "There, this is much better." She turned to the attendants. "You may leave. Please return with lunch at precisely twelve forty-five."

Con Ma studied the three as they left, looking for any sign from them that something was out of the ordinary. Seeing none, he turned back to the Chairwoman. She was busily clicking buttons on a control panel that had risen out of the table. At one point the windows turned opaque, and he heard a nearly imperceptible hum in the air—eavesdropping, even by laser microphone, was now impossible.

"Good morning, gentlemen," the Chairwoman said. "Welcome to this year's first quarterly meeting of Dark Star Security. Thank you all for attending. I would like to introduce Con Ma, one of my, and our, most trusted operatives."

He looked at the men flanking the table.

They were all ruthless businessmen. Some ran their own international corporations, some steered powerful regional gangs, and others were senior members of the Red Army. The Chairwoman had brought them all together by, as it was said in an old American movie, making them offers they could not refuse. Through Dark Star, their diverse business interests had profitably expanded across China and the world.

"Gentlemen, Con Ma was responsible for successfully retrieving documents in Zurich last year. Mr. Chin is now using them to modify his products." She nodded to one of the men. "Our return on this investment is twenty percent and will be an ongoing return through the product's life. Mr. Chin, we of course hope that it is a long life. Con Ma has been primarily responsible for many of your various companies' products and their technological advancements."

She looked down each side of the table, and each of the men acknowledged her attention.

"I will not bother you with many of the other successes of Con Ma," the Chairwoman went on. "Be assured he is working diligently on all of our behalf."

Con Ma kept his eyes focused on the far wall and Zheng. In his periphery, however, he could feel the men glancing at him but avoiding direct eye contact. They knew he was an assassin.

"As per our bylaws," the Chairwoman said, "your lists of leads and acquisition opportunities are due in three weeks. Please submit them through your secured email accounts." The men nodded in assent, and, satisfied, the Chairwoman moved on. "Last year your various needs required us to expend over fifty-three million yuan in research, materials, and transportation costs. Our profit was just over one hundred and thirteen million yuan, an excellent margin. At midnight, profit shares will be wired to your designated accounts."

Con Ma continued to sit stoically as the Chairwoman looked again down the table. While not privy to the details, he knew that the profits the Chairwoman referred to were accomplished through the application of stolen information, designs, products, and technology—much of which Con Ma himself had procured—that had been licensed to the companies these men controlled or influenced. Each member's profit share was linked according to the product or technology acquired and its value. These men were parasites living off the work of others. Con Ma didn't care. He lived off that work as well. Theirs was a symbiotic relationship—why kill the goose as long as it still laid golden eggs?

The Chairwoman opened a folder, removed a small piece of paper, and handed it to Con Ma. He read it and with no expression stood and took a step back from the chair and waited.

"Gentlemen, we have a problem, an extremely vexing one. It seems that one of you has decided to circumvent our contracts and enlist the services of another security firm. They are an excellent company and have, within their own circle of business interests, competent personnel and resources. I admire them. They are exceptional. Unfortunately, you and I have contracts between us, and I do not accept one-sided terminations. Proper procedures must be followed, and you all know there are no exceptions. Isn't that correct, General Liu?"

The general jumped. His chair flew backward and slammed against the wall. Before he could say anything, Con Ma had walked up behind him, seized him across the shoulders, and driven a thin, six-inch blade of razor-sharp steel upward into his head just below the hairline on the back of his neck. In one motion, Con Ma grabbed the dead man by his collar, pulled the chair back to the table, and sat him in his seat. He left the blade, with its jade-green handle, where he had implanted it. He then returned to his seat.

The men around the table were stunned. Each, in turn, looked at the Chairwoman, Con Ma, and the deceased general. None moved.

"The general and I disagreed on this point," the Chairwoman said. "I do not like violations of our business arrangements. We have contracts; I expect my partners to honor them. The next item on my agenda is General Feng's request"—she nodded to the man seated immediately to her right—"for information and designs about the latest drone technology being developed for NATO. As you know, NATO does not have its own military, or its own weapons, but relies on its state partners to provide such men and facilities as required. The exception to this is their new drone program, which is a derivative of the United States' Predator program. NATO is making modifications to this system and adapting it as their own. General Feng has requested this information and has offered an excellent percentage once he has the data and plans. I have decided to accept this request on your behalf, General. I will, when the time is right, pass on information ensuring that you understand the magnitude of the contract. This technology is different from the system we acquired earlier in the year that allowed the development of the cycle-drone."

She looked at the man seated next to General Feng. "Mr. Deng, after viewing the prototypes, I am pleased. You have created a beautiful machine. And thank you, Con Ma, for actions in regard to that acquisition."

The Chairwoman smiled at Mr. Deng, then looked at Con Ma and nodded. He rose from his chair, and the room grew quieter. As he walked to the door, the four men to his immediate right twitched one after the other. When he reached the door, he was certain he heard a collective sigh. He quietly closed the door behind him.

CHAPTER 10

Ho Chi Minh City, Vietnam

Detective Tran Phan stood on the riverfront overlook that had a sweeping view up and down the Saigon River. He finished his cigarette and crushed it on the paving stones.

With a dozen active cases on his desk, his most troubling was over the intransigence of Como Motors and their lack of assistance. Two dead Americans, a fire-damaged property, and probably something valuable stolen, and still the Italians and Americans were not forthcoming. He was also disappointed by his own department's inertia. The dead were not Vietnamese and as such fell into an investigative limbo. When these dead became important for political reasons, they would become important for legal reasons. He'd seen it before, and it did not make him happy. But then again, he could not remember the last time he was happy on the job. He wanted to find this vulture—as he called him—and throw him in jail. Close the case and move on. It gnawed at him.

All he had were the victims' names; the name of the facility owner, Como Motors, a business connected to a new motorbike manufacturing plant in Vietnam; and the website of the American security company, Teton Security and Defense. TSD had eventually handed over fifteen minutes of poor surveillance film and grainy photographs of the thief and murderer, whose face was hidden behind a motorbike helmet. The partially melted device found in the pot of plastic flowers was a dead end. His people could make nothing of it. One of his technical staff said it had a Chinese appearance about it, but then again most everything nowadays was made in China. Phan could not directly connect the device to the murders, and the warehouse owners declared it was theirs. At their insistence, he returned it to them.

He lit his third cigarette. He had other cases: a couple of murders in District 3 that looked gang related, an unidentified body found a few weeks ago in the river with a fatal knife wound on the back of his head, and a dozen others assigned to his office and staff. Each day new folders were added to the pile on his desk. Why the warehouse case irritated him more than the others, he wasn't sure. Maybe it was the fact the dead men were *tâys*—the old term for Westerners or Europeans—and he was half-Western himself. Or maybe it was because this TSD had thrown a blanket over everything. How to pull that blanket off had become as much an issue as the case itself.

His phone vibrated. It read *Jess*. He smiled and answered. "Good morning. Sorry I had to leave so early."

"Is everything okay?" she asked. "I wanted to make you breakfast."

"Nothing but the usual. Admin has dumped a few more cases on my desk. You can make me breakfast tomorrow."

"You'll be fine. Don't forget that Kha has his recital tonight. You promised to be there."

"I've not forgotten, but if I hear that Vivaldi piece one more time—"

"Don't say it. He loves the violin, and besides, it's all your fault."

"I should have gotten him drums," he said. "Will Kim be there, without that weird boyfriend of hers?" He looked at his watch.

"Yes, and probably yes. He's okay. You don't like him because he's studying ecology."

"There're better jobs."

"She likes him. Be thankful he doesn't have tattoos up and down his arms."

He took a drag of his cigarette, exhaled. "Small victories. I should be home at six. We can go together."

"Good, love you. And stop smoking so much."

Phan clicked off, took one last drag, and crushed the cigarette butt with his heel next to the others. *Twenty-six years married,* he thought, almost as long as he'd been with the HCMC police department. Jessica Nguyen was, like him, an Amerasian. Her father, an American GI from Montana, had been killed a month after he'd promised to marry Jessica's pregnant mother. Like Phan, Jessica had grown up in the tough times of racial hatred after the war, but nevertheless they were lucky: they had strong mothers and support from the local Catholic church. And a cop on the beat in Phan's neighborhood had taken an interest in him, kept him out of the local gangs. When he was old enough Phan had joined the police. His ability to speak three languages—Vietnamese, French, and English—had helped.

His phone vibrated again. It was a text; the coroner would call him in twenty minutes.

The drive along the Rach Ben Nghe canal took Phan past the new high-rises under construction across the waterway. Throughout HCMC, gleaming new residential towers emerged from the middle of the old districts. To him, the massive complexes spelled trouble. The city's character was being pushed away, ripped down, or subsumed by this new development. Indiscreet and intrusive, these complexes did not look like Vietnam. They looked more like the exploding coastal cities of China. And the glassy surfaces of HCMC's rivers and canals were now bridged by bizarre concrete structures, beneath which were moored wooden houseboats that were old—ancient, even—before the war. He did not like any of it.

His phone rang: the coroner. "Phan." He clicked to the speaker.

"How are you this morning, Detective?"

"Grumpy."

"Good, normal for you. I've analyzed the wounds from those two Anglo killings in the warehouse district. Very interesting. Can you stop by later?"

"Interesting how?"

"The residue and fragments. Haven't seen anything like it. Hard to explain over the phone. You need to see it."

Phan looked at his watch. "Two o'clock?"

"See you then." The coroner clicked off.

Now what? Some exotic poison? Secret death-ray stuff?

He parked the Toyota police cruiser in front of a favorite pho noodle joint across the street from the police station and sat at a small table. The incessant buzz of motorbikes filled the canyon of buildings on Tran Hung Dao. It was like every other street in HCMC—an annoying burring that never quieted. He treated himself to a midmorning beer with the noodles. The restaurant, which was really just a few tables along the street, was smaller than his mother's noodle joint on the other side of the city.

At precisely two, Phan stood in the tiled hallway of the Center for Forensic Medicine and waited. The coroner's assistant had said he would find the doctor.

Ten minutes later the double doors at the end of the corridor opened, and a small man in a white lab coat appeared, peeling latex gloves off his hands. When he stopped before Phan, he extended his right hand.

"Good to see you again, Detective. Sorry I'm late. The wagon dropped off two bodies; I had to log them in. Unfortunately, they were not recently departed."

Phan thought he'd noticed a distinct odor that arrived with the doctor.

"I understand. What do you have on the two Americans?"

"I need coffee. Follow me to my office—we can talk there."

The two men walked through the forensic center, the largest in HCMC. Two of the side corridors were lined with gurneys and mounded sheets. It was no mystery what lay underneath. The doctor pointed to a chair in the corner of his office, then popped a Nespresso pod into the machine behind his desk.

"Love this thing," he said as he sat. "At least I can expect the coffee to be good."

The machine swooshed and gurgled.

"Would you like a cup?"

"I drink tea."

"I know that, but this could change your mind."

"I'm fine. About the *tâys*?"

The doctor spun on his chair, removed the cup, and grabbed a folder on the credenza behind him. "I think you will find this interesting. The two bodies were finally released and transported back to America a week ago. Before they left, I took tissue samples and detailed photographs of the bodies, as well as X-rays. An explosion caused the wounds, a blow easily a thousand times more powerful than a mere bullet's. Analysis showed crushed and burnt tissue, most from intense explosive pressure and heat. The X-rays revealed minute shards of steel in the wounds, plus high levels of nitrates and other explosive residues, some my equipment can't identify. There were also remains of some type of electronic device—circuits, the kind found in a silicon chip. But this chip was the size of a pinhead. Whatever its purpose, it was destroyed in the explosion. I assume this circuitry may have triggered the explosion when it contacted the body. Different from anything I've seen—and I've seen a lot of bullet and explosive wounds in my career." He handed Phan the folder. "Whatever it was, it packed a fatal wallop. Even if the victims were just winged, the trauma would most likely be fatal."

Phan looked through the pages and the photos. They brought him back to the morning at the warehouse, reminded him of the severity of the wounds. At the time he'd thought they were from something larger, like a grenade. The doctor was telling him it was a bullet, high-tech to be sure, but a bullet.

"Incredible, and you say you've not heard of this type of weapon?"

"That was going to be my question to you, Detective. No, I haven't seen or even heard of one. And from the look on your face, you haven't either."

"None that I can think of. A science fiction movie, perhaps. Maybe this cartridge and weapon is a military experiment."

"It doesn't change my findings of homicide, and it certainly doesn't get you closer to finding this killer. The one thing I can tell you: he is not your garden-variety assassin. This man has serious backing from some government, and it is not Vietnamese—at least I don't think so. This technology can only be found in six or eight countries."

"What are your first two guesses?"

"The Russians and British may be interested in these things. However, here in Vietnam, my guess is the US and China—I lean toward the Chinese."

Phan pushed the folder back across the desk. "Can you send me a copy?"

"This one is yours. What else do you need?"

"To keep this information quiet. I'll let you know when to release it. If it's lost for a while, I wouldn't mind. When I interviewed the employee from the on-site security company, he didn't seem as alarmed as he should have been. I wonder why." He tapped the top of the file. "Excellent work. Thank you."

"That's why I'm paid so well."

"At least they gave you that fancy coffee maker," Phan said.

"I bought that myself."

CHAPTER 11

Dallas, Texas

The plane lurched to a stop at the gate of Dallas Fort Worth International Airport, and the seat belt sign dinged. Rain left streaks on the small window next to Alex's seat, and flashes of lightning lit up the darkening sky above the runways and taxiways. She slipped her phone into her backpack and put away her headphones. When it was her turn, she pulled the single bag out of the overhead compartment and trundled down the airplane's narrow Jetway and into the concourse. Less than a month earlier she'd done the same thing in Venice.

What am I getting myself into this time?

A man in a dark suit, with a chiseled, tan face and military haircut, stood at the bottom of the escalator from the gates. He held up an iPad whose screen read "A. Polonia." Alex walked toward him.

He smiled before she could say anything. "Welcome to Dallas, Ms. Polonia. I'm Jimmy Cortez."

"Mr. Cortez, a pleasure."

"Bags?"

"Just the one," she said, pointing to the wheeled bag at her feet.

"Good; please place your hand on this iPad."

Alex set her backpack on the floor and placed her right hand on the screen. The glass flashed, and she removed her hand. Cortez looked at the screen, then smiled.

"The SUV is at the curb, assuming that they haven't made Bostich go once around the airport."

"Bostich?"

"He's our driver this evening and one of the probies. Everyone works when they get here."

"Probie? God, I haven't heard that since the academy."

"Get used to it, because once you step into the SUV, that is what you are: a probational."

The rain continued as they drove north and darkness fell. When the sign said "Denton," they exited and, without the freeway lights, lost themselves in the black night. Cortez said nothing as Alex stared at her reflection in the window as they negotiated a series of highways and back roads, each narrower than the last. They turned off the two-lane road and onto what looked like a driveway. Five minutes later, the SUV slowed and a gatehouse appeared. The gate ahead was iron and looked as if it could withstand the impact of most lightweight vehicles. A guard stood at the entry.

Bostich lowered the SUV's window. "Three, sir."

The guard walked to the vehicle. The windows all lowered, and rain splashed in on Alex's face. A bright light flashed through the interior. She turned and saw another guard on the opposite side of the SUV, an AR15 clipped to his chest. His flashlight provided a crosslight of the interior.

"You are good to go, sir," the guard said.

"Thank you," Cortez said as the windows closed. The gates ahead swung open.

"Tight security," Alex said.

"We've been under surveillance since we crossed onto the property a mile back. This vehicle has been infrared scanned, had its onboard sensors checked, and has been sniffed for explosives. The works." A big ranch house came into view. "Here we are. Bostich will take care of your bag."

Bostich parked the vehicle in the circular courtyard that faced a well-lit porch. Alex and Cortez walked through the entry's double doors and into the foyer. Chris Campbell stood on the slate floor, a tumbler in his hand.

"Ms. Polonia, welcome to Texas."

Two weeks later, the Jeep lurched hard to the left, then the right, and a second later Alex's butt rose and fell two inches off the rear seat. Lucky for her, her seat belt kept her from banging her head.

"You drive like my mother!" she yelled to the front seat. "Potholes are her specialty."

The driver didn't respond, but he did slow down a bit.

Alex settled back into the seat. She was alone with the driver. She rubbed her arm—she'd lost count of the number of injections. A tetanus booster, a flu shot, a pneumonia and zoster shot, and a series that included hepatitis A and B, typhoid, polio, yellow fever, and rabies. And God knows how much blood they'd taken.

"Rabies?" she had asked the nurse. "Why the hell would I need a rabies shot?"

"That's up to the boss," the nurse had replied. "I just give 'em. Be careful. Your arm will be sore for a week."

The physicals and initial training at Campbell's ranch lasted two weeks. After the physicals, blood draws, and cardiac tests—first a treadmill from hell to measure endurance and recovery analysis, then some demented running and weightlifting combination—she was exhausted. No slack was given. She was sure—after what the psychologist asked about her past, her time in the police, and her family issues—that her head was now shrunk three sizes. Her greatest thrill was the loss of ten pounds.

If Javier liked me before, he'd kill for me now.

The Jeep's next bump and lurch forced Alex to grab the front seat and made her glare at the driver in the mirror. A veteran TSD team leader, Jake Dumas had arrived two days earlier.

"Kandahar was ten times worse," he said as he swerved to avoid the next hole. "And there, the Taliban were shooting at us, and I was going twice as fast, hoping to avoid the party gifts they left along the road."

After the training she'd been through, she was pleased that her forty-two-year-old body could still function, even though in the morning it protested loudly and with pain. Her mile time was just shy of eight minutes—not bad—and she bench-pressed eighty pounds. Sure, the other boys and girls—as she called them—pressed three times that and ran six-and-a-half-minute miles, but she was still pleased. After all, it wasn't as if she ever aspired to be an avenging Amazon cop or Wonder Woman.

The night before, she had read through a thick manual the weapons officer had handed her. The cover simply read "Weapons" at the top. At the bottom: "Property of Teton Security and Defense, Ltd." A quick perusal of the table of contents was daunting: pistols, M9, M11, M17; submachine guns, MP5; assault rifles/carbines, M16, M4, HK416; shotguns, 500 MILS, M1014, M870; machine guns, M249 SAW, H&K MG4; Browning M2, Mk14, M110, M2010, M107. Under "Miscellaneous" were grenade launchers, grenades, smoke grenades, flash-bangs, and an assortment of antitank weapons. She checked again and was disappointed that there was nothing on mortars, tanks, Howitzers, self-propelled rocket launchers, or low-yield tactical nuclear weapons.

"Holy hell, what did I get myself into?" she had whispered to herself as she fell asleep.

"The Country Club, as Mr. Campbell calls it," Dumas said now as he navigated another swale cut through the road, "is two miles ahead."

"What do *you* call it, Jake?" Alex asked.

"The playground." His eyes twinkled in the mirror.

The terrain changed from flat to hilly to rugged and nearly treeless. Scrub growth dotted the dry hills. A rusted sign on Highway 82 read "King County." As far as she could tell, she was on the far side of the moon.

"There are fewer than three hundred people in this whole county," Dumas said. "That's one person for every three square miles. It can be a quiet and lonely place. Except when the wind blows—then you hold on to whatever you can."

The road curved around another hill covered in dried brush. A few cattle stood idly in the wash to Alex's right, their horns six feet across at least.

"Those are some of the boss's longhorns. He has a couple of hundred scattered about the ranch. There's some Hereford and Brangus out here somewhere as well. It's a working ranch as well as our training facility."

On a rise, Dumas pulled the Jeep to the roadside and got out.

Alex followed. "Where the hell are we?"

"The center of the ranch. It goes about three miles that way and four the other. North to south, it's about ten miles. Seventy square miles total, or about forty-five thousand acres. A fair size by Texas standards, but it wouldn't make the top fifty." Dumas pointed into a wide wash that split the range of hills and formed a valley, where there was a cluster of red-tiled roofs. "The ranch complex is down there. It used to be a cattleman's ranch built in the 1880s. The boss has improved it. You will have full access here; nothing is off-limits. Two things to be careful of, though: snakes and wild pigs. The rattlers will let you know when they're pissed; the pigs will just run you down and slice you open. Climbing a tree is the best defense, but there are barely a dozen trees on the whole ranch. If you're armed and one of those porkers charge you, don't be afraid to take 'em out. They're mighty tasty." He smiled. "There's also the usual scorpions, coyotes, fire ants, and wasps. Alex, it's the Wild West here—so be careful."

Early the next morning, Alex, after finishing her kitchen duties, stood on the terrace of the main house of the Country Club, which was a lot different from the house she'd arrived at when she landed two weeks earlier. All was silent. A spring chill still sat in the air, and she breathed it in. The day before had reached eighty degrees yet quickly cooled after sundown. Above, the lights of a jet plane flashed red and green among the million stars that still filled the sky.

"Up early?" Dumas asked.

"Yes, chores done and a little keyed up. I've never seen so many stars. There's too much light and junk in the air around Cleveland. We see the big ones, but not all this."

"I've been around the world, Polonia. Fought in some tough spots, but this is the most peaceful place I've ever been. After an operation, I look forward to coming back. Compared to the world, this place is clean and simple. And when there's a light zephyr, you can almost feel your heart sing. I like that—it's the sound of peace."

"You said you were an Army Ranger. Why did you leave?"

"What I tell myself is that I was getting too old to beat the bushes and wander the streets of Afghanistan, Iraq, or some other shithole. I like my independence, and the only way to stay in the army was to shoot for an oakleaf."

"Oakleaf?"

"Major and higher rank. I'm here because I couldn't stand the thought of sitting in an office all day. I met the boss in 2010, during one of our joint military and civilian operations in Afghanistan. His people were guarding a trio of businessmen from Pittsburgh who were trying to sell steel pipe to the Afghans. The boss and I hit it off. He said when I was ready, come and see him. I did, and here I am."

"Sounds like it'd be hard to settle down," she said.

"No, I'm not the settle-down type—always on the move. Someday, who knows?"

"You're not married?"

"No. Sorry about the problems that your ex piled on you."

"You know about all that?"

"I know everything about my people. I don't like surprises. They put people in danger. You good with all that crap your ex left you?"

"Other than wanting to shoot the son of a bitch, yes, I'm good."

"I like your thinking. There's some fun stuff we'll be training with today. Imagine him at the business end of a Browning." A chime rang through the complex. "Breakfast. I'm buying."

The Country Club's dining room held forty people. Alex was introduced to four other team members that were at the facility for additional training and rest. Dumas also introduced the range officer, the weapons officer, and other support staff. She had been assigned to KP. She'd already met the cook and some of the custodial staff. She began to realize the serious scale and scope of Teton Security and Defense.

A pyramid-shaped array of photos was displayed on the wall at the end of the dining room. Christopher Campbell's picture was at the top. In descending order were ten others, eight men and two women, and under them more photos. At the top of these photos were the teams' names: Black, White, Red, Green, Blue, Violet, Orange, Charlie, Baker, and the last, Flashlight. Some of the teams had two subgroups under them, A and B. Each team ranged from fifteen to thirty members. None of the photos had names. Two of the photos under the Red Team had a black ribbon pinned to them. She leaned in and looked at the two photos.

"Dead," Dumas said. "Actually, murdered."

She looked up at the pyramid. Jake Dumas's picture was on th second tier, over Red Team, Group A and Group B, as well as Charlie Team.

"Murdered?"

"Yes, in Saigon. A man broke into a facility we were guarding, our people were killed. We're working on it. The boss will bring you up-to-date when he thinks the time's right."

For the rest of the week, they fired hundreds of rounds in the morning, then thousands in the afternoon. This was very different from the police pistol range in Cleveland. Alex relearned how to break down and rebuild her weapons, reload magazines in the dark, and shoot from every imaginable and unimaginable position. By the end of the week, her hands were swollen and her shoulders ached.

When she wasn't at the range, she was taking a crash course in digital technology. That was interesting, but sadly most was wasted on her because she was so tired in the evening. They flipped the order the following week, and the tech stuff was first on the daily agenda and resulted in a much higher absorption rate. TSD did not want their tactical people to become programmers or hackers—those were skills reserved for others in the company—but they did want them to be able to recognize the software and tech they saw and know how to interpret what they found.

The device that the killer used in Saigon was discussed. The instructor described it as a storage device, a key, and a transmitter. "It has a high-speed USB plug that, when inserted into a specific device, such as a server port, floods the system with a virus that extracts everything and places that data in the unit's hard memory. When removed, the device would, through a satellite connection, automatically transmit the data. It's fast too, like downloading ten digital movies in one minute. That's where the greatest advance is—its speed. We assume that when the data receipt was acknowledged, the device was told to self-destruct. As you can see from the photo, it melted using a thermal implant. However, much of what the device does is based on assumptions. This is extremely sophisticated and dangerous."

"Do we know what the information was?" one of the men asked, a question Alex also had.

"Here at Teton it is not our place to ask that question of our clients," she continued. "We failed here, and two operatives and friends lost their lives. The client was extremely upset. They're now doing everything they can to prepare for possible attacks and product compromises in the future. We're helping as much as we can. This was unacceptable and may cost us dearly."

"Is there a way to disable the device before it destroys itself?" Alex asked.

"We're working on it. It used a small thermite plug—smaller than a hearing aid battery—and igniter. It burned at more than twenty-five hundred degrees. Once the thermite starts, there's no stopping it."

"Did you retrieve the device?" another asked.

"No, the local police found it. When they reached a dead end, we asked for it back. We claimed that the device belonged to our client."

"Whoever it was, he killed our people!" said another.

"Yes, with what appears to be a new type of weapon. Evidence and forensics say a large-caliber bullet with an explosive tip. The explosive is of the tetryl family as well as another compound we are studying. Casings were not found, so we assume, like with a revolver, the casing remained with the weapon. It is an extremely dangerous weapon."

That evening, Alex studied the wall of photos and wondered why men and women took on a job like this. In fact, she wondered why she did.

CHAPTER 12

As they finished breakfast the next morning, the familiar *whoomp-whoomp* of a helicopter's blades filled the chill Texas air. Alex watched the landing through the large plate glass windows of the dining room. She smiled when she saw Chris Campbell walking toward the complex with the training director at his side, Jimmy Cortez.

She finished her breakfast and headed to the other side of the room and out onto a porch that overlooked the wash that spread out below the complex. A diminutive and wiry Latino man was leading two horses to the porch from the stables. He stopped at the railing and expertly flipped the reins over the top bar.

"Good morning, Senor Diaz. How are you?"

"Very good, Senorita Alex."

"Someone going for a ride?"

"*Sí.*"

"Beautiful horses."

"*Gracias.* The gray is called Excalibur, the bay Lucifer."

"That's ominous."

"Oh, they are good boys. But you have to keep reminding them who's the boss."

Alex turned to the sound of the dining room door sliding open. Chris Campbell stood on the porch.

"Good morning, Alex. You're enjoying your stay?"

"Yes, but I hurt in places I've never hurt before."

"Good. I'll add some new ones. Saddle up."

"What? On those?" She pointed.

"Yes, on those. You take Lucifer. I'm going to give you a crash course in horse-a-nomics. Besides, we need to talk, and I need to ride. It's been a month since I've been here, and I want to look around. José will give you a leg up and explain the basics. After that you're on your own."

Alex looked at the bay and thought the week could not have gotten any worse. Chris took the reins of Excalibur and nonchalantly landed himself in the saddle. José led Lucifer to the edge of the porch and instructed Alex where to place her foot and what to do next.

"Seat belt?"

Chris smiled. "Senor Diaz, lead her around a bit, and let her get the feel of the seat."

Alex looked down at the porch, where four other people had gathered.

"Just don't let him get ahead of you," one woman said with a laugh. "Remember you're in control. You have the leads."

"Thanks," Alex replied optimistically, and then, holding the reins, sat as still as possible as Diaz walked the horse in circles. After each lap, she felt a little more comfortable. She did the last two on her own.

"A natural cowgirl," another said.

"Follow me, but hold on tight to the horn," Chris said, and spurred his horse and trotted out of the courtyard—Lucifer in pursuit, Alex in panic.

For the next ten minutes, Chris led the way. Alex had settled in, and the panic had subsided—some. Chris slowed his horse up to Lucifer's right flank and trotted alongside Alex.

"Not bad. I've seen grown men who'd faced the Taliban quake with fear riding a horse. Nice seat, nice job."

"I once rode a pony when I was a kid. This is the first time since then."

"Well done, city girl. After the next few hours, your ass will be as sore as a bad boy's bottom."

"Nice."

Alex rode silently for the next half hour. Chris pointed out features and landmarks on the ranch. An arroyo here and a steep cliff there—each seemed to have a story behind it. He told her about the longhorns and why he'd bought them, and how many head of cattle were living on the spread.

On a high ridge that overlooked the ranch, Chris climbed down and held the reins as Alex followed. Together they walked to the edge of a ragged cliff of sharp rock and gray-green juniper. A delightful fragrance filled the morning air.

"What's that I smell?" Alex asked.

He seemed to think on it a moment. "Juniper, for sure. Sage. A bit of sumac too. This morning's humidity is just enough to perfume the breeze. Can't get enough of it."

"You're proud of what you've done," Alex said. "I can see that."

"I am, thanks. I've had a little luck and a lot of help from good people—who, I've discovered, are hard to find."

"Being a Cleveland cop reinforces what you said. I've given up trying to figure out why people are bad. I now take it as a given and work accordingly. Many deserve a cage, and I've sadly come to the conclusion that some of them deserve to be dead. But that's not my call."

"Do you mind?" Chris asked, holding up a cigar. "Bourbon and cigars are my worst vices."

Alex thought of her father and smiled. "No, I don't mind. Just as long as you keep them to once or twice a week."

"Yes, Mother," Chris said with a laugh. "But truth be told, I do a good job of keeping it in check." He lit the maduro. "A few weeks ago, I consoled the parents of the two men killed in Saigon. Heartbreaking.

I hate that part of the job. The insurance never makes up for the loss. Mercifully, neither were married or had children."

"Jake told me about it and the device that was left."

"If I find the killer, he's dead." Chris took a long draw on the cigar and blew the smoke out into the breeze that rose up the face of the canyon. "But that's not what I want to talk to you about. We have a new client—actually an old client, but the individual within their company is new to us. I'm putting a team together for him."

"The people in your company are tough," Alex said, unsure where Campbell was headed. "I admire them."

"Yes, they are, and don't forget that they're your people now. Nonetheless, they are warriors learning to be guards and facilitators; it's hard for many of them. They need to learn patience. There's not enough excitement, as I say. Your mindset is different; patience is built into a cop. They deal with soldiers and an enemy; you deal with civilians and bad guys. Big difference. You would have a hard time learning to kill on command—you are both different folks learning different jobs."

"I saw that in the academy, especially with ex-military applicants. It's hard to overcome."

"I brought Javier out here," Chris said, the smoke from his cigar snatched away by a gust. "I was trying to get him to join me for the umpteenth time. He turned me down, again. I understood, but he would be an incredible asset."

"He is a Texan, after all," she answered.

"Yes, there's that. Alex, I'm offering you an offshore assignment. You'll be working with one of my most experienced men, Harry Karns with the Southeast Asia Red Team, which Jake Dumas oversees. The initial assignment and commitment is for six months and may go longer if they exercise the various options in the contract. The thirty-days-on-then-off policy doesn't apply here. Your first break will be after ninety days. It's also a babysitting job."

"Okay."

"The overall client is Como Motors out of Milan, Italy. They're building a new motorbike plant in Saigon. The plant manager is Nevio Lucchese. Seems like a good guy, hardworking. Has come up through the ranks of the company."

"You said he's new?"

"New to us. We've worked with his boss and other managers in Taiwan and South America. This is Mr. Lucchese's first management job in Asia. The company's owner has always committed to his managers a high degree of personal security, at least for the first year of an assignment. By then, the business will have trained local people to handle the security."

"This needs two people?"

"Lucchese is bringing his wife and two children," Chris explained. "It's one of the company's benefits in politically stable countries. She is Ilaria Lucchese. The kids are Paolo, fifteen, and Gianna, twelve. Her family has a significant controlling interest in Como Motors."

"You weren't kidding when you said babysitting. Saigon? Venice was the first time I'd even been out of the country. Now you're sending me halfway around the world. When will I meet Karns?"

"When you reach Dubai."

"Dubai?"

"It will be while you're in transit with the family. He'll come in from Vietnam and help you move the family into Ho Chi Minh City. But the family's security is your job. Karns will be focused on Nevio Lucchese. Karns is a year older than you. Grew up in LA. A SEAL, left the navy with the rank of commander. He was bored and applied to us. Speaks fluent Vietnamese—he's an Amerasian, in fact, half-Vietnamese and half–African American. Speaks some Pashto too, and some Arabic. He, unlike you, has traveled the world on Uncle Sam's dollar. Over a beer, he'll tell you his whole life's tragic tale. My guess is that he's only telling half of it."

"You said this is Dumas's team."

"Yes, Jake runs Southeast Asia. He's one of the few team leaders with two teams, Red and Charlie. Charlie includes Australia and New Zealand. Red is split into two groups, A and B. Hong Kong divides the region east and west, with Vietnam in Group A. His home base for both teams is Hong Kong. You may get to meet some of the team members during your deployment."

She paused for a moment. "So, this is real?"

"Yes, Alex. Very real. Are you interested?"

Alex looked out across the canyon to the opposite side, and her eye caught movement. A coyote loped through the scrub, stopping every dozen steps to look around. It froze when one of the horses whinnied. Alex wondered whether the scruffy animal might think the horse a possible meal. Then the coyote turned its snout up into the air, sniffed, and continued its ramble along the ridge until it disappeared.

She took a deep breath, and then thought of the Air and Space Museum. "As someone once said: there's a time when you have to learn to fly."

CHAPTER 13

Cleveland, Ohio

Alex stood in the chill of the early-May morning, looking through the front window of her parents' home. The view was through the living room into the kitchen. Her father's silhouette crossed the room, a cup in his hand. He was heading for his toast, a ritual that never varied for as long as she could remember.

After the rough late-night drive across Texas, and an early-morning flight from Dallas to Cleveland, her stomach grumbled. She needed some home cooking, badly. She climbed the steps, took a deep breath, and rang the bell. The chimes rang with the soft sounds of church bells; she remembered when her father installed them some twenty-odd years ago. Beyond the door, she heard footsteps on the oak floor. She took another breath as the door opened.

"Well, don't just stand there," her father said, reaching for her bag. "Why didn't you use your key?"

"It's at the house. I came directly from the airport. Mom up?"

"In a while. Always me, then her—never changes. Coffee? You want breakfast?"

"Yes, famished. First coffee. I just landed an hour ago. Early flight. I'm exhausted."

They crossed the living room to the kitchen doorway. The smell of toast and warm peanut butter filled the kitchen. Her father stuck a white mug in her hand.

"They make you drink your coffee with cream in Texas?"

"No, Dad, but I did learn to stir it with a strand of barbed wire," she said with a smile. "Some bread left?"

"Toast it is." He dropped two pieces in and pushed the black handle down. "Nice tan—was it warm?"

"Warm enough, but the real heat doesn't come for another month. We were outside a lot."

"Your face—the color suits you. You look good. Lose a little weight?"

"A bit, yeah."

A minute or two later he dropped the toast on a plate and slid it to her along with the jar of peanut butter.

Alex raised her cup. "To old times and another pennant for the Tribe."

"Not good when the day starts out so maudlin." He took a bite of his toast and sipped his coffee. "They treat you right?"

"Dad, I've only had a couple of jobs in my life, and half my life has been with CPD. I didn't know what to expect going to Dallas. They seemed all mysterious and secretive. But I think I'm going to like it. My boss is great, and the people around him are serious, direct, professional, and actually nice. I was shocked. I expected some type of testosterone-fueled military organization with all sorts of tough-guy attitudes. I was mistaken."

"Your friend from the CIA didn't steer you wrong?"

"Javier? No, Dad, he didn't steer me wrong."

"Look who's home," a voice said from the hallway. Pulling her housecoat tight, Alex's mother smiled and walked into the kitchen.

She hugged her daughter, then shot a dozen rapid-fire questions. Alex answered the last first: "I have a week and a half before I report."

"Report?" her father asked. "Report where?"

"Milan, Italy. I've been assigned to protect a family that's transferring from Milan to the Far East."

"Protect?" her mother asked. "Are you now a bodyguard or something like that?" There was an edge to the question.

"Yes and no, and I can't tell you much more than that. I'm to assist and make sure everything goes smoothly. The assignment is six months. Then I'll see what happens."

"You said the Far East," her mother said. "China? Japan?"

"No, not those, and that's all I can say."

Her father stared at her, and a strange look grew on his face. "Saigon? You're going to Saigon?"

"Yes, Dad, Saigon, but that's it, no more. I have a little more than a week to get my things together, take care of the house, buy some clothes and a few other personal things."

"You know your father spent time there during the war?"

"Yes, Mom, I know. From what they tell us, it's changed."

"What's the name of the company you'll be working with?" her father asked.

"I can't tell you—in fact, I might have said a little too much already—but you need to know some of it."

"Are there kids?"

"Yes, two, a boy and girl. They have a nanny, and when we reach Saigon there will be a cook and a housekeeper. My job will be to keep them safe."

"A babysitter," her father said with a snort. "You, once a detective on the Cleveland police force, and now, all due to that fool you married, a babysitter."

"I'm okay, don't worry."

"For God's sake, it's Vietnam," her father said. "It's a hot and fly-ridden place. From day one, I hated it."

Alex wanted to ask about the girl in Saigon, but she wasn't sure what her mom knew. No sense in asking a question that might cause her mother pain.

Her father refilled his cup and raised the pot to his daughter. She held her cup up, and he topped it off. He took a seat at the kitchen table. Then he surprised her.

"Back in 1971," he began, "I lived for nine months in an apartment in a part of Saigon they call District 1. I was with the First Logistical Command Unit. The port was a few miles away, and my bunkmates and I rode our bikes to the port for the first six months. We were handling the incoming and outgoing supplies for the army. By then, the war was winding down, and the equipment was mostly outgoing. Then a couple of GIs were shot dead by the Cong as they pedaled down the street. From then on, we were picked up by a jeep and driven to the port. Strange city, crowded with refugees and corruption—not sure what there was more of. A dozen times Vietnamese businessmen approached me with propositions. All I needed to do was divert some supplies to their businesses, and I would get a nice bundle of American dollars."

"Well, why didn't you, Roger?" her mother asked with a laugh. "We could have used it when we started out."

"A twenty-one-year-old kid thinks about a lot of things, and money's certainly one of them. But the word had gotten out that they'd caught a GI selling food and clothing to a local warlord or someone. He was court-martialed, spent five years in Leavenworth. If he'd sold weapons, I don't know what the army would have done to him. I wanted to go home, but not that bad."

"How long were you in Vietnam?" Alex asked.

"Just a little under a year. I was injured and sent home."

"I didn't know that," Alex said.

"It was nothing. I got well, your mother found me, and here we are."

There's a large gap in this simple summary, Alex thought. But their life was theirs—no reason to ask if he didn't want to tell.

"Saigon," her father sighed. "I've wondered what happened to that city after the communists took over. Not that they could be any worse than the local police, the ARVN, and the politicians back then. Probably deserved what they got. The last thing any of us GIs wanted was to die for the sons of bitches. You be careful."

"First thing on my list," Alex answered. She finished off her coffee in one big gulp. "If you don't mind, I'm going to shower and crash here until this afternoon. Then I'll go to the house. I'll pick us up something for dinner on the way home."

"Need some things washed, honey?" her mother asked.

"A few things. They're in my bag."

"You go and take your shower. I'll put some clean sheets on your bed." Her mother took her hand. "It's good to have you home."

"It's good to be home."

CHAPTER 14

As Alex was drying her hair, a piercing scream came from down the hallway. She wrapped a towel around herself and ran toward the yelling. It continued in quick panicked bursts. Reaching the end of the hallway, she almost knocked her father over. Her mother stood in the utility room, a look of terror on her face. The heel of her father's boot twisted on the floor.

"What the hell happened?" Alex asked.

"Nothing much," her father said with a laugh. "Just this." He raised his shoe. Crushed on the linoleum floor were the remains of the largest scorpion Alex had ever seen.

"That thing fell out of your bag," her mother said. "It could have killed me."

"Not that poor fellow," Alex said. "They were everywhere in Texas. Maybe a sting, but it wouldn't kill you. Sorry, Mom. I'll shake out the rest of the clothes just to make sure."

"You might put some clothes on first," her dad said.

Later, after Alex took a nap, there was a tap on her door.

"You decent?" her father asked.

"Come in."

He pushed the door open and leaned against the frame. Alex sat on the edge of her old bed, tying her jogging shoes.

"Going for a run? It's a beautiful day out."

"I can be easily discouraged."

"That thing gave your mother a fright."

"She okay?"

"Yeah, she went out shopping. She said that if you're spending more than a week at the house, you'll need some things." He paused and then rubbed his hands together. "I saw some scorpions in Vietnam that were as big as my hand. Mean suckers."

"You trying to convince me that I shouldn't go?"

"Not at all—I know you can handle yourself. Better than I did. I was young and naive. I'm amazed I survived." He walked into her room and pulled out the chair at her old school desk. "Do you have a few minutes? I don't want to stop your run. Do you need to get to the house?"

"No, I'm good. What's up?"

He removed a folded envelope from his pocket and set it on the desk. "You don't know the whole story about Vietnam. And now that you're going to Saigon, I think you need to know."

"You don't have to, Dad."

"There are things you need to know—and understand." He cleared his throat and took a breath. "Your mother and I never had secrets. There are things we kept to ourselves, away from you kids. And for the first few years of our marriage, there were things that happened in Vietnam I didn't tell your mother. When I finally did, it was as if a dark cloud had been finally brushed away. It helped me get through the bad times. She was my rock."

"I understand."

"You never asked me about any of it, but I knew that you knew something was going on. For the first few years after I came back, I was suffering, real bad. I hated the nights—my dreams kept coming back. She was there to help me through them. They call it post-traumatic stress disorder now. Back then they didn't know what to call it."

"Yes, even the CPD has therapists to help us get through the tough days after a shooting. Some try to tough it out. Usually it doesn't work. Even I have talked to the police shrink, so I think I understand."

"I didn't know."

"I tried to keep you and Mom away from it."

Her father took another deep breath and slowly let it out. "I was stationed in Germany, a good posting. I was handling shipping and receiving—pretty good at it. Almost a year. As close to a regular job as you could get. Every month, though, somebody was reassigned to Vietnam. Everyone was looking over their shoulder. We'd been fighting there for five or six years then. Nixon was now sending everyone home; the war would soon be over.

"I got my reassignment papers in December 1970. I went directly from Germany to Vietnam, with only a two-day Christmas pass to see your grandparents. The army wanted my butt in Saigon so fast even I was shocked at how quickly the army could process me. I landed on February the fifth, 1971, the first day of Tet, the Vietnamese holiday. For the Vietnamese, Tet is like Christmas and New Year's all rolled into one. But since the 1968 Tet Offensive by the Viet Cong, three years earlier, everyone was on edge when the holiday arrived. My command at the port handled everything for the troops, and I mean everything. The US was pulling out of the war. A lot of what we were doing then was collecting equipment and supplies and sending it back to the States. Some of it was transferred to the ARVN—that's the Army of the Republic of Vietnam. For us the war was over, or so we thought. There were still fifty or sixty thousand of us Americans in the areas around Saigon and maybe another hundred thousand in country. It was far more than the available housing could hold on the base. So, some of us had billets in town; I shared a place with maybe a dozen other guys."

"Sounds crowded."

"You have no idea. The apartment building was a few blocks from the church the French built. Notre-Dame Cathedral it was called. I must have gone to Mass there a hundred times. Looking back, I think it was all that kept me sane. We had help keeping the apartment up—a cook came in, two housekeepers. I can't remember the one girl's name, but the other was Yvette. She was knock-down gorgeous, and as a naive and culturally ignorant kid from Cleveland, I was taken in—exotic oriental girl and all that.

"Yvette lived near us and would come every day. I started walking her home, to keep her safe. Thinking back, I guess I was making her a target, walking with a GI. But she didn't mind. She spoke English and French. I learned a little French from her. In time, I asked her to marry me."

Alex stiffened and stared at her father. "Marry?"

He smiled. "Yes, marry. I had just turned twenty-one. I was head-strong, full of myself, and to be honest, somewhat good-looking. I wanted to get her out of Vietnam. I could see that there was not going to be a good end to this war, particularly for the Vietnamese that had anything to do with us Americans. So, I decided to marry her and take her with me. Well, the army had other ideas and dragged out my request for months."

"Did they approve it?"

"I never knew. Yvette asked me to take her to her village and help bring her mother into Saigon to stay with her. It was about fifty miles north of the city. Their story was like hundreds of thousands of others. The Vietnamese had been fighting somebody for almost fifty years—the French, then the Japanese during the big war, and then, after they threw the French out, America. Many of their relatives died during those wars. Four years earlier the Viet Cong murdered her father, the mayor of the village. One night they just took him away. Two nights later they dropped his body in the village center. They had tortured him before cutting his head off. A note pinned to the body said that the village must leave him where they left him. If anyone touched the body, the same thing would happen to them. Yvette and her mother ignored the order and took the body to the cemetery and buried him. From then on, she would have nothing to do with the Viet Cong or any of the South Vietnamese politicians either. She hated all of them for what they were doing to her country. She asked me to help move her mother into the city so she could take care of her."

Tears formed in his eyes. Alex smiled at her father.

"I borrowed a jeep from the motor pool. Someone there owed me a favor. It would take less than a day, up and back. We headed north on Highway 13. We passed thousands that were fleeing the highlands, all trying to get to Saigon. It was chaos, and there were no police or army troops providing any type of security. About twenty miles outside Saigon, we ran into a barricade put up by South Vietnamese soldiers. I could tell they were all deserters. They had that vacant stare of fear and defeat. Two of them came up to the jeep and stuck a rifle in my face. They demanded money. I gave them the few dollars I had, but it was not enough. One of the soldiers was ogling Yvette, talking to her in Vietnamese. She slapped him. The man grabbed her arm and tried to pull her from the jeep. I reached for my pistol, but before I could do anything, somebody shot me."

"My God," Alex said.

"The next thing I remember, an American GI is sticking his nose in my face and asking what the hell happened. I couldn't recall a thing, nothing—why I was there, where the jeep was. I couldn't even remember Yvette. The bullet just missed my skull—left a scar, though. Knocked off my helmet, which was still on the ground next to me. My pistol was gone. Everything was gone. I found out later it was traumatic amnesia."

Her father lifted the thick, dark-gray hair on the left side of his head, revealing a thin white strip of skin. "This is the scar. I was taken back into Saigon, and over the next few days I tried to remember what happened. That's a feeling I don't ever want to have again. When the guy from the motor pool came in asking about his jeep, I began to piece together the story. My bunkmates helped, and it slowly came back. I never saw Yvette again. She never came back to the apartment. The wound was serious enough that I was evacuated through Okinawa. By winter 1971, I was home. I sent messages to my bunkmates in Saigon, asked if they'd heard anything from Yvette—nothing. I was at your grandparents', a total basket case. Physically, I was good. My head—that was a whole different story."

"Gram and Gramps never said anything."

"I asked them not to. Hell, if I walked the street in my uniform, I was spit on and called a killer. Those were bad days here in America. I heard through some guys in the VA hospital that the ARVN and the Cong attacked the region where Yvette's mother lived. After the battle of Loc Ninh in 1972, nothing remained. I gave up—I assumed she was dead."

"I'm so sorry, Dad."

"Then I met your mom. She helped me through the bad times, and finally, I put most of it behind me. The VA began to get a grip on what we were going through, but it was a shrink here in Cleveland that did the most good. He helped soldiers from World War II and Korea. I got lucky. My logistic work did have some benefits. I found my job with UPS. With your mother's help, and with you on the way, I grew up and kept my head about me, and eventually it all faded away."

"Mom knows?"

He smiled. "Yes, she knows everything. When you yell out the name of your Vietnamese girlfriend in the middle of the night, she kind of wants to know who it is."

"Yeah, I guess that would need an answer," Alex said. "Is there anything I can do in Saigon?"

"Like trying to find Yvette? Please don't, sweetie. It was all so long ago. Nothing can come of it."

"Maybe give you some closure?"

"I am a happy man with the usual pains of age. Please don't. Call us often. Tell me about the city." He handed her an envelope. "Inside are photos of the apartment I was staying in and one photo of Yvette. It's the only one I have. At one point, I was told that someone put a bomb in the apartment building we lived in and blew it up. They killed four GIs. But if you can find the place, send me a picture. I've wondered what happened to it."

"It sounds like you *do* want me to try and find her, Dad."

Her father took in a deep breath and sighed. "No . . . but, if you have the time . . . I don't know."

Alex placed her fingers on her father's weathered hand. "I'll see what I can do."

Chapter 15

That afternoon, Alex wished the long nightmare of the previous year, and all the crap that her ex-cop ex-husband had left in his perverted wake, would just disappear. The furniture in her house showed the scratches and damage that the cops—her own department, for God's sake—had inflicted during the raid. Her closet was still a mess; she'd not had the ambition to clean it after the chaos.

She hoped, deep in her soul, that Ralph was dead. If there was anyone that deserved to be dead, it was Ralph Daniel Cierzinski. She thought of the last email she'd received in Venice, where he called her Sandy, from the play *Grease*. That had been their thing, long ago—he'd call her Sandy, and she called him Danny, for the male lead, Danny Zuko. It was all a game to him, a game that had left at least a half dozen dead in his psycho wake. But while she hoped he was dead, she knew, in her detective's heart, he was alive and still playing games. She knew she was the object of his desire and his taunts. The next time she saw him, she hoped to God that she had a gun.

She put the bags of groceries and toiletries, the tray of mail, and a Barnes & Noble bag on the kitchen counter. After putting away the perishable groceries, she sorted the mail. She neatly stacked the travel guides and books on Vietnam and pushed them to the back of the counter before taking the rest of the mail into the study. There she organized the envelopes and began to pay the bills, including a small late penalty on half of them. The cash advance from Chris came in handy.

Two hours later, she returned to the kitchen and put away the rest of the groceries in the pantry. It was no longer as empty as Ralph's heart. She smiled.

In the garage sat two cars and her motorcycle. The first was Ralph's pride, a 1972 yellow Dodge Challenger. She hated the thing. Job one was to sell it. Next to it against the wall was her premarriage Harley-Davidson Sportster, one of the few personal things she'd kept from her days before Ralph. The most practical vehicle in the garage was the five-year-old black Ford Escape. It surprised her by starting on the first turn of the key.

Ten minutes later she was sitting in a diner on Detroit Avenue sipping coffee and writing out a list of things she needed to do. It would be a busy week and a half.

"Haven't seen you in here for a while, honey," the waitress said.

"I've been traveling," Alex replied.

"Honey, what they did to you was wrong. I just don't understand it."

"Thanks, Laurie. I don't either. But things are good. Actually, the best they've been in a few years."

"That's good, honey. More coffee?"

Alex nodded. "Thanks." Laurie refilled her cup as Alex asked, "Still cooking breakfast?"

"Twenty-four hours a day. The usual?"

"Yes, thanks. Sausage and scramble, no toast, no hash browns, but fruit, please."

"Got it."

Her to-do list almost filled a whole page. The top item wasn't to sell the Challenger after all—it was to find a Realtor. There was no way she was going to stay in the house if she wasn't sure where she would be from one assignment to the next. Annie, John's wife, said she would help to sell the place. The next to-do was finding an apartment, a studio, maybe something near the lake with a view. All this would take more than a week. Then the rest of the big things on the list: storage space, utilities, sell the Dodge. Then again, she hated everything that was connected to that asshole. The list continued with some toiletries, a few clothes, and underwear. She shook her head over all the things—even the simple stuff—that needed to be done to entirely change her life.

She looked at her phone: her ex-partner was late. She'd asked him to late lunch. "Can't," had been his answer, but he said he could stop by for a couple of minutes. It wasn't a strange answer. They had been partners for three years, and even though Bob Simmons was entirely on her side, she knew he needed to keep space between them. He needed to keep his job.

The tinny bell over the diner door jingled. She looked up and waved to Simmons, who wove his way through the tables.

"You're looking good," he said as he sat. "A little sun?"

"Yes," she answered, "and lots of fresh air. Does the soul and the head good. They treating you right?"

"As good as I can expect. And yeah, a new partner. My last partner, the one who passed on the information about where you were to those DEA idiots chasing you in Venice, is riding a desk. Whether he keeps his job is up to IA. I hope they drop him in the river. What he did was so wrong. My new partner, though, she's a rook, but she's smart, top of her class. A ball-breaker too."

"A woman? Be careful—they can get you in trouble."

"Don't I know."

"Katy and the family, they okay?"

"All good. BJ's getting ready for Little League, and Joe got a dog— they're inseparable. It's good for him. It's helping with his therapy. But it's a long road, maybe an endless one."

"You and Katy will be fine—you make a great team. You can do anything, and Joe is tough. He will get through it."

"The tumor's gone—that's one thing to be grateful for. And he's walking again. The doctors say that with time and growing up, it may all be a bad memory. We can hope. The bills, that's another thing. A lot of costs weren't covered. I'm taking on some security jobs just to add a few dollars to the bank. In some ways, I envy you."

"Stop right there. Never envy me. My life is crap. However, there's a thin chance that it might just be turning around. Katy and those boys . . . I'm the one envying you. What's your partner's name?"

"You'll love it—Mary Beth Applegate. I kid you not."

"Not from the Cleveland Applegates?"

"Don't go there. She's from Akron. A degree in criminal science, a black belt, blonde like you, and cute."

"I warned you, stop. This sounds like the devil's work."

"And a lesbian."

"Well there's that—just be careful."

Simmons looked at his watch. "Time to go. You staying in the area?"

"Just through the next week. I have an assignment that will take me out of the country."

"With who?"

"Can't tell you, but it looks good. Good pay and bennies, but I may be gone for six months. John and Annie are taking care of the house. Selling it."

"Good, never liked that place. Didn't suit you. And the Challenger?"

"No, I'll not saddle you with that. So, just get it out of your head."

"It was built before we were born—what's not to like?"

"It will cost you too much, and the boys will just cause you trouble when they want to drive that piece of shit."

"A boy can dream. My treat." Bob threw a twenty on the table. "Call before you go." He leaned in and kissed her on the cheek. "I wish you all the luck and success in the world—you deserve it."

Chapter 16

Lake Simcoe, Canada

Ralph stood at the window of the Lake Simcoe house. The ice had retreated over the previous weeks but still held to the center of the lake. The grass was starting to turn from gray-brown to a color that hinted at life. He was beginning to develop the same thing he'd felt in prison: isolation. An ex-cop in prison had few friends, and more enemies than he wanted to count. He'd been a scalp to be collected, a number to the guards, and a potential bounty to a few of the smarter cons. He'd avoided all of them. They'd had nothing he wanted.

He had grown tired of the laptop, so he'd ordered a larger desktop computer with a huge monitor and had set it up on a folding table in the second bedroom—his operations room, he called it. The wall held taped pictures, notes, photos he'd downloaded, and a calendar he'd mark in red the days he was sure she was at the house. She had been gone for nearly two months, and back for just three days.

Earlier Alex had walked through the kitchen with her sister-in-law, Annie. A witch if there ever was one. No matter how he'd try and charm the family, he could never get past the wives. Alex's two brothers were solid rocks, and they'd married similar women. The women and his ex were tight.

The current image on the screen was of an empty garage. He was pissed. He'd watched his ex-wife and a man, older than her, walk around his yellow 1972 Dodge Challenger. The man had opened the hood, pointed, and then climbed into the front seat. When he got out he was smiling. They had spent a few more minutes together and then shook hands.

His pride and joy was gone. It had taken him two years to find this car, and another year and twenty grand to make it right. Hell, the paint job itself cost five thousand. Now she'd sold it. He didn't even want to think what she got for it. Then again, she got everything in the divorce. Then he thought about the accounts in the Caymans and Zurich—he could buy a dozen Challengers if he wanted to.

He guessed that Alex was selling the house. She'd been moving things to the garage—furniture, boxes, bags, even a couple of rolled-up carpets. Then today, Friday morning, along with her Harley, it was all loaded into a box truck. He assumed that it was going into storage. He considered calling and finding out what was happening, but thought better of it.

He ran the video back to when she'd dumped her mail, grocery bags, and a Barnes & Noble bag on the counter. He watched as she flipped through the mail, setting the usual keepers to one side and the toss-outs to the other. Then she removed the books and stacked them next to the mail. She left for a moment to make herself a cup of coffee.

Ralph took a snapshot with the software and enlarged the image. He could read the spines of the three books: one was yellow and black and read *Vietnam*, the next was green and read *Ho Chi Minh City*, and the last, with a blue spine, read *Lonely Planet: Vietnam*. He printed out the enlarged image.

Why the interest in Vietnam? And old Saigon too. Years before he'd married Alex, and before he'd joined the Cleveland Police Department, he'd spent a few years wasting his youth in Vietnam and Saigon. By the mid-1990s, he'd smoked a lot of dope, experimented a little with heroin and women, met a few characters, and more importantly found associates that shared an interest in the drug business.

Vietnam was different now, very different. Capitalism and business ran the communist country. His old connections were still there, though, and he used them. They had improved their logistics and supply chains. Product from Vietnam, black tar heroin, was easily transported to Cleveland. Millions of shipping containers moved around the world every day, and most people didn't care what was in them. And he also knew, with proper management of drug sales and distribution, it was a road to success and riches. That is, unless you were caught or killed. It was this way all around the world: the business model didn't change much from Saigon to Kiev to Paris to Cleveland. He knew he'd screwed up when he started getting greedy and getting Cleveland kids involved.

He returned to the Teton Security and Defense website. While it was brief and vague, there was a paragraph and a photo on the third page, about international operations. The photo showed the president, Christopher Campbell. Ralph recognized the spot where the photo was taken, a park on the Saigon River in downtown Saigon.

Saigon. Is that it, baby? You took a job with a security company and are going to Vietnam? I think a few calls are in order.

CHAPTER 17

Annie and Julie dropped by Saturday and helped move another piece of furniture Alex was keeping to the garage. There were also more boxes of clothes, linens, and dishware. Alex said that was the last of it. One box held a collection of books, as few as there were, and some serious heavy-metal albums. Julie mentioned how very different a box of her CDs would be from Alex's.

"Remember, I had brothers," Alex said. "Younger, but they had to learn from someone."

"Yes, and their taste in music still sucks," Julie said. "At least I know where they got it. The boys, I have no idea what they're listening to. And if I do, I can't understand it. The music from the eighties is so dreamy, and those Pet Shop Boys."

"Really, Pet Shop? You are an old lady," Annie said. "I'm a Bruce Springsteen girl. What more can be said?"

"One word," Alex answered. "Metallica."

"Really?" both sisters-in-law said together.

They finished separating out what would be moved to the garage. Rick and John would move the rest of the furniture and boxes from the garage into the storage unit after she left.

Her brother John thought the Escape would make a good car for his oldest in a year or so, so she sold it to him. But she didn't give it to him just yet, as it would come in handy for moving her things. She was glad she wouldn't be here. Julie said she would want to keep more stuff than she should.

◆　◆　◆

Two days before Alex was to leave for Milan, she sat at the kitchen table. The contract to sell the house—through a broker friend of Annie's—was signed. All she needed to do was drop it off at the real estate office. After she returned from the Saigon operation, she would find an apartment. There was something about all this that gave her a feeling of peace. One more reminder of Ralph gone.

The door chimed. It had to be her mom. But she opened it and found Chris Campbell on her doorstep.

Alex looked at her boss, perplexed.

"Nice neighborhood," he said. "May I come in?"

She moved to one side. "Yeah, sure."

He breezed past her and walked into the living room, looking around at the furniture. Pink tags were stuck to many of their surfaces.

"I remember when I did this with the CIA. It was after one of my tours. God, that was more than twenty years ago. Tagged stuff to sell and moved with the leftovers. Each assignment after that, I took less. The government was a stickler about how much you could move. You learn not to value things. Then I got married and settled down." He looked at the boxes and labels. "It's people that you can't put a tag on. You have a beer or a drink around here?"

Alex kept staring at Chris as she crossed the living room and went into the kitchen. He followed. She took two Rolling Rocks from the refrigerator.

"I haven't had one of these since college," Chris said.

"Nostalgic and cheap—they've been in there awhile," Alex answered. They clinked bottles, and she took a long pull. "Why are you here, Chris?"

"I heard from Javier. He's still in Milan. He said to say hello. He said he'd like to see you."

"You could have sent an email or something." She took another swig, squinted. "I never told him I'd be in Milan. Is that why you're here? You think I broke your trust, told someone something I shouldn't have?"

"No, I told Javier where you'd be," Chris said. "I'm not here to question your loyalty or integrity."

"All right then, what's so important that you would come to Cleveland to talk to me face-to-face?"

Chris stalled a moment, then took a long pull of his beer. "I have a problem. I hired you because you have the skills to be a good operative. As I've said before, your years as a cop and detective are talents that most of my recruits don't have. I value those abilities more than you can imagine."

"Then why the babysitting job?" Alex said. "Doesn't seem like the best use of my skills. I took it out of gratitude and maybe for the adventure, but you seem to be implying something else."

"Yes, the Luccheses are your official charge and assignment. But there's something not right in Team Red. Too many coincidences. Too many thefts and data breaches. Some were our clients, some were tangential. I can't go into detail, but there are enough compromises that I'm very concerned. The real reason you're going to Saigon is simple: I want *you* to find out what's wrong and report back to me so it can be fixed. You're the only person I can trust in this operation."

"Me? I've barely cashed a TSD paycheck, and you're telling me I'm trusted." She pulled two more beers from the refrigerator. "You want me to spy on my own team?"

"Yes, and this is not one of my tests. I lost two friends a few months ago in Saigon. You saw their faces on the wall at the Country Club. They were good people. Experienced too—for someone to get the drop on them, to surprise them, was almost impossible. It had to be inside information. I believe they were set up and murdered, plain and simple."

"What happened?"

Chris told her what he knew and speculated on the rest. "This infiltrator knew what to expect, knew exactly what time no one would be in the facility, and where everything was. He was fully prepared. He wore a type of night-vision goggles that we've never seen and was armed with a weapon we haven't heard of. It fires bullets that, on contact, explode with the force of a hand grenade. He was also equipped with a drone, one that performs like an airborne motorcycle. During his escape, he outmaneuvered a helicopter and forced it down."

"A drone? Large enough to carry a man?"

"Exactly! Jake and Harry have been trying for months to figure out what went wrong."

"One man managed all this?"

"Yes, our Far East sources believe he's a Chinese agent of Vietnamese heritage. He is on every wanted spy list across the world. Some have issued orders to shoot to kill. The others, including the CIA, want to break him down and find out what he knows. Our people believe he's working for the Chinese army or a similar organization and is primarily used in industrial espionage. We determined that he downloaded everything that was on the server and transmitted it to his people. You saw in Texas the curious high-tech merchandise he left at the site, the item that destroyed itself after it transmitted the data. We still haven't completely cracked it."

"He has a name?"

"Some in the governments of the Far East call him Con Ma, the Ghost."

Alex looked at Chris. "Really? The *Ghost*! Jake talked about the intruder in the Saigon facility at the ranch. So, there really is this person?"

"There's a superstitious vein that runs through Eastern religions, particularly Buddhism. This man has struck at least a dozen times, probably more. The victims do not want the authorities to learn that their security was breached. Just like this incident—we too are keeping it close to the vest. Just a few people outside of Teton Security and the client know. I've never been fired, and I hope to change their minds. That's my problem."

"But it wasn't our fault."

"In for a penny, in for a pound. We should have stopped it."

"You said someone may have passed on security information, someone within Teton?"

"Yes, the operation in Saigon was compromised. Everything about the technology facility was under our care. Outside of the client, only we knew anything about it. Someone said something. My immediate reaction is that it can't be anyone on our team, so it must be someone on the client's. They want to blame us. That's the easy way. I convinced them that they needed to also consider their own house. A few months before the break-in, one of their senior engineers failed to show up for a meeting. He was on the team developing a drone-like product. He was found floating in the Saigon River, a small knife wound to the base of the back of his head. The Saigon police are investigating, but no one has been arrested."

"These guys play for keeps," Alex said.

"Yes, and I need to find out who did this. First, you will be babysitting—that is your cover story. However, I also want you to find out what the hell is going on and report back to me. Only me. Do not let anyone else know what's going on. Probe and question. You're good at that. Second, do not take any action. Contact me, and I'll direct you."

He pulled a phone from his pocket and handed it to her.

"This has a high-security scrambler built into it. It cannot be cloned and cannot be compromised. The access code is taped to the back. Memorize it. Then destroy the code. Failure to get the code right twice will crash the device. Use it anytime to reach me, and I mean anytime. I will not call you unless under dire circumstances."

"Do you have any ideas?"

"Some, but you're the detective. If I say anything, it might make you look the wrong way. Everyone is a suspect. Talk about this with no one. My fear is that this goes far beyond the Saigon operation. I cannot have any of the other operations screwed up."

"Can you tell me what was in the facility?"

"Software under development for NATO. The tech facility is owned by Como Motors, our client. The warehouse location was temporary and known to just those working for the company and to me. Our people didn't know what they were guarding; they thought it was next-generation technology for autonomous automobile software. Data worth something commercially—not military technology affecting NATO security. I wanted them to keep it in the cloud or in some type of blockchain, but NATO and Como were unsure. They didn't trust the systems. Now they're just pissed."

"You said this Ghost escaped from the scene on a cycle-drone type of vehicle?"

"Yes, not long after the break-in and the murders. We assume he stayed on an adjacent roof because he was wounded. We think one of our people hit the man; they found blood in the warehouse and on the roof. There were also bits of paper and empty vials of antibiotics, painkillers, and even a stimulant on the roof. He knew what he was doing and was cool about it. He later knocked a Saigon police helicopter out of the air with a weapon similar to the one he used on our men. The drone-like vehicle is sophisticated and advanced technology. Como Motors was working on such a system. The murdered engineer was one of the chief designers. And according to the helicopter pilot, he would give it a lot more room next time."

"This Ghost, do you know what he looks like?"

"We're still reviewing internal CCTV footage. He wore a helmet during most of the operation, but we have his build and height, plus a few grainy face images that appear to match the other images we have from thefts in Hong Kong, Singapore, and San Jose."

"California?"

"Yes, in San Jose it was proprietary data from a company that develops guidance systems for the air force's Predator drones."

"This is a big deal."

"The biggest, and if one or more of my people are involved, I must know."

"Then what?"

"That's for me to decide."

Ralph's computer pinged. After logging in, he checked his video feeds. For the next ten minutes, he watched a man talk with his wife in the kitchen. They both walked in and out of the camera's view. Based on their body language, he could tell that they were discussing something serious. Both his wife—ex-wife, he corrected himself—and the man seemed on edge, even as they drank his Rolling Rock.

He reminded himself of how cheap he'd been not to include microphones with the installation. The man looked familiar. Something about his professional appearance said *authority*. He snapped his fingers and went to the bookmark bar in his web browser. He scrolled down and clicked.

The website for Teton Security and Defense opened. He clicked to the personnel page and smiled: the top photo was of the same man in his kitchen, Christopher Campbell. The same man standing on the dock in Saigon.

"So, Mr. Campbell, you are my darling Sandy's boss. This adds a whole new meaning to the word *two-timed*."

CHAPTER 18

The morning before leaving for Milan, Alex was having another break-fast at the diner when she received an unexpected, yet welcome, phone call. The screen read *007*.

"Good morning, cowboy," she answered.

"And good morning to you. It's in the middle of the afternoon here. Chris tells me that you're coming to Milan the day after tomorrow. Do you need a lift? Glad to pick you up."

"Working for Uber now?"

"Cute, but if you want to pay me, I'm sure we can work something out."

"Now you're just being a boor. It will be nice, though, to see a familiar face in a strange city."

"I've missed you," Javier admitted.

"And I've missed you . . . a lot. And yes, I get in early Saturday morning. After customs and luggage, I should be out around ten o'clock. You can buy me breakfast."

"Done and done."

A few minutes later, she called Campbell. "Javier wants to pick me up in Milan. I thought you should know."

"I told him when you would arrive. I could tell there was something irritating you. Maybe seeing him may help get your head right."

"Chris, my head is right. I appreciate your telling him. However, from now on, can we keep my business and personal lives separate? I like the guy—a lot. But if you want to keep my head in the game, let me control it. Is that acceptable?"

There was a pause on Campbell's end. "Got it, and I appreciate your candor. Thank you. He's an old friend; I believed I was helping."

"I understand. Just stop for now. If I need help, I'll ask. That okay? Are we good?"

"Five by five. Got it. See you Monday."

"Monday, boss."

The paramount directive driven into her and the new recruits during their training was secrecy. Only management, the team, and the client were to know scope, schedules, and itineraries. No one else. And now—with what Chris revealed in her kitchen—she needed to manage the flow of information as well. Everything else surrounding the operation was outside the box, and that box had a lid. Nonetheless, she now had to define the boundaries that even a helpful boss might push.

Alex's premium-economy seat was significantly roomier than the steerage seat she'd had to Venice. A two-hour flight from Cleveland Hopkins to JFK, a two-hour layover, then nonstop to Milan—two flights to Europe in less than six months. She felt like a jet-setter.

Chris's visit nagged her. Her years as a cop had given her a jaundiced view of the human species. She'd come to the sad conclusion that many would do anything for a buck, some for even less. But to turn on your own people, to set them up to be killed, that was debased. There had to be more behind this treachery.

Waiting in the JFK lounge, she received a confirmation text from Campbell that he would meet her in Milan a few days after she arrived. He had meetings in London and Munich first. He'd meet her at the

Hilton early Monday morning. They were scheduled to visit with the Luccheses later that day.

An hour into the eight-hour flight, Alex opened the new satellite-enabled laptop that had arrived at her house by messenger. Access to the computer was through her fingerprint and a temporary password that was sent to the phone Campbell had given her. She memorized the fourteen random digits and letters and rebooted the computer. The text on the phone disappeared. There were four folders on the desktop, one each for the Luccheses, Teton Security, Ho Chi Minh City, and Vietnam.

She clicked on the Lucchese folder, and four new folders appeared: *Como Motors, Nevio Lucchese, Ilaria Lucchese*, and *Lucchese Children*. She opened the Como Motors file and the ten-page Word document within it.

She read about the history of Como Motors since its founding in Milan after World War II. Included were addresses of its worldwide manufacturing operations in Italy, Brazil, Taiwan, and China and of the newest facility in Vietnam. Worldwide sales approached two billion euros, well ahead of other motorcycle manufacturers, such as Harley-Davidson.

The document then went into the company's management team and board of directors. She recognized a couple of the names from the news and their connections to international manufacturing companies and banks. The last section outlined the company's future, and one paragraph—headed *Future NATO Prospects*—caught her eye.

> *Our analysis and contacts within the domestic and international defense industries of Europe have confirmed that Como Motors is a subcontractor to NATO. This contract may include the development and manufacture of data management and helmet controls for the new NATO swarm drone program. These control systems are an offshoot of their motorbike helmet*

control systems that are being developed to assist the motorbike driver. These systems are based on swarm theory and dealing with unlimited data input. They are expected to help augment safety, peripheral visibility, and communications.

Per NATO regulations, these systems must be manufactured within NATO countries in highly secured facilities. TSD is not sure that this contract has been signed, but we believe that it is possible over the next few months. TSD also believes that this software system may have military value, that it can be weaponized for both defensive and offensive purposes. The goal would be to overwhelm enemy defensive systems or provide an offensive capability that cannot be easily compromised.

Alex noted that the last paragraph about NATO had been inserted by Chris—his name was posted at the bottom. She read, with special interest, the documents on the Lucchese family. Nevio Lucchese was fifty-eight and had been with Como for fifteen years. He managed the expansion of facilities in Italy and set up the Como manufacturing facility in Brazil. It was also speculated that he may be heading up the research for the swarm defense system.

Ilaria Lucchese was thirty-six. She was Nevio's second wife, and based on the photo, pretty. His first wife died eighteen years earlier in a solo car crash in the mountains above Genoa. It had been declared an accident due to excessive speed and road conditions. Ilaria was the complete opposite to the first wife. The biography noted that she didn't drive. She was the daughter of an old political family from Milan with manufacturing and industrial roots. Apparently, her grandfather had been involved with Mussolini's fascists, and his company had manufactured tanks and other military vehicles for Italy's war effort. He merged the firm with Como Motors after the war. Her father, Enzo Giordano, had controlled the company until it became public in the early 1990s. He was still alive.

As for the two children, Paolo and Gianna, the files gave their ages, school test scores, and little else. Their photographs showed handsome children with bright eyes. Something about Paolo's look reminded Alex of her brother John. It was the look of a troublemaker. She smiled at the thought. The girl had the childish grin of an ingenue and the eyes of a starlet. She would have to watch out for the boys with this one.

She restudied the TSD folder. It contained everything she learned from her weeks at the Country Club. She rubbed the sore point in her shoulder from the butts of the assorted rifles. She then waved at the attendant and ordered another Belvedere on the rocks.

The folders on Vietnam and Saigon were the most interesting. She scanned through the pages on Vietnam's history, old and recent, as well as those detailing its current political structure and climate. In the section on its economy, she learned that the nation was becoming an economic powerhouse in the region, and not just for its cheaper labor. The documents included articles, photos, and maps that showed a country far different from the one her father had left fifty years earlier. Saigon, relabeled Ho Chi Minh City by the communist victors, was even more surprising, especially its population. In Cleveland and Cuyahoga County, there were one and a quarter million people. Saigon and its surrounding countryside held more than eight million.

As she drifted off to sleep, thoughts of overcrowded streets, a million motorbikes, and oppressive heat and humidity drifted around in her head. Let the fun and games begin.

Alex cleared customs and walked into the Milano Malpensa terminal expecting to see Javier standing there with a grin on his face and a paper sign saying "Polonia." She was greeted with the sign, but it was held by an older man whose tailored black suit and chauffeur's cap gave him a distinctly British look. She pointed at him.

"Ms. Polonia, I'm Dugan McCorly. Mr. Campbell sent me to collect you." The accent confirmed it: British indeed.

"Collect me?" she answered. "Why am I being collected, by you?"

"An unfortunate word. I'm sorry, Ms. Polonia. I am to drive you to your hotel. I expect you're tired after your trip." He took the two bags from Alex and began to roll them toward the door.

"Stop," she ordered. "I'm just fine, Mr. McCorly. So, stop right there. I do not like surprises, and this is a surprise. You will wait."

"Certainly, Ms. Polonia." He stood next to her two bags, an extension handle in each hand, and waited.

She extracted the phone Campbell had given her and punched in a number. After four rings, it went to voice mail. "Chris, I have a McCorly collecting me. This was not in the program. Call me now. I'm not leaving the airport with this man until you do."

"Mr. McCorly, I need a drink," she said as she ended the call. "Is there a bar somewhere in this airport?"

"Not on this side of the security gates, unfortunately. Just a couple of small delicatessens. Sorry, lass."

Alex followed McCorly until they reached a sign that read "Restaurant Gourme." At ten in the morning it was half-full. A few people from her area of the plane were there drinking wine. This would have to do.

She threw her backpack on one of the plastic seats and pointed McCorly toward an empty one. As he sat, so did she. "Who are you, and why are you here?"

"Mr. Campbell said you would be suspicious. I am who I said I am. Dugan McCorly: Milan liaison for Teton Security and Defense."

"Were you some kind of spook in an earlier life too? Or military? Everyone at Teton seems one or the other."

"British MI6, yes. I met Mr. Campbell in Mumbai. He offered me a position, so here I am—your personal chauffeur and Sherpa. Today anyhow. Airport collections aren't my normal route." He took off his hat and set it beside him. "Red wine, or white?"

"White. And cold."

"I'll be right back." McCorly stood and walked to the counter. Alex heard him order in Italian. A few seconds later a glass of white wine sat in front of her.

Her phone pinged. Christopher Campbell's text message sat on the screen:

Had to change the plan. I'll tell you why later. Ask McCorly what his favorite color is. If he says red, he's good. If he says blue, shoot him.

She looked at the British agent. "What's your favorite color?"

McCorly smiled. "Red, of course. Now you won't have to shoot me."

She took a long sip of the wine. "My loss."

CHAPTER 19

Alex sat uneasily in the rear seat of the BMW sedan. She appreciated the luxury, but she was still annoyed by McCorly's surprise "collection." What happened to her original driver, the Texan from Waco? She looked at her phone every five minutes hoping for a text or email from him—nothing.

Milan was hectic, even on a Saturday morning. Trolleys and taxis filled the streets. She didn't know what to expect as they drove through an industrial area, which, with its brick buildings, looked like one of the older neighborhoods of Cleveland. Not a good thing.

"Ms. Polonia," McCorly said, his eyes in the rearview. "I fear we got off to a bad start. I apologize. This was a last-minute request by Mr. Campbell, who is in London. Other arrangements must have fallen through. I was free this morning, so he sent me."

"To *collect* me?"

"Precisely."

"I understand, I think."

"You're at the Hilton? The one near the train station?"

"Hilton, yes. The train station I don't know. This is my first time in Milan."

She removed the paperwork from her bag. "Is it the one on Via Luigi Galvani?"

"*Sì, sì, quello e l'unico.*"

"Now you're just showing off, Mr. McCorly."

"Sorry, I've lived here a long time. Some days I won't say a word of English. And please call me Dugan. Only my wife calls me Mr. McCorly, and that's when she's vexed."

"Now why would someone be vexed with you, Dugan?"

"Some weeks my address is the doghouse. The hotel is not far. And the train station is across the street from it. You can be in Venice or Florence in just a few hours, Rome a little more. North is Switzerland. The train station is central to northern Italy."

"Do you know why I'm here?"

"Not my place to know. Excuse me, ma'am, I have a call." He tapped something on the steering wheel. "Dugan here."

Alex watched an enormous and ornately carved white cathedral pass on their right. It was bigger than anything she remembered in Venice.

They build big cathedrals in Italy. Then again, I guess they've had a long time to do it.

"Change in plans, Ms. Polonia. I've been instructed to take you to another hotel; the Hilton has been canceled. Our travel director tells me the new location is the Hotel Principe Di Savoia. It's not my place to comment, but it's one of Milan's best. Just a few blocks from here."

"Great, another surprise."

Standing under the porte cochere to the hotel, she looked up at the white stone-faced building. At each arched window, a flower box over-flowed with spring flowers. It all screamed *expensive*. She assumed it was Campbell's idea, but why?

McCorly handed her bags to a bellman, who gave him a receipt. McCorly walked over and passed the slip of paper to her. "All you have to do is check in. Everything is taken care of. I must go. I hope to see you again, Ms. Polonia."

"I apologize for being rude," Alex said. "There was no reason. I was surprised. I hate surprises, and I was expecting someone else."

"In my line of work, I don't like surprises either. I completely understand. Until later." He extended his hand, and she took it. "By the by, there's an excellent bar just inside the door."

As McCorly drove out between the white columns of the hotel's entry, she wondered what other surprises her boss had for her.

Inside, a dapper man in a beautiful suit met her. "Ms. Polonia, I am Signor Mazzetti, the manager. I have your key card here." He handed her a stylish cardboard envelope. "Your bags will be taken to your room. Is there anything else I can do for you?"

She stared at the man for a moment too long. She wasn't sure whether she was jet-lagged or just plain tired. "Thank you, Signor Mazzetti. I think a cocktail, then a nap."

"*Eccellente.* I hope you enjoy your stay with us. If you need anything, please ask. *Buongiorno.*"

"And *buongiorno* to you, sir."

It was a quarter to noon. She had been traveling for the last twelve hours, and it was a toss-up between the room and the bar. Her stomach growled as she walked through the lobby and turned into the bar. It took a moment for her eyes to adjust to the dark, wood-paneled interior. Tables, mostly unoccupied, populated the main floor. Overhead, a crystal chandelier glowed. Her eyes lazily drifted to the bar, where, on the center stool, sat Javier Castillo, an ice-filled tumbler at his side.

At first she thought she ought to walk over and dump the drink on his head. Instead, she marched up to the Texan and gave him a kiss. After thirty seconds, he mumbled something about not being able to breathe.

"Too bad," she said into his ear. "Maybe I should strangle you while I'm at it."

"That will wreck the rest of the weekend I've planned." He patted the stool next to him and handed her the drink as she slid onto the seat. "Your Belvedere on the rocks."

"This will not get you off the hook, but it's a start. Why weren't you at the airport?"

"Government business. I couldn't reach you; you were in the air. I texted Chris, and he said he'd take care of it. Did Dugan McCorly pick you up?"

"Yes, strange man."

"He's an old spy. He plays the role of the dandy snoop just for fun, but he's a serious player in this part of Italy."

She looked around, took in the grandeur. "I don't think I can cover this place on my expense account."

"I've worked it out with Chris. I had some American government officials staying here, all paid up through next week. They went home yesterday, no reimbursement, so it's yours until Monday. Then, I'm afraid, Cinderella's pumpkin turns into a Hilton. That's when Chris gets you back."

"You mean it's just you and me?"

"For the entire weekend."

"I'm not sure what to do for an entire weekend."

"It's Italy. I'm sure we'll find something."

"I'm famished."

"They have a menu somewhere around here," Javier said, looking at the bartender. "Can we eat here at the bar?"

"*Sì, sì,*" the bartender answered.

Alex stood. "Room service will be just fine." She slung her backpack over her shoulder, picked up her drink, took his hand, and headed to the elevator.

CHAPTER 20

Two days later, Alex exited the elevator and crossed the marbled lobby of the Hotel Principe Di Savoia. McCorly stood at the BMW just outside, holding the door open for her. Her bags nestled into the spacious trunk, its lid still open.

"Good morning, Mr. McCorly," she said, stepping into the car.

"Good morning to you. The boss will be here momentarily."

She settled into the back seat and smiled at her reflection in the window. For the first time—in so long she couldn't remember—she was happy. The surprise of meeting Javier and the stay at the hotel, their Sunday trip to Florence, the wonderful meals, the evenings, the lack of expectations, the comfort of his shoulder in the mornings. What they had discovered of each other in Venice, they had found again in Milan.

"Welcome to Italy," Chris said, hopping in next to her. "I hope the change in plans was acceptable."

"More than acceptable, and thank you. Javier says he will call you later in the week, something about NATO. He had to leave early this morning. Other than that, I'm reporting for duty."

"There's a cup of black coffee in the holder, Ms. Polonia," McCorly said as he handed a manila folder and a manila envelope to Chris, one thin, the other thick. "The boss said that's how you like it."

"Thank you, Mr. McCorly," she answered, then turned to her boss. "So, it begins."

"It begins," he said as McCorly started the car. As the Englishman steered away from the hotel, Chris opened the thin folder and handed Alex a sheet of paper. "This is the schedule. For the most part, today is a get-to-know-each-other day. We'll meet Signor Lucchese at his office, which is about twenty minutes away at the Como Motors plant near Cinisello Balsamo. After that, we'll meet with the family for lunch at their villa in the hills above Monza. The children are home from school. I've been told they're not happy with this move. They do not want to leave their friends."

"My brothers have had the same problems with their kids, and those were merely moves from one neighborhood to another in Cleveland. The children may be confused and puzzled. But I'm prepared."

"Ilaria Lucchese moved with her husband a couple of times early in his career, but that was before the kids. His last overseas assignment was Brazil, and she stayed with the children here in Italy. They're older now."

"From what you included in my packet, Saigon seems reasonably safe. Is this additional protection necessary?"

"Yes, they feel it's even more warranted now after the tech facility incident. His position with Como and their corporate-safety policies for their employees at certain international locations require it. Como Motors also has contracts with governments and international agencies. I'm told the NATO contract is the most important. They do not want their employees to be put into positions where they might be compromised."

"Like the threat of being kidnapped and held for ransom?"

"Yes, that's one of the issues. Or extortion, intimidation, even terror. Our job is to prevent these incidents from happening." He handed her the thick, padded envelope.

From its weight, she immediately knew what was inside.

"When on the job, all my operatives are armed. I'm not one who believes in nonviolence. If there is a threat, you will be prepared to meet that threat with equal or greater force. Please open it."

Inside the envelope were concealed permits for Italy and Vietnam, a box of nine-millimeter bullets, and a Glock 43. The firearm was comfortable in her hand, and compared to other Glocks, including her old service pistol, small and more easily concealed. The pistol was in a black belt holster.

"I don't have to tell you to think first before using it," Chris said. "Your training and experience should take care of that."

Alex nodded.

"On Friday, you're flying to Saigon," Chris went on. "But there will be a two-day, one-night stop in Dubai—the Luccheses do not want to subject their children to the long flight from Milan to Saigon. You're flying Emirates. The adults are in first class; you and the kids are in premium economy. Once in Dubai you and the Luccheses will be staying at the Four Seasons Resort."

"Are you or anyone else from TSD flying with us?"

"No. I'm going back to London, then Miami, then Dallas. For the first leg, you're on your own. Harry Karns will meet you in Dubai. He's handling logistics for the stopover. He'll be coming in from Ho Chi Minh City."

"Is that necessary? It's only a couple of days."

"Since you're new, Harry offered to help. I had no problem with it. The children will have their nanny, Maria. Other than that, it's just you on the first leg. Harry will provide added security from then on."

"Is there anything more about the tech facility break-in?"

"Jake and Harry are checking DNA against databases, and we're trying to isolate as many people as we can to see who may have leaked information that led to the Como warehouse massacre."

Alex removed the pistol from the holster. She dropped the magazine, checked it—empty. She pulled the slide and confirmed an empty chamber.

"May I?" she asked, holding up the magazine.

Campbell nodded.

She loaded the magazine, inserted it into the weapon, reholstered it, and secured it to the waist of her slacks. "It's been a while. I feel dressed again."

◆　◆　◆

McCorly stayed with the car in the visitor parking area outside Como Motors. Inside the lobby, Alex and Campbell greeted Nevio Lucchese. He was late.

"Please, follow me," Lucchese said after introductions. "We can talk in my office."

They passed through long corridors lined with offices. Lucchese stopped and directed them into a rather inconspicuous office. The view out of the large window at the back was of another Como parking lot. A beige desk, a sofa, a chair, a bank of file cabinets, and two bookshelves were the sole pieces of furniture in the office. Lucchese pointed to the couch, and the Americans sat.

"Coffee?"

Campbell shook his head, and Alex politely declined.

After pouring himself a cup, Lucchese took a seat in a matching chair. "Ms. Polonia, it's a pleasure to meet you. Mr. Campbell has told me a great deal about you. My family is also eager to meet you. Ilaria completely understands the need for security, especially these days. However, she is concerned about the children. They are defiant, stubborn, and confused about this move. Paolo is fifteen and is into soccer—his grades are excellent. He doesn't understand why he must go. He wants to stay with his grandmother, Ilaria's mother. Gianna is almost a teenager. She's twelve and worships her older brother. They're close. She doesn't want to leave her friends. In fact, she told me that one of her girlfriends offered her a room until we return. When I told them about you, they seemed, how you say, unimpressed."

"Teenagers can be like that," Alex said.

Lucchese smiled. "Paolo asked all about you, your name and what sports you played—guy things. When I told him you were a woman, and a police officer, he seemed disappointed. I think he thought that Alex was a man's name. Gianna said she hopes you like horses, because she loves them. She has a mare she rides at the equestrian center. She will miss that horse."

Alex paid attention, as this was all new information about the children. Gianna's fondness for horses was interesting. Paolo's passion, when not studying, was soccer. Then again, what teenage boy, in most of the world, was not passionate about soccer?

"Mr. Campbell, my family is the most important thing in the whole world. I will do anything to secure their safety and happiness. You are here to ensure that. I will accept nothing less."

"We completely understand," Chris answered.

They spoke for another twenty minutes about the roles Teton Security and Defense staff would play during their time in Vietnam. Lucchese appeared comfortable with the scope and depth of the team and the personnel. Alex knew he had complete veto power over the people assigned to his family—so far, she had survived the interview.

Lucchese looked at his watch. "We have time for a tour of the facility. Would you like to see what it takes to build a motorcycle? The plant in Ho Chi Minh City manufactures smaller motorbikes and scooters. Here in Milan, we build larger and more powerful motorcycles—our primary competitors are Ducati, BMW, and Harley-Davidson."

The tour took an hour. Afterward, Alex was impressed by both the cleanliness of the plant and the professionalism of the managers. "You said that the facility in Saigon was already open," she told Lucchese. "I was under the impression that you were going there to build the plant and make it operational."

"We call it Ho Chi Minh City, so as not to be rude to our government supporters. Yes, it rolled out its first motorbike five months ago," Lucchese said. "Since then, it has been running nonstop. Our products fit well in the Southeast Asian marketplace. Our Vietnamese customers like the fact that the motorbikes are made in their own country. We're also expanding the technology facilities inside the plant, and I'll be there to oversee those as well. I have, as you might say, a full plate."

"The plant in Vietnam—is it as large as this?" Campbell asked, looking across the large manufacturing floor.

"Ho Chi Minh City is significantly larger. We will also employ twice as many as here. Labor costs are lower, so some of the automated tasks we do here are done manually in Vietnam. We also ship motorbikes to Cambodia, Laos, and Indonesia. After the expansion, we intend to increase sales to other Asian countries."

"And the animosity by the Vietnamese to the war?" Alex asked.

"I have found little, if any. Most Vietnamese are too young to even remember your war. Some, academics and politicians mostly, still have issues about past colonialism, and primarily with the French, but it was an American war, not Italian. Today, our communist partners and friends enjoy money and profit as much as the next Westerner."

The drive to the Lucchese villa took twenty minutes. The eighteenth-century stone structure sat along the ridgeline of hills to the north of Milan. Ilaria Lucchese met Alex, McCorly, and Chris in the soaring entry to the villa and invited them in. Tapestries hung on the walls.

"It is a pleasure to meet you, Ms. Polonia. I was drawn to your name. It's Italian for Poland, am I right?"

"Yes, and thank you," Alex answered. "I'll tell you the story behind it sometime."

Ilaria gave them a tour of the main rooms and took them out onto the terrace that overlooked the gardens and, to the south, the skyline of Milan.

"It can be very pretty here in the evening," Ilaria said to Alex. The men were admiring the small garden that Nevio had planted alongside the house. The early tomatoes were just turning red. "Nevio will miss his garden."

Alex nodded. "Yes, it must be hard to give this up."

"This house and the property have been in my family for almost three hundred years. Mine is an old and respected family. We have been industrialists since the founding of modern Italy more than a hundred years ago. We've survived two terrible wars. Some days, with the state of European Union politics, I'm not sure we will survive the peace. That's why we're building in Vietnam."

"You're part of the company too, aren't you?" Alex said, remembering the information in the dossiers she read on the flight.

"Yes, I sit on Como's board, and my family retains a significant part of the company. Nevio is an experienced manager who, as I like to joke, married into the family business. We're not selling the villa. It will be cared for during the two years we're gone. We will be coming back—that was one of the promises to the children. My business connections and involvement with the company will require us to return quarterly to Milan. That helped to mollify the kids, a little. It's not so bad."

"You are aware of what my job is?"

"Yes, Ms. Polonia. However, I'm not sure why we need two people watching us. Knowing the thoroughness of Mr. Campbell, I would have thought one was more than enough. And it's Nevio who is the primary target—don't you think?"

"Signora Lucchese, I was a cop. I've seen many things that would say one thing but are really another. My job is to protect you and the family, and that includes Signor Lucchese. I don't expect trouble, and if there is a threat, it will be deterred by our presence. However, we are trained to protect and respond as necessary. It's my hope that we never have to exercise that training. We intend that you and your family go about your lives as you like."

Ilaria paused for a moment as she looked across the garden at her husband. "Nevio is my life. He is a good father, an excellent provider, and a wonderful husband. Our children are strong and healthy. What more could a woman and a mother want?"

Alex thought about the madness she'd been through during the last year. *Yes, what more could a woman want?*

Two children left the villa and walked across the lawn toward them.

"Alex—may I call you that?" Ilaria said.

"Certainly."

"And you can call me Ilaria. And these are my two most favorite people in the world," she said as the children stopped a few paces from their mother. "They both speak English, and quite well. Paolo and Gianna, I would like you to meet Signora Polonia; she will be helping, along with Maria, to take care of us."

The two children extended their hands, and Alex shook each in turn. Gianna seemed shy and kept close to her mother. Alex thought the child seemed a little unsure. Paolo stared at her and puffed up like a teenager trying to impress his teacher.

"I know what you really are," Paolo said with a touch of defiance. "You are like the police. We don't need you. Do you carry a gun?"

"Paolo, that is impertinent and rude," Ilaria said. "Apologize to Signora Polonia."

The boy hesitated.

Alex's work had given her experience with countless troubled and confused youths, rich and poor alike, so she knew what Paolo was doing: he was asserting his role as the oldest. She was after all an interloper into the tight Lucchese family. But she was not about to let him take the high ground.

"Paolo, I am here to protect you, your sister, and your mother and father from the bad guys. I am a trained professional, and I have the tools necessary to do that. These tools require years of training. I do not, and neither should you, treat them as something from an American cowboy movie. I hope you understand."

"I can take care of myself."

"That may be true, but who will take care of your sister? Things will be strange and confusing. The cities, the travel, the food, and jet lag may make you feel out of sorts. You are a strong and tough kid—I see that. I'll need you to help us get through this. We all have our jobs; my job is watching all of you. Your job will be to take care of your sister and yourself. Can you do that? Can you help me make this work?"

Paolo's defiant look softened, yet his eyes sharpened. He looked at his sister, who was standing next to their mother. He reached out and took Gianna's hand. "I can do that."

"Excellent. On a ship, the second in command is called Number One. Paolo, can you be my Number One?"

"Like in Star Trek?" he said.

Alex smiled. "Yes, like Will Riker in Star Trek. So, you're a Star Trek fan?"

Before Paolo could answer, Ilaria said, "You have no idea. Paolo, you can show Signora Polonia your room later. She will then understand."

"Can I be Number Two?" Gianna asked.

"I think that's a brilliant idea," Alex said. "So, my Numbers One and Two, shall we go see your father?"

The two children walked ahead of them, whispering to each other and laughing.

"You could not have been a bigger hit," Ilaria said. "How did you know about his love for Star Trek stuff?"

"I didn't, but I'm a fan myself. And I have a few nieces and nephews that keep me up-to-date on all things Trekkie."

Alex was introduced to Maria, the nanny. The surprise was that Maria was Vietnamese. She told Alex her parents escaped on one of the boats during the mass exodus in the midseventies. They became part of a small group of refugees that settled in Italy. The forty-year-old Maria Nguyen spoke fluent Vietnamese and English, had been married once when she was younger, and had been the Luccheses' nanny for ten years. She was excited about traveling to Vietnam; she hoped that she would be able to see some of her family.

Lunch was served on the terrace.

CHAPTER 21

Alex's cell phone vibrated not long after midnight.

"Good morning," she said. "This is way too early. You okay?"

"Maybe," Javier said. "I don't know. We need to talk. Something's come up. Can we get together for breakfast?"

"I'm up now. Once up, I'm up. The cop in me just won't go away. How about now?"

"There's a small breakfast place at the train station, north end. When can you meet me there?"

"Fifteen minutes. I need to dress."

"That works. Be careful."

Before she could ask why, Javier had clicked off.

A dozen thoughts twisted around in her head. Javier sounded stressed, out of sorts. She dressed and walked through the small lobby of the Hilton. It was empty except for the young woman standing at the reception desk. She smiled as Alex walked by.

"Can I get you a taxi?" she asked.

"No, but thank you."

"Be careful, signora."

"I'll be fine," she answered, and tightened her leather jacket. The pistol was secured into the back waist of her jeans, hidden under a knit sweater and the jacket.

Milano Centrale train station was a block and a half from the hotel. She crossed the grand piazza that fronted the station. She and Javier had crossed this same plaza early Sunday on their way to Florence. Now it was empty. Beyond it rose the white wedding cake of marble that was the train station. Javier had mentioned that Mussolini built it before World War II.

She hurried inside and walked under the stone-and-glass vaulted ceiling of the main concourse, looking left and right. The great hall was empty except for a few tourists dragging their bags.

"Follow me," a voice said from behind.

Startled, she turned and faced Javier. "What's happening?"

"This way." They walked to the end of the terminal, where a small all-night café filled one of the corners. Signs in red neon offered pizza, drinks, and espresso. He pointed to a small table. Except for three young people at the coffee bar, the other tables were empty.

They ordered double espressos.

"Are you okay?" Alex asked.

"One minute. I need caffeine. It's been a crazy eighteen hours."

After the small cups and saucers were placed on the table, the disinterested waitress left them.

"Cloak-and-dagger stuff?" Alex said, sipping. "What?"

She looked at his eyes. Bloodshot.

He took a deep breath. "I've been in meetings all day, meetings that deal with NATO issues. Issues that I can't discuss with anyone—especially you. But they're issues that concern you and your assignment."

"What do you know about my assignment? You know I can't talk about any of this with anyone. I have a contract. Other than people with TSD and you, no one knows exactly where I am. I told my folks about Milan and Saigon—all they know is I'm on assignment, but they don't know who I work for. You're the only one who knows who my employer is. And I'm here because of you and your friendship with Chris."

"I know. That's why this is so important."

"What is?"

"Information came up in my meetings that someone is involved with the illegal distribution of military information, and the recipients are associated with people not friendly to the United States."

She looked at Javier, hoping he would say more. "And . . . ?"

"I'm in a precarious spot here, both professionally and personally. I've learned about things that are both a great concern and a possible personal disappointment. Things I can't talk about."

Alex thought for a moment, then waved at the waitress and pointed to the cups. The waitress turned and walked back to the coffee bar.

"I think I get it. You have your duties and responsibilities, and I have mine. You can't talk about your work, and I can't talk about TSD. Hell, it was like that with Ralph and me—and look what it got me." She stopped while the espressos were delivered.

She tapped the table and looked around the concourse that spread out toward the long platforms that split the incoming train tracks. A red-and-silver locomotive was easing into a slot between the platforms; a dozen or more carriages stretched out behind it.

"Okay," Alex said. "Let me say a few things, and you can nod yes or no. Looking at you, I can tell if I'm warm. There's something about my assignment that's hinky . . ."

"There's that favorite word of yours. Must be a Cleveland thing."

"Shush. Hinky, and that I should be concerned. I can't tell you what my assignment is—I have a contract. However, I'll assume, and for now just nod, that it may have something to do with my assignment and the company I work for."

Javier nodded.

"Something that you may have an idea about but can't confirm or even ask me about. You can't tell me anything more than that; I get that. Based on all this crap, I assume that you're warning me to be careful."

He nodded again.

"I can and will do that—but this all sucks. What if I discover some-thing during my assignment, something that's wrong? How do I know? What do I do?"

"You'll work it out," Javier answered. "I know you. It's a lot better than me losing my job and going to prison."

"Yeah, there's that. I get it—this is serious."

"Yes, extremely serious. People have died."

"And hypothetically, Agent Castillo, what happens if I find out something? Again, what do I do?"

"You'll figure out a way to deal with it, I'm sure."

"Shit."

"Yeah, there's that too."

Javier stood, then leaned over and gave Alex a kiss, turned, and walked away.

"You stuck me with the bill?" she called out.

He waved his hand in the air and disappeared around the corner toward the exit.

Alex sat in the terminal for another five minutes, wondering if she had been followed, or whether Javier had been followed. She'd regressed to stakeout mode and undercover cop.

What the hell was all that?

She stood and followed the same route that Javier had taken, her cop eyes and brain working. Now, everything and everyone was suspect, and it pissed her off. At one o'clock in the morning, she was not happy with Mr. CIA agent Javier Castillo for adding to her paranoia.

CHAPTER 22

That afternoon, a sleepy Alex slowly walked through the Lucchese villa, admiring the tapestries and paintings that hung on the stone and stucco walls. Her vision of the Italian countryside was all based on the movie *Under the Tuscan Sun*. She imagined most Italian buildings as old and shattered, with peeling paint, and exposed brick under the cracked stucco. The Lucchese home was a dramatic mixture of old and new: modern furniture; thick, elegant carpets; gigantic oil paintings of nymphs, goddesses, and armored men with ancient weapons. A few of the paintings were quite revealing, in a Renaissance sort of way.

"Many of these paintings were collected in the last century by my great-great-grandmother," Ilaria said, joining her. She offered Alex a cup of coffee. "Our family has always had a connection to the arts and literature. We were manufacturers. Nevio's family is also old, certainly by Italian standards. They come from the guilds and banking. They're from a bastard line of Medicis, one rumor goes. Then again, half of northern Italy believes they come from the Medicis or some other important fifteenth-century family."

"You have a remarkable and beautiful home," Alex answered.

"Thank you. We are just caretakers. I hope that my son will inherit this and carry on the family traditions. We also have a house in the mountains above Turin. That one is in Nevio's family. The children love to ski there. I spent my winters and many summers in a nearby village as a child. I didn't meet Nevio until I was much older, and it was after his wife died. He took that hard. They had no children, which was probably a blessing. I think that's why he dotes on Paolo and Gianna so much. I love him for that."

The two women walked a long corridor. Alex was surprised that the wall was unadorned; she saw brackets that might hold tapestries, but there were none. They came to a library that smelled of old leather, musty paper, and lilacs. A double door was open to a cloistered garden.

"I could spend the rest of my life in this part of the villa," Alex said.

"I spend a lot of my time here. The garden is what I'll miss the most. The roses are coming along, look. I'll miss their first bloom. And can you smell that? Lilacs. I wish I could bottle it up."

For the next three days, Alex's fondness for the Luccheses grew. She and McCorly helped the family finalize everything for their two years in Vietnam. Most of the packing had been completed before she'd arrived in Milan, but the family still managed to fill three large trunks with additional items. McCorly would see to it that the shipment would follow the family in a few weeks.

When Gianna discovered that there was a pony club not far from their Saigon apartment, she wanted to take her saddle. Alex listened in as Ilaria explained to her daughter the need for other things, but that if she were a good girl, she could later send for the saddle. Gianna reluctantly agreed, but it gave Alex a chance to talk to the child about horses and riding. She did not let on, even after her adventure with Campbell in Texas, that the expert was Gianna, not herself.

Paolo was the most economical when it came to packing. He announced that he would not be staying the full two years. He would return to school in the winter, he confidently told Alex, as there was a class ski trip to Switzerland. He was not going to miss it.

Javier had texted her but had mentioned nothing about their early-morning coffee, just that he was called back to Washington, DC, and wished her a good trip. Not an hour went by that she hadn't thought about their late-night conversation, which had made her even more suspicious than the job required.

Alex and Ilaria spent one afternoon shopping, just the two of them. Alex learned more about style and fashion than she had in the previous thirty years of buying clothes for herself. Ilaria bought her stylish jeans and an expensive blouse woven with gold threads. Alex sensed that Ilaria was not entirely happy about the move, in fact almost nervous. The signs were there: slight tremors in her hands when talking about the relocation, nervous glances at the crowds in the Galleria Vittorio Emanuele II. She talked about what they would do when they returned to Milan, never about what they were facing in Ho Chi Minh City.

During a quiet moment, Alex talked with Maria Nguyen. Maria told her that she had never been back to the country her parents fled in 1976 and confided that she was a little afraid. Her father, a government bureaucrat in Hue when the Tet Offensive swept through the city in 1968, was one of the few public officials in the ancient capital not to be summarily executed. After the North's victory in 1975, her parents fled as soon as they could. Eventually, they found space on an ancient wooden junk. After three weeks drifting in the South China Sea, an Australian destroyer rescued these boat people. Maria was born in a refugee camp near Rome. She considered herself more Italian than Vietnamese.

On the final day in Milan, once they'd finished the last of the packing, Alex was waiting for McCorly to pick her up when Nevio cornered her.

"Do you like automobiles?" he asked.

"As long as they get me where I want to go and don't cost a lot to run, I'm fine."

"Let me show you something."

They walked through the house and a courtyard that extended toward a low building that Alex guessed were the stables at some point. When Nevio opened the door, she was surprised to find a spotless garage and a dozen automobiles displayed like in a museum. Interspersed were more than a dozen motorcycles.

"These are my other children," he said. "They're almost as temperamental as Paolo and Gianna. However, they do cost a lot more." He laughed. "These two are pre–World War II Italian Bugattis, those two are Ferraris, and the bright-yellow one is a Lamborghini. Those two"— he pointed—"are Alfa Romeos I store for friends. That Ferrari won the Le Mans twenty-four-hour endurance race in the early 1960s. They're toys, but in my line of work, they do keep you grounded. The coming wave will be electric, sadly. And they don't get your blood pumping."

Alex knew little about cars but appreciated their beauty and the style. They were certainly easier on the eyes than Ralph's Dodge Challenger. Most were from days when mass production did not exist.

"There's a gap here," she said, pointing to a spot where there was room for three automobiles.

Nevio paused for a long moment. "Those spaces are for two Ferraris and an elegant Bugatti Type 57SC. They're out being serviced and tuned. I do that for all my cars once every year. They must be driven, and the garage comes and takes them out. They'll be returned after we leave."

Alex believed there was more to the story. However, Nevio did not elaborate, and she didn't ask.

CHAPTER 23

Dubai, United Arab Emirates

The flight to Dubai was uneventful, and thankfully the children behaved. Once Paolo found the private entertainment service, he disappeared into one of the more recent Star Trek movies starring Chris Pine. Gianna had exhausted herself the day before, riding and saying goodbye to her horse. She slept most of the overnight trip while Maria read.

After clearing customs, Alex recognized Harry Karns standing in the concourse just outside the doors. He held a small sign. Alex reviewed his credentials and asked him three questions provided by Campbell. He answered correctly. The overly cautious formalities complete, two men with pushcarts arrived and collected the luggage.

"I hope you had a pleasant trip," Karns said. He turned to the Luccheses. "It's good to see you again."

"And you," Nevio answered.

"I didn't know that you've met," Alex said.

Both men paused, and then Karns said, "It was during Nevio's earlier trip to Saigon. We met briefly to discuss—"

"Mother, I need a bathroom," Gianna said.

Nevio took the opportunity to ask, "We are at the Four Seasons Resort?"

"Yes, you'll be pleased," Karns said. "You and Signora Lucchese have the large suite, and the children their own rooms. Your plane for Saigon leaves late in the evening tomorrow, more than enough time to become accustomed to the time change. Shall we?"

Signor Lucchese nodded.

"Excellent," Karns said. He said something in Arabic to the two men. They promptly began to move to the exits. A limousine and a large van sat at the curb.

"Any difficulties I should be aware of?" Alex asked Karns. Later she'd ask about his previous meeting with the Luccheses.

"None. The boss wants you to give him a call. Don't worry about the time difference."

Outside, Karns wanted Alex to ride in the van with Maria, but she refused.

"I'm in the limo," she quietly said. "They're my responsibility."

Karns reluctantly agreed.

The drive to the Four Seasons Resort took twenty minutes in the midmorning traffic. Alex was surprised by how wide awake she was. Within an hour of checking in, the two kids had spotted the massive pool and beach behind the hotel. Ilaria agreed to let them use the pool but told them to stay away from the beach.

"Maria, make sure they have sunscreen on," Ilaria said, and looked at the children. "And I want you both to stay in the shade. I do not want sunburns. The next two days will be long, and if you two are even the least bit sunburned, you won't be happy. I want you to look out for each other."

"I'll go with them, and don't worry," Maria said. "I have sunscreen somewhere."

"You'll be all right?" Alex asked Maria.

"Yes, in fact, a little sun will be welcome," Maria said.

"Alex, I'm famished," Ilaria said. "How about lunch? There is a wonderful restaurant near the Burj Khalifa."

"The Burj Khalifa?" Alex asked.

"The incredibly tall building we saw on the drive here. There's some nearby shopping as well. This may be the last civilized meal and shopping we'll have for a while." She smiled pleasantly.

"I think that may be an exaggeration," Alex answered. "Will Signor Lucchese be joining us?"

"No, Nevio has work to catch up on, and he's stuck here for the afternoon. The kids will collapse after the pool, and Maria can take care of them. I want everyone to get a good night's sleep. Mr. Karns is with Nevio—he will be just fine."

Alex thought for a moment. All this was new, so new that she had no idea what to expect. The last six months had been a cultural and geographical hurricane. "Would love to."

The seafood lunch was delicious. If Alex believed that Venice was a challenge, with its old canals, passages, buildings, and history, the modernity of the Burj and its surrounding retail complex was like going to an alien city in some far-off galaxy. Nothing about the Dubai Mall complex reminded her of anything in Cleveland—mall or otherwise. Ilaria led her through the complex of shops and stores like an expert.

"Friday is Dubai's Sunday," Ilaria said on the ride back to the hotel, after Alex commented on the Burj complex's crowds. "It's the day for prayer and reflection. Today though, Saturday, everyone is out. But it's not as congested as the traffic in Rome can be. Tomorrow might be congested, but at least we're leaving late in the day. I have this surprise for the children tomorrow morning."

"Surprise?"

"Yes, something no one will expect here in the desert."

"Hint?"

"That's all you're going to get until tomorrow. We leave at ten, just after breakfast."

When they returned to the hotel, the children were watching a science fiction movie. Alex thought about her nieces and nephews and came to the conclusion that kids were pretty much the same in the United States and Europe. They spent an inordinate amount of time on their phones, watched the same movies, and according to Gianna, liked the same music. When Gianna mentioned a few of the current pop stars, Alex didn't know a single name.

The kids ordered a pizza. When Ilaria told them about a surprise for the next morning, they pestered her for an hour. Alex had to admire her silent determination. Ilaria declined pizza for herself, saying that lunch had been more than enough for her, and she went to bed early. Nevio was already asleep on the couch in the suite. Karns was reading a magazine on a nearby chair.

Alex walked out onto the suite's terrace and watched for a few minutes as the sun reached the horizon of the Persian Gulf.

"How long have you been with the boss?" Karns asked, suddenly behind her.

Startled, she said, "This is my first assignment. I think you call it babysitting."

"My first was a babysitting job as well. A Green Team operation. We went into Yemen to rescue the head of an oil company and his family. My job was to manage a wife and three kids. Why the man brought them, I don't know. It was a hot zone; we fought our way through al-Qaeda on the way to the airport. We lost one of the local guys."

"I don't think this will get that hairy," Alex said.

"It shouldn't. TSD does not like surprises; hence all the preparation. I'm here to help on the ground. When we get to HCMC, Jake Dumas will be a good man to follow. Jake has a lot of experience."

"I've met Jake."

"Good, so when Jake says jump, don't ask how high—it will be too late. Just jump."

"No one from Green here to join us?" Alex asked.

"Chris didn't think it was necessary. We're just passing through."

"Do you live in Ho Chi Minh City?"

"No, Hong Kong. Good airport connections and central to Red Team's piece of the world. Jake lives there too. But the way things are growing in the region, I wouldn't be surprised if TSD opens an HCMC operation."

"Would you like that post?" Alex asked.

"Wouldn't be too bad. There are worse spots, I can tell you that. I understand that you've never been to Vietnam."

"Not been many places. This is all new. Intimidating too, to be honest."

"I get that. Me, this old soldier been just about everywhere— Middle East, Far East, Africa."

"Chris said you grew up in Los Angeles."

"Yes. Got out when I could, joined the navy SEALs—ten years. When Chris offered me a job, I jumped at it. And here I am."

"Your experience sounds a lot like one of those soldier-of-fortune roles in old B movies," Alex said. "Foreign legion stuff. You like the adventure, the jazz?"

"The boss tells me that you were police, so I could ask you the same question."

"My story is a lot different," she answered.

"I know a little of it," Karns said. "When we have time, we'll exchange war stories."

The sun disappeared, leaving a purple haze that gradually faded on the horizon. She looked up and down the beach. A million lights sparkled across the city.

"Care for a drink?" Karns asked.

"I'll pass for now. I need a few items from the shop downstairs—I forgot toothpaste and some other things. Then bed. Will you be here in the morning?"

"I'm here all night. My room is next door. Sleep well," he said as he left the terrace.

She found the small twenty-four-hour shop in the hotel's concourse and collected a few of the articles she needed. The lobby bar beckoned, and she decided, now that everyone was in, to have that nightcap after all.

"Belvedere on the rocks," she said, taking a seat and looking around. The lounge was dark and quiet and looked out across the nearly empty atrium and the reception area. She finally had a chance to look at her phone and emails. Junk mail, mostly. She was hoping for a short note from Javier—nothing—or from her father. Nothing from him either.

In the mirror behind the bar she spotted movement in the lobby. Where she sat, no one could directly see her. As she sipped her drink, she entertained herself by voyeuristically watching the guests come and go. One couple, clearly just arrived, were in the middle of an intense argument. A small mountain of luggage was stacked on a cart behind them, and the bellman with the cart tried to ignore their conversation. Across the lounge, a woman in a deep leather chair, her phone pressed to her ear, waved one arm about. A businessman in a long white robe— she'd forgotten the garment's name—stood in the middle of the lobby, also talking into his phone. Three men talked in the corner of the lobby near the doors to the porte cochere. Two looked Chinese and wore dark suits, and the other was vaguely European, dressed casually, and had spiky, almost-white hair.

Then she saw Karns and Lucchese. They crossed the lobby and walked up to the three men. They didn't shake hands, just slightly bowed to each other. Karns pointed to each of the men, then to Lucchese. A conversation began. Karns looked furtively around the lobby.

Alex raised her phone and clicked a series of photos.

The five men crossed the lobby and exited through the automatic door.

Alex turned to the bartender and pointed to the drink. "I'll be right back."

She walked to the glass doors and saw a black Mercedes limousine under the awning outside, the overhead lights reflecting off its polished finish. The three unknown men climbed into the back seat, along with Nevio. Karns closed the door behind them, then took the front passenger seat. As soon as the door closed, the driver, hidden behind black glass, accelerated and left the courtyard. Alex walked out into the one-hundred-degree night air and quickly took a few more photos before the car turned right and disappeared into traffic.

A taxi idled nearby. Should she follow? Karns was with Lucchese. Her charge was Ilaria and the family.

Son of a bitch.

She returned to the bar, downed her drink, and walked back to the suite, furiously texting Chris the whole time.

CHAPTER 24

After the family, including Nevio, had breakfast in the suite, Alex tilted her head toward the terrace, looking at Karns. She wanted an answer. He followed her out.

"Where did you go last night? I need to know everything that happens with this family."

Karns looked stunned. He turned and stared out at the glassy surface of the Persian Gulf.

"Karns, you may have rank on me here, but this family is my assignment. So, where did you go?"

After a pause, he said, "Signor Lucchese received a phone call from a Como Motor client. They learned that he was in Dubai. They asked for a meeting. He reluctantly agreed; that was all there was to it."

"You came back at two o'clock, hardly an hour for a business meeting. What was it about?"

"I don't know. I remained in the car with the driver. Signor Lucchese was gone about twenty minutes. He returned alone to the limo. He didn't tell me what the meeting was about, and I didn't ask."

"You let him out of your sight for twenty minutes?" Alex said, her voice rising.

"Nevio said he knew them," Karns said.

"I assume that Chris knew about this meeting?"

Another pause as Karns tried to come up with an answer. She'd used this caught-with-your-hand-in-the-cookie-jar confrontation approach before.

"It can't be that difficult to answer," she said. "Did Chris know or not?"

"It was a last-minute thing. They were here in Dubai until this afternoon. I made a judgment call."

She made him stew for a minute. "I get it. Just business, no problem. And we *are* here at the pleasure of Signor Lucchese and Como Motors." She paused. Karns seemed to squirm a little. "We leave for Ho Chi Minh City tonight. Signora Lucchese wants to take the children out for something special this morning. Something they will always remember. Can you have the driver ready for us in an hour?"

She watched Karns visibly relax. "Yes, he will be ready."

"The whole family is going, including Signor Lucchese. I can handle the oversight. There's no reason for you to go. You have, I'm sure, other things to do. When we get back we'll head for the airport. You'll handle the final packing and get the luggage to the lobby. Maria will help. The kids are getting their bags together."

Karns started to object, then stopped. He was obviously trying to get the cookies back into the jar. "No problem, we'll be ready."

"Thank you, Harry. That will be a big help." She checked her phone. Still no reply to the text she had sent Chris the night before.

"Alex," Paolo said from the door. Gianna stood next to him. "We're all packed. I was hoping to spend a few more hours on the beach."

"Paolo, Gianna, your mother has something special planned for just the two of you. Mr. Karns will remain here with Maria and get the bags together. So, it will just be you kids, your folks, and me. So, Numbers One and Two, let's find your mother and get this adventure under way."

"Yes, Captain," Gianna said with a smile, and took the hand of her brother and went back into the suite.

The traffic was light as they drove southwest on Jumeirah Street. They turned south and crossed over a wide freeway. Paolo was the first to see the signs.

"The Mall of the Emirates," he said. "We're going to a mall? I'd have rather stayed at the beach."

"Be patient, Paolo," his father said.

The driver threaded his way among the cars heading into the massive complex whose facade filled the left side of the road for what seemed like a thousand meters. Seconds later they drove into a parking garage. The driver wound his way through the labyrinth and eventually stopped at a drop-off, where attendants stood waiting to valet cars.

Ilaria turned to the children. "There are ground rules. Paolo, I do not want you to lose sight of your sister for one minute. Do you understand?"

"Yes, Mother, but—"

"And Gianna, the same goes for you. I want you to stay near your brother."

The signs over the doorway read in both Arabic and in English "Ski Dubai."

"We're going skiing?" Paolo said excitedly.

"Yes, but it's inside the mall," Nevio said. "If you'd rather go back to the beach, the driver can take you to the hotel."

"This is so cool," Paolo said.

"Skiing in the middle of the desert?" Gianna said. "Really?"

"Yes, really," Ilaria said. "It will be a long time before you get a chance to ski again, and we thought this would be fun. They have all the equipment you need inside. Alex, the children are excellent skiers. Gianna has been on skis since she was two years old. Paolo almost as long. Do you ski?"

"Once, when I was about Paolo's age. I swore never to do it again. I can ice-skate, but I leave skiing to the professionals," Alex answered, and smiled at the children. "Is there a place to watch?"

"Yes, and they serve lunch. Are you two ready?" Ilaria asked.

Thirty minutes later the children were dressed in comfortable ski clothes, boots, and skis. Paolo decided to ski and not snowboard. Alex wished she'd been warned. She stood on the terrace that looked out over one of the weirdest architectural setups she had ever seen or even imagined. She was freezing. Climbing up and away from the restaurant and shops were two brilliant white ski slopes with real snow, ski lifts, and a couple of hundred skiers. Nevio and Ilaria stood side by side just inside the doors of the restaurant, watching.

Alex took Gianna's gloved hand in hers. "You got this?"

"I never even thought about doing something like this in the middle of the desert," Paolo said. "Wait until I tell everyone at school."

"Gianna?"

"Absolutely, we ski in the Alps every winter. These hills aren't as tall or as difficult, but it's also not as cold."

"You two remember what your mother said. Do I have your promises?"

"Yes, ma'am," Paolo said. "We will watch out for each other. You ready?"

Gianna quickly pushed away and left Paolo standing next to Alex. "She's going to beat you to the lift," Alex said.

"Not a chance."

Alex watched Paolo's strong young legs push off and glide effortlessly to his sister. They skied up to the chairlift and expertly dropped themselves into the chair. In seconds, they were looking over the edge of the lift and down onto the skiers schussing down the slope.

Alex hurriedly made her way back through the glass doors and into the restaurant. Nevio and Ilaria were having coffee at a table with a view up the slopes.

148

"They are so excited," Alex said, rubbing her hands together as she sat. "This couldn't have been more of a surprise—and the middle of the desert."

"It is strange," Nevio said. "But it's like this here. Dubai is where money from all over the world collides. As conservative as the Arabic nations are, they are also extremely capitalistic. There is nothing like this city in the whole world."

Alex ordered coffee, and just as it arrived, the two children raced by and back to the ski lift. Paolo raised his arm in salutation, Gianna a ski's length behind him. Her smile stretched from ear to ear.

"They're very good," Alex said. "Not that I'm any expert."

"He's a lot better than I am," Nevio said. "No fear."

"That makes a big difference," Alex said. "All I imagine is tumbling down the slope into a pile of broken skis and bones. My favorite part of skiing is the après-ski lounge."

"I agree," Ilaria said.

"Alex, don't let Ilaria sell herself short," Nevio said. "Years before we met, she skied on her university's biathlon team—almost made the Italian national team. Or that's what her friends told me."

"Biathlon?" Alex asked.

"That's where you ski cross-country and shoot at targets," Ilaria said. "I was very good, even if I say so myself. Father made sure we children know our way around guns. I'm also a good shot during duck season." She smiled.

"She's too modest; she is very good," Nevio said.

The three watched the children make run after run down the slopes. Alex was amazed at their agility and skill, especially Gianna's. Eventually Alex looked at her watch.

"Yes, I know, it's getting near the time," Ilaria said. "We'll have a late lunch back at the hotel. The children should have a nap. In fact, I think I'll lie down for a while."

"I'll go get the kids," Alex said.

Alex steeled herself for the blast of cold air and walked out to the edge of the terrace. It was wet and slippery. She thought about Cleveland winters. This was so different.

"Where's your brother?" Alex said to Gianna. The girl, in her pink parka, was standing next to a low fence that separated the skiing areas. "Gianna?"

The girl turned around, but it wasn't Gianna. Startled, Alex looked around. Off to one side, near where the equipment rentals were, stood another child in a pink parka. "Gianna?" Alex said loudly.

Gianna turned, a strange look on her face. She then looked back to a door that led out of the rental area and the complex. Alex carefully slipped and slid over to her.

"Where's your brother?" The girl was fixed on the doorway. "What's the matter? Where is your brother?"

"He's coming. He said he was going to make one more run. I'm waiting."

"What happened?"

"A man."

Alex dropped to one knee and gently took Gianna's arm. "What man?"

"A man. He went that way." She pointed at the door.

"What did he do?" She instinctively looked for a security officer.

"Nothing. He came up and told me to tell Father that they're watching, and to remind him of his promise."

Paolo slid up to the two with a spray of snow. Alex held up her hand to him.

"What promise?"

"That's all he said. He was scary looking."

Alex turned to Paolo. "You were supposed to never let your sister out of your sight."

"It was just one more run. No big deal."

"No big deal? Someone came up to your sister and said something to her. It was your job to watch her."

Paolo, stunned, stepped out of his skis. "Are you okay, Gianna? I'm sorry, Alex. It was just one more run."

Alex was more upset with herself than the boy. She should have stayed out here watching. She looked at the two children. They were fine, but she was spooked.

"What did the man look like? What was he wearing?"

"He was very strange," Gianna said. "He was thin, had blue eyes like yours and white spiky hair. He wore a motorcycle jacket and a black hood."

"And he said nothing else?"

"No, just to remind Father of the promise he made."

As Alex led the children back into the lodge, the first thing that came to her was they had been followed. Whoever this man was, he'd been watching them, and he'd followed them from the Four Seasons Resort. She would be much more observant from now on.

CHAPTER 25

Ho Chi Minh City, Vietnam

The small screen secured to the back of the airline seat showed that they were over the Bay of Bengal. All Alex saw out the window was water to the horizon. The Lucchese children were asleep in the row ahead of her. The parents were forward in first class, like they were for the first leg of the journey. Karns was in the back, in economy. She had switched seats with Maria—who wanted the aisle—but she still couldn't sleep.

Between Javier's late-night espresso session, the mysterious trip from the Four Seasons by Signor Lucchese and Karns, no response from Chris, and now this man at Ski Dubai, her head was in turmoil. And this man, based on Gianna's scared account, fit the description of one of the men that attended that meeting. After the late-night adventure, her detective brain had clicked on and run scenarios that surprised even her. Clandestine meetings, foreign agents, or customers out for a drink? The list was endless, and some of the things on the list were not nice. They twisted into strange events that she couldn't shake. She felt like she was outside watching a strange movie.

After they had returned to the hotel from Ski Dubai, she'd told Nevio and Ilaria about the man. They were both shocked and wanted to ask Gianna about what happened.

"They're both all right," Alex had said. "I suggest we not make more of it than what it is. No reason to get them upset. Signor Lucchese, do you have any idea what the man meant about your promise?" She included the part about the man and what he looked like, and that she'd seen him with Nevio.

Ilaria turned to Nevio. "What is she talking about?"

"I had a late meeting last night. You were asleep. Some customers. It was nothing."

"You should have wakened me. You should have told me."

Nevio paused, thinking. "There're some contracts to put together, but I'll do that in Saigon. I don't know why the man followed us. I'll tell them that it was unacceptable."

"It was more than that," Ilaria said. "They crossed the line. I will not have my children approached like this, never. Do you hear me, Nevio?"

"I said I will take care of it." He turned away. "I need to finish packing."

Ilaria turned back to Alex. "Thank you for being there. This was unprofessional of these people. I will make sure Nevio tells them."

"The kids will be just fine," Alex said. "Don't worry. I'll keep an eye open."

She did not tell Karns about the strange man at Ski Dubai. If Karns were a part of this—if he was the kind of TSD employee Chris had warned her about—she would find out soon enough. When she landed in Saigon, thirty-five hundred miles from this, she would call Campbell and find out what he knew. His lack of response to her text message was baffling. Did he just want her to mind her own business or something? No, it couldn't be; he'd asked her to keep a lookout for weird shit like this, after all. Regardless, it was what Javier had told her—or hadn't told her—that was the real issue. Something fishy was going on, and these latest events only added to it.

She recalled something about NATO she'd read in the laptop's Como Motors folder. Javier had said that he was working on something with NATO too—coincidence? Were TSD and Como and the CIA working together on something? If so, this was big—she knew that. It could be a hundred other things, yet the thoughts just kept churning.

Maria left for the bathroom. Alex slid the blind to the window down and closed her eyes. A few seconds later she felt a tap on her arm.

"Alex, I'm not feeling well," Gianna said.

"Sit here and tell me what's the matter." Alex was certain that her and her brother's chaotic eating schedule hadn't helped. And even though the meal on the plane wasn't bad, it might not have settled well.

"My stomach just hurts, and so does my head."

"Are you going to be sick?"

"I don't know. I think so."

Maria returned from the bathroom and talked to Gianna in Italian. She then rummaged through a cloth bag that she took down from the overhead. She removed two pills from a small plastic container and retrieved a bottle of water.

Gianna took the pills and water and gave Alex a weak smile. Maria said something else in Italian, and Gianna returned to her seat.

"What were the pills you gave her?" Alex asked, concerned.

Maria held up the small white bottle, which read "Midol."

"This is her second, and she is so young. And now she has to go through all this travel on top of it. Poor girl."

"Ah, the joys of becoming a woman," Alex said.

Entering the Jetway at HCMC's Tan Son Nhat International Airport felt like being slapped with a wet sock—the humidity was that thick. And Alex couldn't place the smells. They walked through the morning craziness of the modern concourse. Tourists and business people filled the aisles. The direction signs were in both English and Vietnamese. She was prepared for an ordeal at customs, but it was surprisingly uneventful.

The interior of the contemporary airport was glass, polished floors, and stainless steel. In many ways, it looked like a modern American airport, except nicer and far more elegant. Alex, Maria, and Karns loaded the luggage onto trolleys, and with the help of the kids, pushed them out of customs. In the middle of the mix of arriving passengers stood a lanky Vietnamese man in gray slacks and a white shirt. Karns walked directly up to the man, said something, then pointed to the trolleys. The lanky man pointed to two men standing near the doors. They both quickly walked to the trolleys and took control.

Alex walked up to Karns.

"Alex, this is Tommy Quan," Karns said. "He handles a lot of TSD's logistics and driving. Kid knows every alley and canal in HCMC."

She put her hand out. "Good to meet you, Tommy. Alex Polonia."

"Ms. Polonia, a pleasure," Tommy said. "Those guys are Bobo and Bing. They work for me. Good kids, my cousins, no worries."

Karns introduced Quan to the Luccheses.

"We go; can't afford a ticket for parking along the arrival curb," Quan said.

They then pushed their way out into the street-side arrival area, where two Mercedes limousines awaited. Bobo and Bing each stood next to one. Behind the two Mercedes sat a black Humvee.

"What are the arrangements, Alex?" Karns asked deferentially, clearly remembering Dubai.

"Nevio and Ilaria will travel with you in the first Mercedes; I'll go with the children in the second. The bags go wherever." She turned and looked at the Humvee. Bobo and Bing had been joined by two others. "Do we need this much assistance, or are they security?"

"No, HCMC is safe, probably better than Dubai." Karns leaned in to her. "But labor is cheap here, so a few extra boys to help is worth it."

Alex ran her hand over the trunk of a limo. "Is it raining?"

"Been raining all day," Quan said. "It's that time of year."

As they left, the rain increased with a ferocity that Alex couldn't believe. The drive through the city was a dreamlike visual through the speckled windows of rain, buzzing motorbikes, neon signs, and congestion. Even in the bright day, there were flashes of overhead neon signs in English mixed with Vietnamese. A road sign read "Cau Thu Thiem," and a moment later they were crossing a bridge. The water below was a confusion of lights reflecting off its surface. Then the chaos of the city disappeared, and a neighborhood of massive high-rises appeared, many like the ones they passed in Dubai.

The vehicles pulled under a porte cochere of a high-rise building. A sign on the boulevard fronting the structure read, "The Pearl." Karns directed the family toward the lobby. From there the bags were sent with Quan and some of the boys to a freight elevator. The Luccheses, Alex, and Karns took the residential elevator.

That evening, empty boxes of takeout were strewn about the apartment's kitchen. Earlier there had been a moment of panic when the delivery boy demanded cash, but Alex had dug through her backpack and found an American fifty-dollar bill—the kid was more than satisfied.

The jet-lagged family and Maria had wandered away to their various rooms. The apartment contained five bedrooms, a large kitchen, a dining room, and two family rooms, one formal and the other for media use. For an apartment in a communist country, the whole place seemed to Alex quite American upper middle class.

Alex and Karns stood on the wide terrace that surrounded two sides of the apartment. It was then that Alex realized the Luccheses had rented half the upper floor of the tower. The view was toward old Saigon and the new high-rise towers across the river.

"I'm confused and exhausted," Alex said. "I didn't know what to expect."

"Ho Chi Minh City has changed a lot during the last forty years and the end of the war," Karns said. "I first arrived twenty years ago. I have a type of dual citizenship. My mother is Vietnamese. She emigrated to the United States after the war."

"I hear a lot of English," Alex asked.

"There's a lot of English spoken here; you'll do fine."

"I saw the airport signs. That surprised me."

"Quite a few Australians and Americans come to visit. The country is gorgeous, and the people are wonderful. You just need to cut through the urban chaos and confusion. Hopefully, you'll get a chance to see all this." He pointed across the Saigon River to the intense concentration of lights that were beginning to come on and light the city core.

Karns removed a cigar from a case in his pocket. "You mind?"

"No, thanks for asking."

The moon cut through the thick clouds as the storm moved away.

"What happened at the tech facility?" Alex asked, finally getting to a subject she'd wanted to ask Karns about for three days.

"We were caught by surprise. The asshole planned it well—quick in and out. My guys were slow. If I ever find that man, he's dead."

"He?" she asked. Chris's conversation rang in her head.

"Yes, he—tall, lanky, and athletic. Went up and down ropes like a monkey. And could see in the dark—some type of night-vision helmet I've never seen or even heard of. The weapon he used fired explosive bullets. They were like miniature guided missiles with enough explosive power to blow a steel door off its frame. Blew my men to pieces."

"Did anyone get a shot off?"

"Yes, and we think he was hit. Left some blood. The police CSIs took samples, and so did we. But two of our associates are dead. I had to take them home to their families. Chris joined me. I missed you in Texas by a few days when I stopped there. From what Jake and Chris say, you should do a good job here with the family."

She wanted to ask Karns more about Dubai and what had gone on, push him. But as Chris told her, it was her investigation. She understood that if she knew something that someone else didn't, she might be holding more of the high cards.

CHAPTER 26

The next few days were a blur. Maria tried to establish a schedule: meals, school preparation, and laundry. Alex sat in on three interviews for cooks. They settled on a woman with French and Italian experience but whose every dish had a touch of Vietnamese. Bobo, one of Tommy Quan's men, chauffeured Ilaria, the kids, and Alex around Ho Chi Minh City and pointed out the more famous landmarks, the shopping areas, and the markets. The children's school would not open for another month. Paolo signed up for his school's soccer team, and Gianna reached out to the small equestrian center she'd told Alex about back in Milan. Alex promised her they would go visit in the next few days.

Nevio began leaving for work at seven, with Karns—his near full-time security detail—in tow. They rarely returned until after nine or ten in the evening, and Nevio would spend an hour or more in his home office on the phone with Milan. It was a five-hour time difference. Three days into the settling-in confusion, a safe and three steel filing cabinets were delivered to Nevio's office. Two of the cabinets were the type that held plans and drawings in large flat drawers. Once, Alex checked the door to the office, and it was locked. Alex asked for and received a small safe to store her pistol.

She had sent Chris another short text message about the night in Dubai, but—to her surprise and annoyance—still nothing. Until now, two full days later. She walked to the terrace, and standing under the broad awning, out of the early-afternoon rain, read:

I need to see you today. Reverie hotel on Nguyen Hue Blvd, room 2640. 3:00 p.m.

Her phone read 1:34. *What the hell? Chris is here, in Saigon?*

She walked into the kitchen where the family was having a late lunch. A tray of sandwiches sat on the counter along with iced tea and sodas. Not feeling hungry, she poured herself an iced tea and took a seat next to Gianna.

"Alex, is it ever going to stop raining?" Gianna said. "I really would like to go see the horses."

"The horses will be there when it stops," Paolo said, looking up from his phone.

"I know, but it feels like jail here. Nothing to do."

"You'll be fine. The school gave you a list of books to start reading," Ilaria said. "You have four of them. You could do that."

"Maybe, but it's still boring."

"Mother, they need a deposit for the ski trip to Switzerland by the end of September," Paolo said.

"We talked about this. You are not going. You will be here."

"Like Gianna said, it's a jail." He took a sandwich and a bottle of Coca-Cola and headed toward his bedroom. It had become his Fortress of Solitude. Gianna followed.

"Ilaria, I'm going out for a while this afternoon," Alex said.

"Alone?"

"I'm sure I'll be fine. And like Gianna said, it's getting a little prison-like here. When we were out the other day, I saw some Western shops in a mall along Nguyen Hue Boulevard. This rain has ruined one pair of shoes, and I need replacements. No reason to bother Bobo. I'll take a taxi and be back before five."

"Be careful," Ilaria said. "Nevio called and said there is a reception this evening at the Sheraton. Some advertisers are in town from Laos and Cambodia. He would like me there. It will be dull, but at least I'll be able to get out of our 'prison' for the evening. I didn't want to agree with Gianna, but both of you are right."

"I'll be back before you leave. Can I get you anything?"

"No, I'm fine. We'll get out this weekend and do something, agreed? I'll get the kids on it. That should keep them occupied for a while."

"Agreed."

Alex retrieved the pistol from the safe. Then, with the firearm snug in its holster in her jeans, she slipped on her lightweight raincoat, grabbed her handbag, and headed to the door.

Gianna intercepted her. "Mother says you're going shopping. Can I go?"

"Not this time, sweetie. Like you, I need a little time for myself. That okay?"

Gianna put a hurt look on her face. "I guess so."

"Your mother wants a family adventure this weekend. Can you and Paolo look through the guidebooks and come up with something? Maybe a boat ride, or a street market, or one of the museums? Look online—maybe you can find a place or two to visit."

She brightened a bit. "I'll try."

"Excellent. I'll be back before dinner. Your parents are going out this evening. Maybe we can find a movie on Netflix or Amazon tonight."

The taxi drove over the Nghe Channel to Ton Duc Thang, then along the waterfront past Me Linh Square to Nguyen Hue Boulevard. Two blocks up from the Saigon River, the taxi stopped in front of the Reverie hotel. Early for her meeting, she spent some time walking Nguyen Hue Boulevard to the old city hall and then back toward the river and Chris's hotel. The city, its aromas, and its sounds were fascinating.

The Reverie's lobby was a rich and colorful mix of crazy French tiles and bizarre, over-the-top decorations and chandeliers. This was not what she imagined when she thought of Chris Campbell. Then again, she hadn't given the personal Chris Campbell much thought. It dawned on her that she was in the most peculiar and whacky situation that she had ever been in. Nothing around her was familiar, nothing seemed real—even the smells were like nothing she'd ever experienced. Now she was going up an elevator to meet a man who said, via a text—not even a phone call—to meet him in a room, in a hotel, in a city that five months earlier she'd never have imagined herself in.

I told the children to find an adventure. It's not going to top this.

She knocked on the room door and waited. She knocked again, and the door opened. To her shock, Chris, disheveled and with his shirt open, stood there with a pistol in one hand. He backed down the suite's hallway, looking at her. He said nothing. He beckoned her in. She followed.

In the main room of the suite, he pointed to a chair at the small dining table. The view was the gray sky over the Saigon River. Through the haze was the multibuilding apartment complex that was now the home of the Luccheses and herself.

"Are you wearing your pistol?" he asked.

"Yes."

"Give it to me."

She did. "What's up, Chris? Why didn't you answer my text?"

"Sit."

She did.

He set his weapon on the counter of the small bar. "Belvedere on the rocks, is that right?"

She watched as he dropped three ice cubes in a tumbler and then filled the glass with vodka. He placed it on the table in front of her, then retrieved his drink and pistol from the bar. He spun one of the chairs around, sat, and placed the gun on the table. She saw that the safety was off.

"Give, damn it! I'm a cop; I'm used to this macho, in-your-face interrogation. I'm good at it, very good. I'd offer a Coke to a junkie, or water to a strung-out tweaker. Anything to make them pay attention to me, or to put them in my debt. Well? I've gotten my drink, but I'd never put a loaded gun on a table in front of a suspect. That's suicidal. What's going on?"

"You tell me," Chris said. He then ran his fingertip over the rough grip of the Sig. "Right now, I have no idea who you are or why you're here. I've told you things I regret. Things that put my people and my company in serious jeopardy."

"Christ almighty, what are you rambling about? Two days ago, I sent you that second text about the strange events I saw at the Four Seasons. I hadn't heard from you. I figured it was something I didn't need to know. Then your message today—and now I'm here. And for all intents, you're pointing that fucking thing at me." She looked at the Sig Sauer. With a light-ning move, she seized the pistol, clicked on the safety, dropped the magazine, and ejected the bullet in the chamber. It rattled across the wooden floor. She flipped the pistol back at Campbell. He caught it in midair.

"Feel better?" he asked.

"Much."

"I didn't get your text for a day; I was out of communication. I barely had satellite phone coverage where I was. When I read it, I was stunned. It took me two days to follow up—and I still don't know what that meeting was about—yet. Then I get this." He placed a large manila envelope on the table.

"And?"

"Open it."

She removed three pieces of paper, the first was an eight-by-ten color screenshot from a video. The resolution wasn't good. It was a man's face. He was lean and angular, American or European, with white, spiky hair. He was dressed in black and in his left hand held a motorcycle hel-met. His head was partially turned, as if he was looking at something.

"Do you know this man?"

She studied the face. There was something vaguely familiar about it, but she couldn't recall what. The eyes, maybe. He looked to be part Asian, and—

Wait, I know that face.

"May I get my phone?" she asked, careful not to make any sudden movements.

"Where is it?"

"In my bag on the chair."

He walked over and picked up the bag. "In the front pocket?"

"Yes."

He retrieved two phones. He looked at them and handed them both to her.

She clicked her phone on and began to scroll through the images. She stopped and looked closely at the photo on the screen, then the one on the table. "This is the man I saw that night in the Four Seasons lobby in Dubai," she told him, holding the screen toward him. "The same man as the one in your photo. He may also be a man who threatened Gianna and the family at Ski Dubai."

Chris's face turned ashen. He reached behind his back and pulled out another pistol, a match to the one on the table. He pointed it at her. "Who the hell are you?"

"Good God, Chris, what are you babbling about? You know who I am. I'm the same person that Javier stumbled into in Venice. I'm an ex-cop now because of him and you, damn it. And someday that man will break my heart." She placed her index finger on top of the photo of the man. "Where did you get this?"

"Get in here, Javier."

She turned and saw Javier standing in the bedroom doorway. "What is this all about?" She stood. "Damn it, Campbell, I punched you in the jaw once, and I'll do it again, pistol or no pistol, if one of you doesn't tell me what's going on."

Javier walked over and gently lowered Chris's pistol. "You won't need that." He looked at Alex. "That is a photo of the man who broke into the tech facility across the river." Javier looked at the image on the phone. "That man on your phone looks like the same man. He's an assassin and foreign agent who met with your client, Nevio Lucchese, and Harry Karns in Dubai."

"Yeah, I know that. I saw them."

"It was a meeting that we knew nothing about until your text. We think the other men you saw are businessmen from Shanghai. There are significant concerns by the company about their legitimacy."

"The 'company' being the CIA?" she asked.

"Yes," Javier answered. He put his finger on the photo. "Like Chris, I want to know what you know about this man."

She slammed her fist down on the picture, almost hitting Javier's finger. "I know nothing about this man. That night in Dubai was the first time I'd ever seen him."

"Really," Chris said. "Is this how you're going to play it?"

"Play what? What is going on?"

"Come on, Alex," Chris said. "Your little game is over. What I can't figure out is why you would tell me about the meeting. What do the Chinese want?"

"Game? Chinese?"

"Yes, this is big-time, not Cleveland party games. People are dying. You and your Chinese partners have stolen millions of dollars in defense secrets and technology and sold it to the Chinese. Secrets stolen by this man—Con Ma—and with your help."

"Javier, what is Chris saying? Secrets? Chinese? My help? I haven't a fucking clue what you're talking about. Two hours ago, I was helping a little girl figure out what she needs for school, not plotting to overthrow the fucking world. And Javier, I thought you were my friend, and right now all I get from you is—nothing." She turned back to Chris. "I don't know who any of these people are. You were there when I met the Luccheses, and Karns is your man. Why didn't *he* tell you about the meeting? You told me to handle this. I'm trying to figure this out, and you keep jamming me up. I don't have any partners, as you call them."

"Are you telling me you don't recognize your own family?" Javier said.

CHAPTER 27

"This is a joke, right?" Alex said as she stared at the photo. "One of your goddamned tests. Family? My family is in Cleveland, Ohio. How did you come up with this ridiculous idea? Javier, what am I, a total goddamned stranger to you? Why are you fucking me over like this?"

"The other papers," Chris said. "Look at them." He stood and walked to the bar and refilled his glass. He raised the bottle to Javier, but he shook his head no.

She picked up the papers and scanned through them, and immediately she knew what she was looking at: a DNA profile. Dozens of them had crossed her desk over the years. A few had helped her put bad guys in jail and, in one instance, had led to the conviction of a cold-case serial rapist. The name on the top of the first page of the file in front of her now said nothing—blank. The name on the second sheet was hers.

"I know what these are, and I know what they mean," she said. "So, what?"

"This profile shows you have more than enough genetic markers to make you and Con Ma related," Chris said. "According to my experts, and Javier's as well, that means you both have the same male parental line."

"No fucking way. Impossible."

"We want to know what that connection is to this operation," Javier said. "We're already watching your family."

"My family? You goddamned son of a bitch."

"It's standard procedure concerning national defense," Javier said. "My hands are tied."

She glared at Javier and took a long pull from her drink. She would have emptied the glass if her stomach hadn't rebelled. She ran to the bathroom and threw up.

"Keep the door open!" Chris yelled.

"Fuck you, Campbell!"

She stared at the mirror and slowed her breathing, hoping to knock down the panic that was rising in her gut. Her mind raced as she threw water on her face and rinsed out her mouth. DNA did not lie, so either the samples were wrong, or it was something else. She patted her face with a towel.

Operation? What operation? Think, think . . . Dad!

The towel against her mouth, she walked back into the living room. Javier was leaning against the kitchen counter. Chris was still sitting on the chair. His Sig sat on the table.

Her eyes shot daggers at Javier, then went to the table and looked diligently at the papers. "There *is* someone else involved," she finally said. "And your so-called experts should have seen it. I've been trained by the best. These say that he's not my brother but from another generation. If anything, this man is a nephew or cousin. Hell, look at him: he's at least twenty years younger than me. I also know for a fact that my father hasn't been out of the country since returning from Vietnam in 1971. Back then he didn't have enough money to do anything but send us kids to college. I know where you got my DNA; I freely gave it in Texas. Where did you get this guy's?"

Chris looked at Javier. "Is what she is saying about the DNA correct?"

"Yeah, maybe. Hell, I don't know. They said there were enough markers to make the connections. Further tests would need to be made."

"Damn it, Javier," Alex said, "you could perform a thousand tests and the result wouldn't change. Where did you get the sample?"

"That man was wounded during the break-in; he left a blood trail," Chris said. "We sampled it."

She lifted her empty glass, gave it a shake, and eyed Javier. "I need a fresh one."

Dutifully, he walked to the bar.

"Chris, I want you to get this in your head, and you too, Agent Castillo. I do not know this man. I am not aware of any family I have in Vietnam or anywhere else outside Ohio. If there is a connection to this man, it must come from one source. And it sure will surprise the hell out of the man responsible."

She told them about her father, the war, and the world of Vietnam in 1971, the same story her dad told her.

"Do you mean that your father may have fathered a child here?" Javier asked, handing her a freshly made cocktail. "That somehow this assassin, this Con Ma, might be his grandson?"

She sipped from her vodka on the rocks. "When you throw out everything else, what other possibility is there? Dad had no brothers, just two sisters. That is the only realistic conclusion, based on what we know and these pieces of paper."

Alex's breath caught in her throat as Chris put his hand on his pistol, but she exhaled when he slipped it into his back holster.

"So, you believe me?" she asked.

"Before you walked into this room, I wanted Javier to arrest you for treason. I had no idea what to believe. That man is your greatest defender. He said to hear your side, then decide."

"Golly gee, thanks for the super support, cowboy," Alex said.

Javier raised his hands in mock surrender.

"And?" Alex asked.

"For now, let's play this out," Javier said. "It's too damn peculiar to be something made up on the run. What do you suggest?"

"You said *operation*," she said. "What operation? Chris has me trying to find out who gave away top secrets that led to this Con Ma character killing two of our associates and transmitting classified data. After Dubai, Karns is certainly on the top of that list. So, what operation is this you're talking about?"

Javier looked at Chris, who nodded. Chris went to the bar, pulled two beers from the refrigerator, and handed one to Javier.

"Our sources tell us," Javier began, "that this Con Ma is working for a Chinese espionage syndicate that steals technical data, patents, software, and anything else worth something and sells it to those that would pay the most for it. The evidence says it's run by a woman; she's called the Chairwoman. They'll stop at nothing to get the information. For the last five years we've come up with zilch on this man, only a few sketchy photos and the debris and death he's left in his wake. What we've learned in the last few days is more than we've ever had on Con Ma."

"Great, just great. And what else?"

"We want this ring," Chris said. "We want Con Ma. And we'll do whatever we can to find them."

"Like staking out a simple man and his family in Cleveland?" Alex said. "Really, Jave? My detective vibes are telling me that there's a lot more going on. NATO? Easy access to a facility with super-important international data? Even in today's world, data can easily be hidden. I may be in my forties, but even I've heard of the cloud and blockchain. It would be easy to keep this information out of the hands of a group like this." She stopped and thought for a moment. "Yeah, I get it. It *is* easy, too easy. My brothers love to go fishing. The one thing I learned is that the bigger the bait, the bigger the fish. This is all a setup, a fishing expedition, all to catch this Con Ma, this Chairwoman, and her gang. But right now, all you caught was . . . me? Am I right?"

"I'm sorry, Alex," Javier said. "All of this caught us by surprise. Chris thought that Karns might be involved, but it's bigger than that. You found that out in Dubai, and we think that we can catch them here in Saigon."

"There's more?"

"Yes, the technology that we helped Como Motors create is real. It has significant importance to both the United States and NATO. It's a five-part software package that works with hardware that can overcome a swarm attack of drones or other massed intelligent offensive and defensive weapons. We've dangled this out there to see what we can catch. Unknowingly, Nevio Lucchese and his behind-the-scenes deals are helping us."

"You're putting his family in harm's way as well," Alex said. "Damn you—and this software is real?"

"Yes, to a point. But he's been passing information to Con Ma and maybe others. There are some built-in glitches, and in a month or two it will fail and eat itself. But it also needs all five of the plug-ins to work. One was stolen by this killer in the technology center. The second part Lucchese passed on in Dubai. As I said, I thought Karns might be involved. But we thought there might be someone else."

"I won't ask who."

"Jake Dumas is clean," Chris said, "if that's who you were thinking of."

"Good, I like him. So, am I still on board?" She looked at both Chris and Javier. Their response wasn't overwhelming.

Alex looked back at the papers and sipped her fresh drink. "Jesus, what a pair of bastards. Things we know: First, that Nevio Lucchese must keep dealing with this Con Ma like nothing has changed. Second, that Con Ma, this Ghost, is somehow related to me. I don't like it, but for now, it seems inescapable. Third, the Chinese have no idea that we know what's going on. And lastly, this Con Ma has no idea about me or our relationship. It also means that he has a father and mother somewhere, dead or alive."

"Where do you think this Con Ma came from?" Javier asked.

"No idea," Alex answered. "Other than something that must have happened almost fifty years ago, no clue. Chris, did you have any further research done on this DNA?"

"Like what?"

"There are dozens of worldwide data banks that collect and share DNA results. Did you check any further than your own DNA match?"

"Our people are still chasing this down."

"That's the first thing." She held up the papers. "And check them against as many databases as possible. We may get lucky, find his father or mother. However, remember that those results will be from people who have posted their DNA. This Ghost may have sisters or brothers, and he most certainly has a mother and a father. Whoever his parents are, one of them is my sibling—my half brother or sister—and they might be in the system. We must find out. It may be one of the leads we need to find this Ghost."

"I'll have my people in Washington help," Javier added.

Alex spun on Javier. "And that brings me to you. Why the hell are you here? To give Chris leverage on me?"

"Not fair."

"Then why?"

"We were meeting on another matter."

"And that is?"

"Top secret."

"Bullshit. Chris was going to shoot me if I made a wrong move. And you would have let him. So, all this top-secret crap is just that: crap. I called this bait—there has to be something else."

"Politics," Javier said.

"Politics, really?" Alex answered.

"Our efforts to cover up these facility deaths have kept the HCMC police highly suspicious. They were all over the crime scene; we couldn't keep them away. First, the port's fire trucks arrived, then a detective and his CSI team. They looked for fingerprints, went over everything. They took the transmitting device. We demanded it back, and they returned it to us a few weeks later. Even the escape ropes this Con Ma used were taken. They haven't shared anything with us. It's my guess that they also have this DNA, as well as data on the weapon."

"This is the weapon with the explosive bullet?"

"Yes, so we need to know what they have."

"That's my first job: find out what the police know," Alex said. "What's the name of this detective?"

"Tran Phan," Chris noted. "I met him with Karns during a follow-up trip I made a few weeks after the break-in. Nice enough fellow, but cagey. He didn't let much out. When I pushed, he rebuffed me and told me to mind my own store. He does not like dead bodies, even if they were *tây*."

"*Tây?*"

"Vietnamese slang for an American."

"If this Ghost is who you think he is," Chris said, "will you have a problem? To stop him will require some serious use of force."

"I don't know. You threw too many balls in the air." She checked her phone. "I've got to get back. I don't want to be late."

"Alex, I'm trusting you on this," Javier said. "My head says one thing, my heart another—and right now, be glad it's my heart."

"Is that a threat, Mr. CIA Agent? Lay off it, will you?"

She finished her drink and took the towel back into the bathroom. She splashed water on her face, then sorted out her blonde hair with her fingers. The curls had a mind of their own in the humidity.

When she returned to the room, her pistol was sitting on the table. She took it, dropped the magazine, inspected it, glared at Chris, reloaded the magazine, and slipped the pistol into her waistband.

"I'll go with you," Javier said.

"No, you stay here with Chris. I don't want to be seen with either of you. I'll let you know what I find. Chris, I'll need that additional DNA information as soon as something pops. Send it to the phone you gave me, not mine. And, Javier, right now is not a good time for us. Give me a day or two to get through this. Okay?"

He gave a reluctant nod.

She slipped on her raincoat, picked up the folders with the pictures and files, and without turning around walked out and into the hallway. What she really wanted to do was go back and punch them both in the mouth.

CHAPTER 28

When Alex returned to the apartment, Ilaria, dressed for the evening, was waiting for Nevio to return from work and take them to the event at the Sheraton. Nevio had told the family that he'd cleared his schedule for the next two days. Gianna was looking at Ho Chi Minh City guidebooks in the living room. Paolo was watching a video. Maria and the cook were putting together a feast.

"Eating all this before going out?" Alex said, entering the kitchen.

"This is for tomorrow night," Ilaria said. "The sauce needs to marinate."

Alex was amazed; fresh pasta sat on the counter in neat curled piles, the smell of tomatoes and seasoning filled the air, loaves of bread sat next to the pasta, and an open bottle of red wine rested on the countertop.

"Need help?" Alex asked.

"Too many cooks already," Ilaria said. "What, no bags?"

It suddenly dawned on Alex that she had no shoes from her shopping trip. "I couldn't find anything in my size," she said, thinking quick. "These Vietnamese girls are a lot smaller." She smiled and said she would be in her room. She took one last look as she turned into the hallway; it was the happiest the family had looked in weeks.

It was four thirty in the afternoon, which meant—she mentally did some calculations—it was five thirty in the morning in Cleveland. She needed more information, information only a man in Cleveland could give. Too early to call her father—he had to be told about this family connection in Vietnam. There was no sense in putting it off. During the taxi ride back to the Lucchese apartment, it had been all that she'd thought of. Assuming the testing was correct and double-checked, this Con Ma, this Ghost, this spy and murderer, was her nephew. No wonder Chris and Javier were upset. She'd have been furious if she'd found this DNA trail in a case she was working on in Cleveland. There was no reason for Chris to fake this—based on his reaction, he was as surprised as anyone. She was beyond shocked. Her father had left a child in Vietnam? A child, now an adult, that sometime, maybe twenty-five years ago, had a son of their own? A son that had become this murdering Ghost? Was this child of her father still alive? Was this person a man or a woman? Did she have a sister or a brother in Vietnam, maybe here in Saigon? Maybe just two blocks away, running a noodle stand?

After the Luccheses left for the reception, Maria put together a quiet dinner for the children and Alex. Later, after watching a movie, Alex said she was going to her room. She said she was tired, but her watch said it was past nine o'clock in the morning in Cleveland.

She closed the door to her room and dialed.

"I was thinking about you this morning," her dad said before Alex could even say good morning. "What time is it there?"

"Hi, Dad. It's almost ten thirty at night. How are you and Mom?"

"We're great! Never a moment's peace around here. We're going to the lake this afternoon. John and Annie and the kids are coming out to the cabin. I was hoping for a relaxing few days, but not this time. The Tribe's in New York tonight, so there should be some good baseball to watch. The kids want to water-ski. They say there's a crappie bite going on. Busy, busy."

Alex didn't say anything for a long while.

"You okay, honey? What's up?"

"Something has come up," she said, "something that I need to talk with you about. I wish I could do it in person, but this is as good as it can get for now."

"Jesus—you okay? You're not hurt, are you? Something happen?"

"No, I'm fine. Is Mom there?"

"No, she spent last night at Rick's. One of the kids has a bad cold and they had this thing last night, so your mom stayed with them. She'll be back before noon. Damn it, Alex—"

"Dad, tell me about Yvette."

"Yvette? Why, what's going on?"

"Dad, I need you to tell me about Yvette and Saigon. You said that you two were in love, and that you believed she died during the war— and that you never found her, is that right?"

The pause was longer on Roger's end. "Why are you asking? What's happened?"

"You mentioned never hearing from her again and wondering if she were dead. There was no confirmation about her death?"

"Honey, how could there have been a confirmation? The whole of South Vietnam was burning. There was no one to go and find out anything about anyone. Now tell me what's going on."

Alex didn't care what Chris and Javier said about national security or that something was rotten in Teton Security—this was her family, her father.

"Dad, I'm in Saigon. I'm assigned to care for a family. There are two kids and a wife and husband. He works for a large international company. My job is simple: provide safety and security for the family. Earlier this year, there was a break-in at a facility that my company was protecting. Important data was stolen, and two men were murdered."

"You told me that this was a safe job. When your mother finds out—"

"Don't say anything. I'll tell her when the time is right."

"She'll know before then. You know her."

"She'll have to wait." Alex stopped and thought for a long moment. "You still there, honey? What does all this have to do with Yvette?"

"A man, an Amerasian man, is the prime suspect in the killings. He fled after he stole the data. He was injured and left a blood trail. My boss had the blood tested, hoping to connect to someone in the international database of criminals. He found a match, or at least a close match."

"It can't be Yvette. She's not a criminal. There was no way they could have made a connection to her."

"No, Dad, it wasn't to Yvette. My boss sampled my blood as part of my training. And the DNA match was to me. This man, this killer, this criminal they call Con Ma, the Ghost, is my nephew . . . your grandson."

CHAPTER 29

After the conversation with her father, Alex was restless. She flashed on the thought of chucking it all and going home. What her father must be going through—all the anguish, the lost years, the questions with no answers. She stood at the window and watched the lights of Saigon. Even at three in the morning, hundreds of motorbikes wove in and out of traffic over the bridges of the Saigon River. Sometime around five, she fell asleep, then woke an hour later with a start. She showered, dressed, and went to the kitchen for a cup of coffee and was surprised to see Ilaria sitting at the table, a cup in her hand.

"*Buongiorno*, Signora."

"Good morning, Alex. I couldn't sleep either. Nevio won't be up for an hour or more. The reception and dinner went late."

Alex sat in a chair. "Are you okay?"

"As good as I can be so far away from everything I know. Thank you for taking care of the kids—they like you a lot."

"I'm more concerned about you. What's going on?"

"Lonely, a little depressed, bored . . . the usual."

"Usual?"

"I got wrapped up in the excitement of the move, the packing, the organization—I even told myself that this one would be different. They never are. I could be in the most glamorous place in the world and still feel this way. It's just the way I'm wired. I'll get through it—takes a few weeks. A little depression. I'll be fine."

"Maybe we can get away for a day or so. Maria can take care of the kids while you and I do something."

Ilaria smiled. "I'd like that."

A few hours later, Gianna offered her plan for the day.

"I found a market we can all go to," Gianna said. "I watched a video, and Paolo helped me find it on the map. Food and all sorts of interesting clothes. What do you think, maybe later today?"

"Where is it?" Alex asked.

"It's called the Ben Thanh Market. According to the internet, they have the best street food, and clothing, and so many other things—they're nothing like our markets in Italy. Even Father said he would go. The whole family."

"That sounds nice," Alex answered. "Since you're the travel director, what are your orders?"

Gianna told her about getting the limo, and that Mr. Karns would do the driving. They would leave at 11:00 a.m. It would be the family's first big adventure together in Ho Chi Minh City. She had even checked the weather. "They say absolutely no rain."

At eleven o'clock, Gianna mustered everyone together, and in one group they headed down to the lobby. Maria begged off. She said a few hours of peace and quiet would be all the therapy she needed. She would go next time. Karns was waiting with the limousine at the front door; all five managed to fit comfortably.

Ben Thanh Market was in the center of the old part of Saigon, almost a direct shot south from their apartment. Gianna, guidebook in hand, pointed out buildings and museums along the boulevard as they approached the massive, two-block-square, red-roofed complex. At its entry, a clock tower faced a traffic roundabout filled with hundreds of motorbikes that circled like a swarm of bees looking for somewhere to land.

"I'll find a place to park," Karns said as everyone climbed out. "I'll wait with the car. Text me when you're ready to leave. If anything happens, call."

"Don't be far," Alex said.

The market, a rabbit warren of narrow walks and paths, was crammed with T-shirt dealers, lacquerware shops, kitchenware—to stay in business, these vendors sold almost everything. Most of the shoppers were Vietnamese, but the place was obviously aimed at the tourist trade. At each food vendor, someone would walk out and shove a laminated card in their faces with photos of dishes, yelling, "Best food, best food. Best price!"

"Isn't this cool?" Gianna said. She took Paolo's hand, and when they passed a DVD dealer with thousands of pirated copies stacked six feet high, she pointed. "See, there's a *Star Trek Beyond* in Vietnamese; I'll bet no one at home has one of those."

After a short negotiation with the dealer, Paolo walked away with the DVD for one euro. "I hope it works in the DVD player," he said to Alex.

As they neared the fish and meat stands, the crowds thickened. Alex was a little above average height for an American woman, yet she towered over the Vietnamese women and many of the men. The Americans and other Westerners wandering the passageways were often a head taller than the Vietnamese; they stood out.

Everywhere Alex looked there was something new and different. Great slabs of meat—she assumed they were beef and pork carcasses— hung from racks to her left. To her right, long, ice-filled displays of fish extended for hundreds of feet. Uncountable varieties of fish, shrimp, and shellfish were stacked and neatly displayed in the trays.

With his camera, Nevio took close-ups and wide-angled photos of the fish. A woman behind one overfilled tray raised a huge fish to show him—she smiled, and he took her picture. Afterward he continued along the fish counters, clicking away.

The crowd pressed in, and Alex spotted a man that was easily a foot taller than anyone around him. His hair was bleached white and stiff, almost bristly, and a hoodie covered the back of his head. The man bumped into Nevio, whose free hand passed something—it flashed in the overhead glare of lights—into the hand of the hooded man. In that split second the drop had been made. Nevio then went back to taking more photos.

The hooded head of the man moved toward the exit. There was something familiar about him—something strange. As he reached the end of the fish counter, he turned his head; it was Con Ma.

Alex leaned down to Gianna, whose hand she was holding. "I'll be right back. Go to Paolo, okay?"

Without waiting for a response, Alex pushed her way through the crowd, trying to keep the man in sight. She saw his head for a moment, and then it disappeared out an exit. Reaching the street, she scanned left, then right, while a hundred motorbikes buzzed by. On the far side of the traffic circle, the white-haired man climbed aboard a blue motorbike and sped away.

"Everything all right?" Karns said from behind.

"Yes, everything is fine," she said, her eyes never leaving the Ghost as he disappeared toward the river. "There was a man inside. I thought he dropped something. I followed to tell him. But now he's gone. Are you parked near here?"

"I'm over there." He pointed to a taxi stand. "A few of the locals are pissed about my taking up so much space. I bought them a few beers. We're fine now."

"I'm going back in. It was close in there, stuffy—good to get a little fresh air."

Alex returned to the family. Paolo and Gianna had purchased T-shirts that read "Ciao Saigon."

"Where did you find that?" Alex asked Paolo.

"They made them for us." He pointed to a booth. "Just a few euros. I had one made for my girlfriend. I'm going to send it to her."

Alex smiled. She didn't know that Paolo had a girlfriend. "I think she'll like it."

She was positive that Con Ma hadn't seen her follow him out. His movements next to Nevio had shown skill and patience, and a practiced sleight of hand to take from Nevio what she assumed to be a thumb drive and then leave. He never looked back—a professional drop.

Nevio's expression never changed. The exchange was obviously planned. Once Gianna had decided where they were going, Nevio must have gotten the word to Con Ma. The Ghost was still in Saigon, waiting.

Ilaria found a table at a noodle shop, and the family ordered.

"I need to use the restroom," Alex said, and headed toward a sign. The place was as evil smelling as any restroom she had ever been in. She just needed a few minutes to send Chris a text:

Con Ma at Ben Thanh Market, a data drop by Nevio. Too strange.

She returned to the family and leaned into Ilaria. "The bathrooms are disgusting. I suggest we wait until we leave here if you or Gianna need to use them."

Nevio never said a word other than to point to things for the kids. He continued taking photos.

"He's very good," Ilaria said, seeing Alex watch her husband. "He has an eye for the interesting."

"Second stop today is the zoo," Gianna said. "That will be enough for today."

Alex was not a fan of zoos. Something about them reminded her of police work. While some people needed to be in jail, animals didn't belong in cages. Most animals looked contented, but being locked behind bars made some people crazy. She could only imagine what it did to an animal once free.

Her phone pinged. Chris: *Meet me 8:00 at Me Linh Square.*

"Can I borrow your map?" Alex asked Gianna, who was studying her guidebook. She found the half-round public square along the Saigon River; it was not too far from Chris's hotel.

By the time they left the zoo, it was late in the afternoon. The rain, contrary to the forecast, began in earnest. They hopped into the limo and made it back to the apartment just as the sky opened up.

Nevio was more involved with the children than Alex had seen since they left Italy. He asked what they were doing, wanted to see their schoolbooks, the latest video games they were playing. The day ended with the best Italian dinner Alex had ever had. The cook helped serve. Alex complimented her and Maria a dozen times. Each course was a treat. Nevio said it was in celebration of Gianna and Paolo's successful adventure.

After dinner, Karns left and Alex told the family she was going for a walk. The rain had stopped and cleared. She would be back in an hour. Nevio told her to be careful, and she said she would be fine. She returned to her room, slipped both phones into her pockets, and secured the Glock at the small of her back under a fresh silk shirt.

She walked out of the apartment building and looked out over the roadway for a taxi. A warm, humid breeze ripe with the smells of gasoline exhaust and the Saigon River filled the air. A seagull squawked and dipped low over the river.

"Need a ride?" a voice said from behind. Javier straddled an old motorbike. "Chris has changed the venue."

CHAPTER 30

"Why am I not surprised?" Alex lifted her leg over the ripped seat and settled in behind Javier. He lurched off onto the frontage road. In a few minutes, they were crossing Cau Thu Bridge.

"A little rusty, aren't you?" she said into Javier's ear as he jerked the shift up and down.

"Been a while, and this toy has a lot less get-up-and-go than my brother's BMW."

"Where are we going?"

"The scene of the crime."

They drove through the new developments along the Saigon River in District 2 and then crossed Cau Phu My Bridge. Javier then turned into the port area of District 7, and ten minutes later they pulled up in front of a row of nondescript warehouses. A ten-foot block wall surrounded the buildings. The iron gate was open, and parked in the alley was a pale-blue Hyundai. Chris was standing by the rental car. Javier stopped next to him.

"Not what I had planned," Alex said. "I can be away an hour, no more. They may get concerned."

"Won't take that long," Chris said. "I wanted you to see the facility where the Ghost broke in. I want your opinion."

Thirty minutes later, Alex was sure it was all a charade set up by Chris. "There's nothing here. It was months ago. Why am I here? What's going on?"

Chris turned to Javier. "Tell her."

"We needed to see if someone was watching the apartment. To see if somebody would follow you."

"And?" Alex said.

"Jake says no."

"Jake Dumas is here?"

"Trust is a hard commodity to find these days," Chris said.

Alex's eyes flashed. "Is that a dig at me?" She took a deep breath, calmed herself. "I haven't seen anyone watching the apartment either."

"It was Javier and me in Milan," Chris said. "When you were in Dubai, it was supposed to be Karns."

"That didn't work out so well, did it?" Alex said.

"I know that, now. Since no one here, other than Karns, knows Jake, he'll also keep an eye on Lucchese."

"But you don't trust Nevio either."

"And that's why you're here," Chris said. "Sometimes the watchers need to be watched."

"I thought you didn't trust me." Alex looked at the door of the office, which hung on a single twisted hinge. "I talked with my father. He was shocked that he may have a child here in Vietnam, and even more astonished that he may have another grandchild."

"We thought that you would talk with your father; that's okay. A lot of GIs left children here," Chris said.

"Yes, but he may be the only one whose grandchild is an assassin and spy for the Chinese," she added. "He'll have a tough time with all this. This is so against his sense of right and wrong. It will eat him alive."

"I understand," Chris said.

"I don't think you do. I don't think either of you do. Something like this is so unbelievably traumatic, especially for my father, who went through years of PTSD. No one can understand. You spend two-thirds of your life believing one thing, and with one phone call, it goes all upside down. My father, the greatest man in my life, thinks he's walked away from his responsibility—a woman he loved and a child he didn't know. How would that make you feel? Then to learn that his grandchild is a psychotic killer. It's way too much—too much for both of us."

"You had nothing to do with any of this," Javier said.

"Small consolation—and that's not what you thought earlier. I'm up to my ass in it now." She turned to Chris. "Anything more on the DNA?"

"No."

"Anything from the police?"

"No."

"Why should they, I guess? You certainly haven't been forthcoming. They haven't seen all the files, the photo of Con Ma. Maybe they took DNA or not. So, if you haven't helped them, why should they help you?"

"We can handle this."

"Really? It's a fucking disaster, Chris. You think you've got this bait dangling out there in front of the Chinese, but how do we know they aren't playing us? Hell, we could unwittingly be providing security for them," she said, looking at Javier.

"Not fair, Alex," Javier said.

"Be careful, Jave," she said. "Life isn't fair when it comes to things like this—you know that. I may have been a cop, but I saw things that were exactly like this during turf wars and gang fights. The battles are the same. International politics is just a difference in scale. Tomorrow, I'll contact this detective, Tran Phan, and find out what he knows. Where can I find him?"

"The District 1 police office," Chris said. "Just a few blocks from the market you were at today. I told you I met him briefly with Karns." He handed her Phan's card.

She took the card from Chris and stared at him. "I only told you afterward about where we were. Were we being followed?"

Chris glanced at Javier.

"Really? You were following me? Has it gotten this bad? And if you were following me, why didn't you go after the Ghost?"

"No," Javier answered. "I was following Nevio. He's the man on our radar, not you. I lost you in the market. And it seems our fears were justified."

"And good job on following Con Ma," Alex said. "I spook him out of the bushes, and you lose him."

She looked at the business card. "I'll call Phan and set up a meeting—just me. I'll find out what I can. He doesn't know me from anyone; I'll cook up some cover story. Then we'll see. I'm trying to understand whether you want to find out what happened or are just hoping that you can keep a lid on all this. I can go either way." She looked at both men. "You said there are five parts. They have three now, right? Keep them on edge about the last two. Maybe it will draw them out. And I need to keep the rest of the Lucchese family out of this looming disaster. Chris, if you want me to investigate, then stay out of my way."

Alex climbed on the motorbike. With luck she would be at the apartment in less than a half hour. She wrapped her arms around Javier's waist and couldn't help but breathe in his aftershave. It was one of the first intimate things she'd learned about the man that first night in Venice. His was a muskiness mingled with a touch of lime—exotic as the streets they were weaving through. After they crossed back into the old city of Saigon, Javier slowed the motorbike and pulled off to the side into a small park, where a statue stood. They both got off.

"The DNA, the Chinese, my job, you," Javier said. "It got all twisted up. I'm sorry. I know you can't be a part of this."

"Do you have any idea where this is leading?" she asked.

"I'm trying to stop the Chinese from creating systems that can defeat—"

"Not Nevio and the Chinese. Us, Javier, us! Do you have any idea where this is taking us?"

"No, I don't know where this is taking us," he said, then paused. "I have my duty—a sworn duty—that I'm trying hard to fulfill without getting my ass thrown into a federal penitentiary. I have my friendship with Campbell that goes back years. And I have my mother nagging me about whether you're the right person for me."

"Your mother?"

"And to be honest, she scares me more than the government. We will catch this Ghost. We will stop this Chinese organization. We will stop the spying and international intrigue associated with all this. But overall, I have to make my mother happy."

CHAPTER 31

Detective Tran Phan's secretary handed him a note with a phone number scrawled on it. He saw the area code, according to a quick check on his computer, was from Cleveland, Ohio. He did not know anyone from Cleveland, Ohio. Why was someone from the United States calling him? Then again, he could easily share a bottle of scotch with all the Americans he knew in HCMC. He tapped the note with his pencil. Curiosity got the better of him. He punched in the number.

"This is Detective Tran Phan with the Ho Chi Minh City Police Department," he said in English. "You called me?"

Over the speaker, a woman's voice responded, "Detective Phan, thank you for returning my call. My name is Alexandra Polonia; I'm calling about the incident at the Como Motors technology facility earlier this year—where two Americans were murdered."

Phan paused, surprised. "Ms. Polonia, how can I help you?"

"I work for the company that employed those men. I'm trying to find out what happened. Our investigation has missing parts. I'd hoped that you might be able to fill in the blanks."

"Fill in the blanks? I think I understand what you're asking, and the answer is no. We do not share our evidence with anyone. Sorry."

"You don't want our help solving this crime? I find that hard to believe."

"We are a city of eight million. There are murders and suspicious deaths every day. My job is to solve them. I'm sure that I don't need help from someone who's in Cleveland, Ohio."

"I'm here in Saigon."

He tapped the note again. "We Vietnamese prefer Ho Chi Minh City."

"I'm sure you do. In any case, my boss ordered me to find out who killed our associates. And my boss always gets what he wants."

"Sounds like a nice guy. I met some of your people. They were not that cooperative. You didn't want to help us then, so why now?"

"New evidence has been found."

He paused. "New evidence? What would be more helpful is the truth. We still don't share our evidence. And we're pursuing our own leads."

"And these are . . . ?"

"Again, Ms. Polonia, I am not one to share information."

"At least a conversation," the woman said. "What we have might be considered a gift."

Phan retrieved his coffee from his new coffee maker and sipped. He nodded. While he preferred tea, this coffee was very good. "I'm always open to a conversation. Is there someplace you would like to meet?"

"Your office? Is that acceptable?"

"My office is a disaster. There's barely enough room for another chair."

"Where do you suggest?"

"The Sheraton hotel has a nice rooftop bar that looks over the city—say in one hour. You can buy me lunch."

Phan's walk was exactly thirty minutes. Three-quarters of the way, breathing heavily, he decided for the hundredth time to quit smoking.

As he walked through the lobby of the Sheraton, the air-conditioning chilled his damp shirt, extracting a shiver. The elevator to the twenty-third floor opened near the restaurant and bar. He liked this restaurant. From sixty meters in the air, the city looked deceptively serene; he knew differently. He ordered a beer, a Budweiser. After about twenty minutes, three crushed cigarette butts sat in the ashtray. A blonde, clearly an American, walked through the bar, casually studying the patrons that filled the barstools and tables. A large bag hung on her shoulder. When she passed by for the third time, he asked, "Are you Alexandra Polonia?"

The woman stared at him and scrunched her forehead. "Are you Detective Phan?"

"Yes." He stood and offered her the opposite chair. "You looked surprised."

"I didn't expect a European." She offered her hand. "I'm Alex Polonia. It's a pleasure to meet you."

"The pleasure is mine. I'm half-American and half-Vietnamese. My father died during the war, before I was born."

She looked at his beer. "Budweiser?"

"Very fancy—until a few years ago, it was imported. We now have a brewery here in Vietnam." He looked at the waiter and pointed to his bottle. A second Budweiser appeared a moment later.

"Ms. Polonia, why are you here and not that insufferable Mr. Karns or his boss, Jake . . . something?"

"I work for their boss, Christopher Campbell. It's his company, Teton Security and Defense. I understand that you've met Mr. Campbell."

"Yes, a brief visit. You're not very good, are you?"

"I'm sorry, what?"

"If you're such a big-shot international security firm, how come it was so easy for someone to break into your client's facility and kill two of your people?"

He grinned. He guessed she was not pleased with his comments.

She smirked in return. "I used to do that; I was a cop. I'd badger and poke the bear, looking for a response. All to see if I could get something to use."

The waiter returned to the table.

"Let me order," he said. "Just a few dishes to nibble. I usually eat a light lunch."

He spoke in Vietnamese with the waiter, who nodded and left.

"The food is good here," he went on. "Not great, but more than just edible." He lit another cigarette and saw the disapproval on her face. He took one long drag and then crushed it next to the others.

"I didn't mean to make you put it out."

"I'm trying to quit."

"That's what my father said," she said. "Just a few weeks ago, in fact."

"My kids pester me almost daily."

"How many?"

"Two at home, Kim and Kha. Kim is in college. She's nineteen. Kha is finishing high school this year. He hopes to go to college. They're both good kids, considering."

"Considering what?"

"Being Amerasian. There's still resentment to mixed-race children here. My wife and I had a tough life growing up and dealing with it. The kids are still dealing with some of it."

"Your wife?"

"Yes, Jessica is also half-American. We fell in together, probably because we were both outcasts—that's not the right word. More like on the fringe. We Amerasians are called *bui doi*, the dust. And it's not meant to be complimentary. We're okay; we both had good parents raise us. Jessica is an interpreter working for American Express."

"You said *at home*. There're others?"

"Am I being interrogated, Detective?"

"Ex-detective. And it's for your rude behavior when I sat—payback."

He raised his hands in surrender. "Yes, we have another son. We've not seen or heard from him in years. He had a difficult time dealing with the street gangs and the racial taunts. Beat up a few kids when he was a teenager. We did what we could. Then one day he disappeared. I've looked for years. We hope someday he will return."

The waiter returned and left plates with chicken wings, egg rolls, skewers of meat, shrimp, and scallops, and some pieces of sushi. Detective Phan described each of the items.

"Looks delicious," Alex said.

He ordered two more beers.

"Now, what do you have that would help me with this investigation?" Phan asked.

"How about a trade? I may have something you need."

He bit off the end of a fried shrimp. "Need? I'm curious. So, being magnanimous and since you're paying the bill, I will start."

For the next ten minutes, he told her about the evidence that was found at the crime scene, the residue left by the bullets, the speculations about the man based on the grainy data files that TSD had handed over. He offered his explanation about the theft. He believed that someone, probably Chinese, wanted something in the facility but was interrupted before they could finish the operation.

"Why Chinese?"

"My coroner and crime-scene investigators believe that the weapon used was sophisticated and high-tech. We have nothing like it, and neither does anyone else—as far as we know. Here in Vietnam, we immediately suspect the Chinese. Two thousand years has burned our suspicion of them into our DNA."

"You haven't a suspect?"

"No, the modus operandi is like other break-ins. In fact, last fall there was a robbery at the Bitexco Financial Tower—it's that building there—where, we were told, software was stolen that allowed financial organizations to manipulate bitcoins. A security camera caught the back of the man; he somewhat resembles the man in the video we were given by your company. That's one piece of this crime that I don't understand: the thief acted as if he knew where every camera was located. Now how do you think he knew that?"

"We're investigating that ourselves."

"It's too bad that your company didn't have better surveillance videos; it would be a great help."

The woman's phone began to ring. Annoyed, he looked at her.

"Sorry," she said. "One moment." After saying hello, she listened, then said, "I'll be home in an hour." She clicked off.

"You have your family here?" Phan asked.

"No, it's my other job. I'm security for a foreign family living here. My client is a manager with an Italian manufacturing firm."

"You wear lots of hats. You said you have something for me?"

She reached into the large bag she'd brought, removed a brown envelope, and laid it on the table. "We were not all that forthcoming, Detective."

Phan pursed his lips. "I'm shocked."

She slid the large envelope to him. "We did have additional footage from other cameras, data that we didn't turn over. We attempted to independently try and find out what this was all about."

"And did you?"

"Our firm has resources around the world and is closely aligned with some governmental agencies."

"American agencies?"

"Yes, and others. Based on this, we've determined that this thief and murderer is a man who works for a Chinese company that's involved in industrial and governmental espionage on an international level. He's a sociopath. Many have died; the two at the facility were added to his crimes."

"Do you have any idea who this killer is?"

"Various international agencies call him Con Ma."

"Con Ma? Vietnamese for 'the Ghost.' How creative."

"The bodies he leaves behind and the information he's stolen have cost countries millions of dollars, not to mention the pain of the families of the dead."

"That's not my problem. However, I do not like it when people are murdered in my town. I'm a simple policeman."

"So was I, until the world fell out from under me. Now I'm working for TSD and trying hard to discover Con Ma's real identity."

"And I assume who is also behind the thefts of data and technology. That is more to the point. Some days, I think that people value information and their cause more than lives. Vietnam's history for the last hundred years has proven that over and over." He put his hand on the envelope and pulled it toward him. "Inside?"

"A clear photo of Con Ma, the Ghost. We hope that the police have information that will help us find him."

He opened the envelope, slid out the photo, and stared at the picture. His stomach turned, and he thought he would retch. He removed a handkerchief from his pocket and wiped the sweat away from his forehead. He then set the photo back on the table.

The woman said something, but he didn't hear what. It was as if his ears had filled with the buzzing from the street sixty meters below. He ran the handkerchief over his face again. He reached for a cigarette and tried to light it. His fingers wouldn't work the lighter, and his heart pounded heavily in his chest. The woman said something again. All he heard was, ". . . you, are you all right?"

CHAPTER 32

"Are you okay?" Alex asked, seeing Phan's distress. "What's the matter, Detective?"

The cigarette finally lit. He took a long drink from his beer, then set it back on the table next to the photo.

"I'll be all right," Phan answered as he continued to stare at the photo. "Where did you get this?"

"A low-light digital video camera attached to exterior of the facility. I'm authorized to apologize for not handing it over sooner. There's a thumb drive in the envelope as well—it has the entire video." Alex looked around for their waiter. "You don't look well. Let me get you some water."

He held up his hand and waved her off. "Ms. Polonia, are you positive that this is Con Ma?"

"Yes, Detective. In fact, I saw this same man in Dubai a week ago and yesterday at the Ben Thanh Market. He had contact with my—"

"Yesterday? You saw this man yesterday?"

"Yes, he's involved in an operation that may be compromising NATO security. I saw him. He wasn't more than twenty feet away."

Alex watched as Phan turned his face back to her. She had never seen such pain. In fact, it wasn't pain—it was anguish. It was as if everything was being twisted out of the man. The agony was obvious.

"Do you need a doctor?"

She watched as the detective placed both hands on the edge of the table and took a long, slow breath.

"What is this, some kind of sick game you Americans play?" He looked again at the photo, then turned it over. "I do not appreciate this—this ambush. Yes, I know who this man is, but it's a Vietnamese national security interest. We will handle it from now on. As far as I'm concerned, if you pursue this any further, I will have you and your entire organization tossed out of the country—or worse."

Stunned, Alex asked, "So, he is who we think he is? Do you have a name?"

"National interest! I can't add anything more to this conversation." Phan stood, and his hands visibly shook. He motioned to the waiter, said something in Vietnamese. The waiter removed a vinyl folder from his apron pocket. Phan looked at the bill and stuffed it with some cash, then turned and began to hurry out of the restaurant.

What the hell? Alex thought.

She collected her documents and followed the man. He was waiting at the elevator, pounding his fist into his hand. Then he took his fists and began pounding on the elevator door. Alex reached out and grabbed him by the shoulder, pulling him away.

"Damn it, what's the problem, Detective?"

Tears were running down the man's face. The door opened, and four businessmen pushed their way out. Phan slipped in between them and hit the lobby button. She followed him in.

"No—you, out. Go."

"No, not until you tell me what's happening."

His glare scared her. He then put one finger up in front of his nose. It vibrated like a tuning fork. "I know I will regret this—follow me."

The ride to the lobby seemed to take forever. Alex never took her eyes off the man. Phan hurried out the hotel doors to Dong Khoi Street and turned toward the river. He said nothing as Alex quick-walked alongside. She knew something was going to burst—her skills said so—but the man needed time to pull it together. She waited, said nothing. They passed the rear entry to Campbell's hotel. She thought about calling him but decided against it. They crossed Duron Ton Duc Thang that paralleled the Saigon River and went into a park that overlooked the river.

Chess tables were scattered under the trees, three with players. A carousel full of children turned to a tune she didn't know. Benches lined the walk, and boys and their girlfriends walked hand in hand.

Phan looked out on the river, and Alex followed his gaze toward a small fishing boat that motored slowly upstream.

Eventually he pointed to the envelope. "Show me the picture again."

As he sat at an open table, she spread the photo and two others on its weathered checkerboard surface.

He looked at the photo a long time, then tapped it. "This man, this Ghost, is my son, Lin Van Phan. What do you know about him?"

Now it was Alex's turn. Her stomach rolled over. At the same time, her heart fluttered. She felt the immense pressure of a thousand pounds on her shoulders. She looked again at Phan and felt her face harden. The confusion on his face grew.

"Are you having an attack?" he asked. "You look terrible."

She took a deep breath, deliberately exhaled, and steadied herself. "I cannot believe this. In fact, I won't believe this. After the break-in, this man—who you say is your son—was wounded. Our people took DNA samples from the blood he left at the scene. The profiles matched another profile that was in our data bank."

"It matched me? I've never had my DNA tested. Are you saying you knew this was my son, and until now, you wouldn't tell me?"

"No, that's not what I'm saying. I'm not saying that at all. The DNA was a match to . . . me."

"You? How the hell could it be a match to you? There is no way \ . ." The impact of the realization hit Phan so hard, he jerked to his feet.

"Now, I know this is a trick," he exclaimed. "A trick by you Americans—a trick to force me to turn over my son."

"Sit down," Alex demanded. "Now!"

Phan reluctantly sat.

"This concerns me as much as it concerns you," Alex said. "I came to you hoping to find the answer to a question: Who is this man—this man who, it seems, is my nephew? And now I find out that I have a brother that I never knew existed, that he is a policeman, and that my father's family has grown—significantly."

Phan shook his head. "I cannot believe this. My father is dead—I will not believe it."

"No, he's not dead. He's alive and retired, living in Cleveland. His wife's name is Alice. I have—actually, we have—two brothers. They are John and Rick. You have five nieces and nephews. Our father did not die when he and your mother were separated. I know that side of the story. He tried to find Yvette."

"You know my mother's name?"

"My father never forgot her. He was told her village was overrun and assumed she was dead. He doesn't know you exist." Alex nervously reached her hand across the table to his.

He jerked his hand away. "This is too hard to believe. Too bizarre. This is all wrong." Slowly, he reached out and gently squeezed her fingers. "And my father's name is? My mother would never say."

"Oh my, yes, of course. His name is Roger Thomas Polonia."

Phan, a tear rolling down his cheek, stared at Alex. He said nothing for a long time. "Tell me about him."

Alex and Phan forgot all about the time. She told him about their father, her brothers, the nieces and nephews. She told him about Cleveland, Roger's time in the army, his wounds, his UPS job, even his boat and Lake Erie. She couldn't stop. He told her about growing up Amerasian, his mother—she owned a noodle shop—his grandmother, who was still alive, and his children. The one person never mentioned was Lin.

Alex was jerked out of their reverie by her phone vibrating. "Oh my God, the children. Hi, Gianna . . ." She listened, said she was sorry twice, then finished with, "I'll be there shortly."

She looked at Phan. "I have to go. Can I reach you at the number I called?"

"No, don't call me on that line. Here's my cell phone number. Call me tomorrow. It seems that we have a serious problem to deal with, and I'm too numb to even think about what to do about all this. I'll stay here for a few minutes. I need a smoke. You go on."

Alex stood and touched the back of his hand. "In all the days of my life, I have never had a day like this."

"Me neither."

◆　◆　◆

Lin sat on his motorbike, hidden in a copse of trees a hundred meters away, wondering what his father could be talking about with this woman.

He'd followed his father from the police station to the Sheraton hotel. He'd done this before, tailed his father. It was a game. While he hated the man, he was fascinated by him. Then Detective Phan had gone into the hotel.

Lin had waited patiently across the street and was surprised to see the woman that was supposed to be guarding the Lucchese family exit a taxi and walk into the hotel. The woman that Nevio Lucchese had told him about. Curious, he had thought. Not long afterward his father had walked out of—more like fled—the hotel, looking back over his shoulder, the woman following after him. They had walked down the street and crossed into a park on the Saigon River, and had been talking for over an hour. He was too far away to hear what was said. He wished he had his laser microphone with him.

Just a minute ago the woman had answered her phone, said something to his father, touched his hand, and walked away. His father didn't take his eyes off the woman until after she had climbed into a taxi and left.

His father continued to sit at the low table and smoked two cigarettes before walking back up the street. Lin slowly followed until the detective disappeared into the police station.

Chapter 33

Late that evening, Nevio asked Alex to follow him into his office.

"Why weren't you here when the family went to church?" he said. "It had been planned. You disappointed both the children and Ilaria. This, Ms. Polonia, is unacceptable. Where were you? You're not here to go wandering around Ho Chi Minh City and have a vacation."

"I'm sorry, Mr. Lucchese. Mr. Campbell has me looking into something here in HCMC. It took longer than I thought it would."

"You and TSD are here to protect the children—especially after what happened in Dubai."

Alex wasn't sure which event Nevio was talking about. Was he was talking about the man at Ski Dubai, or something else—his meeting with Con Ma? She wanted to know everything that happened at the meeting and at the market the day before, but she couldn't ask, or at least not yet. After what she now knew, she was certain he would not tell her. She needed to keep up her charade. He didn't need to know what she knew.

"Your family is more important to you than anything in the world—I understand. And they are important to me, as well. In fact, family is all we really have. My family and I have been through a lot over the last year. It's the reason I'm here."

"How do you mean?" he answered.

She told him about Ralph, and the problems after the divorce. His escape from prison, her leaving the Cleveland police, and what happened in Venice.

"I'm not looking for sympathy, or even pity," she said. "These are my problems. And they're not an excuse either, but sometimes I need to get away for a bit. This matter, as I said, was for TSD. My family is still in Cleveland, and they're going through a tough time."

Nevio, his irritation softening, said, "I didn't know, and I'm sorry for what you went through. But you are also a professional. I know that you know what's right, and what needs to be done. Alex, I need you here with the children. Can you do that? Or do I need to talk with Mr. Campbell and find someone who can remain focused?"

"Yes, I can do that. All I ask is for a little flexibility."

"Yes, I can give you some, but if it comes into conflict with Ilaria and the family . . ."

"It won't happen again."

After everyone went to bed, Alex stood at the railing of the terrace. She rubbed her thumb over the face of her phone, then tapped in a number. Three rings later, he answered.

"I've got to see you. It's extremely important. Can you? . . . Fifteen minutes? . . . I'll be downstairs."

Soon afterward, Javier rolled up on the motorbike, removed his helmet, and combed back his black hair with his fingers.

"Someday I'll ask you where you found this contraption." She took the second helmet he offered, and they rolled into the street.

"Where to?" he asked.

"Anywhere, I don't care. We need to talk."

"Ominous."

They cruised along the Saigon River for about a half mile until they came to a small pimple of a riverfront park. Javier dropped the kickstand, and the two wandered along the narrow overlook to an unoccupied concrete bench. The other benches were filled by young people doing what young people do at eleven while overlooking a river. On the waterway, a party boat—ablaze with lights and rock and roll—leisurely drifted past.

"I'm glad someone is having fun," Alex said.

"I've known you to get into a funk," he said. "Good God, sometimes you're as moody as a jilted teenager. But what the hell is this about?"

"Really, you have to ask? Besides, it's not really a funk, but more like all confused and irritated at the same time."

She told him everything that happened with Phan. Javier said "Damn" a half dozen times, and finished with an "I cannot fucking believe it!"

"You? Detective Tran Phan is my half brother. *I* can't believe it—I want to believe it, but something is holding me back. Half of me is thrilled; the other half, the detective half, says, 'Hold on—not so fast! Maybe it's a trick, some game.' I'm not sure if he is even my brother. Short of a DNA test, there's no way to tell. Suppose this is all a setup? Suppose this Lin, this Ghost, isn't his son, and he's used my information to ferret him out or, even more strange, help him hide the man."

"Slow down. This may make your work easier."

"How? And now Nevio is on my case about my time away from the family. Jesus, I get that. We know he has a role in this, an important role, and he obviously knows this Ghost."

"All this helps. I'll get back to Langley and Chris with the information."

"Be careful. It's all tainted. I need to know a lot more before I'm satisfied. Chris is going to have a heart attack. He's forced me out onto thin ice with this case. Each step, I hear the cracking. I need to move fast, or it all breaks. He won't believe me when I tell him that Detective Tran Phan is my half brother, that the Ghost is his son, and that this is all one big fat Vietnam War hangover."

They walked farther, and the never-ending noise of motorbikes continued from the boulevard behind them. Another party boat powered up the river, blasting hip-hop. The colored lights in the boat's interior hypnotically flashed to the beat—a surreal perpetuation of the chaos in her head.

"Have you told your father?" Javier asked.

"He knows about the Ghost, but not his real name—I didn't know it. I called him before I met with Phan. All he knows—hell, all I know—is that his girlfriend, Yvette, survived the war. He thought she died. He also knows she had a child, and I know now that child was a boy—his son, Tran Phan. God, I wish I was there with him. He shouldn't be doing this alone."

"Your mother is there."

"It's going to be tough on her. She's built a family that's strong and hardworking. She minimized surprises and made sure all us kids made it."

"To think they survived that war," he said. "Amazing."

She changed the subject. "Anything more with Como and Nevio?"

"Yes, but it's more about Karns. He's been spending a lot of time behind closed doors with Lucchese."

"I've seen that."

"Chris isn't sure what to believe about Karns. They go back a long time. Chris has confidence in him, but he's seen a few little things. Karns doesn't respond to emails as fast; cell calls go to message. And he has a new one-hundred-and-fifty-thousand-dollar Porsche in a private storage locker near his home in Hong Kong. Jake ferreted that out before he came to Saigon. Karns is a Ford F-150 guy. All out of character."

"Interesting. We look for those things during drug investigations. Drug dealers and high-paid athletes all do the same thing: buy stupidly expensive cars. It's like a big sign that's stuck on their back that reads 'Arrest my fucking ass!' What is Chris doing?"

"Just watching," Javier said. "If Karns is playing for the wrong team, Chris wants to be sure. Then all holy hell will drop. The CIA has engaged Chris and TSD, on the down low, to seriously pursue this Chinese connection. That's why Jake came to HCMC. When Karns asked Chris about Jake, he told him Jake was in Singapore. You'll have to ask Chris about what else Jake's doing—that's all I know."

"With the potential of TSD being compromised, why would the CIA engage us? Seems like asking for trouble."

"Yes, there's that. But my ass is out on the line here as well. I vouched for Chris and TSD. We understand the risks."

"I hope you do," she said, and looked at the motorbike. "I haven't driven my Harley for over a year. Let me take you for a ride."

"You have a Harley-Davidson?"

"Middle age crisis. I got it at a police auction. Paid a quarter of its street value. It may be the one thing I keep after I clear everything else out. It's a solid bike."

An hour later, Alex was positive that Javier had left bruises on her midsection where he'd held on for dear life. She was glad he hadn't seen the smile on her face as she wove in and out of traffic and heard the fear in his voice after every near collision.

"You scream like a little girl!" she yelled over her shoulder.

CHAPTER 34

Con Ma sat on his motorbike in the shadow of a statue in the park near the Lucchese apartment building. For the last hour, after the two Americans had left the waterfront park, his mind and soul had twisted in turmoil. He had disconnected the laser microphone from his helmet and stuffed it into his backpack. He wished he'd never eavesdropped on the woman and the man. He pulled a cigarette from a pack, lit it, inhaled deeply, and blew the smoke toward the river.

The past two hours had turned his paranoid world into a seething morass of self-doubt and hate. His grandfather—if this woman were to be believed—had a real name, Roger. His father, the man who refused to understand him, was the brother of this American blonde. He could no longer trust anyone. Were the Italians going to turn against him and the Chairwoman? Would he have to atone to the Chairwoman for being the son of a policeman (a small detail of his old life that he'd kept hidden for eight years)? He was replaceable—would he feel the sharp point of a blade to his neck?

He now understood why this woman intrigued him—not in some personal, sexual way, but in a clear, professional way. He'd seen her in Dubai and in Ho Chi Minh City with the family. Lucchese had said she'd been a cop. That was nothing; he'd dealt with cops since he was twelve. They were either inept, thugs, or on the take. His father was the exception. His father could look into his soul; even he himself didn't look into his soul. Everything there, misshapen and confused, scared him. When he was on drugs, sometimes at night the shadows would completely enfold him. He found it hard to breathe, to swallow. When fear filled his mouth, it stopped everything—even his screams.

Bui doi, children of the dust. Even the second generation suffered at the hands of the xenophobic Vietnamese. It wasn't his fault. It was the fucking Americans! They came and destroyed his country, they destroyed his family, and they destroyed him. They made him into what he'd become. The American now had a name, Roger. His own name came from the Chairwoman. "I will call you the Ghost—in Vietnamese, Con Ma," she had said one evening after months of training. "It suits you. I want you to become one."

Con Ma was close to the reality of *bui doi*, a ghost hidden in the dust. He now reveled in it. It was sweetly perfect. It was his way of not looking into his soul.

The man on the motorcycle was CIA—interesting. She'd called him Javier. He needed more. He thought that the man was just a boyfriend, but now he knew better. He was a *tây*, a Westerner and American agent.

And what about the other *tây*, what would he do about him? Could the TSD man be trusted? The Chairwoman said he'd been helpful, but how helpful? He was sure that if a man was bought, he could be sold. It was only a question of how much.

He looked up to the top of the apartment building. Karns had said that Mr. Lucchese lived on the top floor. This woman had to be there.

He'd wanted to follow the CIA agent, but decided against it. There would be time later. Their affection for each other was obvious—the agent would be back. Now he knew why Lucchese and Karns in Dubai hadn't told him about this man—they didn't know. If this woman was here for security for the family, as Mr. Lucchese had said, then why was the CIA also here? Did the Chairwoman know?

Now his father, the man he'd hidden from for eight years, most likely knew he was alive. This was something that he'd not counted on, or wanted.

206

The Chairwoman had texted him that he had less than a week to finish; again, did she know? They had another assignment for him in Guam and Hawaii. He hated American food—greasy, tasteless, and unimaginative. After the next operation, he promised himself, he would return to his island in China, where at least everything was clean and simple.

He crushed his cigarette into the coarse grass of the park and started his motorbike. Five minutes later he was in the swarm that filled the streets of District 1. He was hungry.

Javier sat on his decrepit machine and watched the man in the park. He'd picked up the tailing motorbike as he and Alex left the apartment building earlier. Now that tail was a lone figure waiting in the darkness across the road. Even after an hour walking along the waterfront and then Alex's scary joyride, Javier never lost sight of the man and his motorbike. He said nothing to Alex. After dropping her off, he drove around the block and found a vantage point where he could watch the man. When the man removed his helmet and lit a cigarette, the white hair of Con Ma surprised him.

Ghosts should be better than that.

His phone vibrated in his pocket. He smiled at the ID.

"Did you see the man on the motorbike?" Jake asked.

"Yes, I saw him," Javier said. "I'm going to stay with him. Can you remain here and keep an eye on the apartment?"

"Yes, I'll let Chris know."

"Thanks." Javier clicked the phone off.

Javier reversed his thin rain jacket, turning it from bright blue to black, and put on Alex's yellow helmet. He secured his black helmet in the lock case mounted on the back of the motorbike. He watched the Ghost leave the shadows and head back toward District 1.

After being in Ho Chi Minh City for five days, he had regained an appreciation for the ancient city. It was his third trip, all under orders by

Langley. The city seemed freer of the paranoia of the other so-called communist countries in the Far East. In some ways, it reminded him of an oriental Houston, a place where everything and anything goes. Entrepreneurs—from shop owners to high-tech moguls—led the way, money their first goal.

As he kicked the engine on, a body dropped into the seat behind him, startling the hell out of him.

"So, you saw him too, cowboy," Alex said in his ear. "Do you think I'd let you go chasing after the son of a bitch without me? I also assume it was Dumas you were talking to?"

"Don't you miss anything?" Javier said as they slid into the traffic.

"I'm the cop, you're the bureaucrat."

"So romantic."

"Faster, he's getting away."

Ahead of him, the Ghost wove through District 1's droves of two-wheeled machines. A bizarre lightshow of red taillights, bright headlights, flashing overhead neon, and fluorescent-lit billboards rolled past. Some motorbikes had pigs tied to the back of them, some were packed with three or four people, and still others dragged behind them small trailers filled six feet high with broken-down cardboard boxes. Drivers jockeyed for position at one of the infrequent stoplights, then, in a roar, flew off in a cough-inducing smog. Block after block of street vendors and their ten-by-ten-foot shops lined the narrow streets. Even at night, commerce ruled.

Twenty yards ahead, the Ghost veered out of the surge, stopped, and leaned his bike against the wall of a noodle shop. In the glow thrown by overhead fluorescent lighting, a thin and beautifully delicate woman stirred a large pot over a gas burner. Alex and Javier cruised by, not turning their heads. In his mirror, Javier watched the man approach and kiss the woman on both cheeks. Javier then found an assembly of motorbikes parked behind an electronics shop a half block away. Between the outdoor shelves, with a radio blaring the sound of the Clash's "Rock the Casbah," they watched the Ghost eat his dinner.

"Culture, ain't it great?" Alex said in his ear.

"You must see your father," Yvette Phan said to Lin as he ate his soup. "Your sister and brother have missed you, and your mother is sick in her heart. They don't know whether you're alive or dead."

"Thank you for keeping our secret, Grandmother. I asked too much of you. Only a short time more, and then you can tell them."

"Yes, you have asked too much. They have a right to know."

"They know."

"They know? How?"

Lin told his grandmother about the conversation he'd heard that evening, about the man named Roger and the woman. He didn't tell her about the CIA agent, or the reason he was spying on the couple. They were part of an investigation he was conducting. His grandmother believed his story that he was a member of the state police, an undercover secret agent—that was the reason she couldn't reveal him to her son. He did nothing to dissuade her from the belief. He wasn't sure what she would do if she were to learn his real profession.

"Roger is alive? This woman, this American, is his daughter?"

"Yes, Grandmother. All of this is a shock to me as well."

"And you say that your father knows?"

"Yes, he knows about his father."

Yvette removed a small cloth from her pocket and began to cry in small, heartrending sobs. Lin didn't know what to do. His sociopathic callousness made it almost impossible to empathize with anyone. He now realized how bad it had become when he couldn't even feel the grief or happiness of his grandmother. He truly hated himself.

"After all these years, may I tell your father about you?"

"Soon. I will tell him first, Grandmother. But be careful. There are some who would exploit this knowledge. It would put me in danger. I'm not sure about this American, this woman who claims to be my father's half sister."

"God will provide."

"Yes, Grandmother. He has done me many great favors and kept me safe."

Lin finished his dinner and kissed his grandmother goodbye. He looked up the street to the electronics store, mounted his bike, and turned into the flow of late-night traffic. He went slowly for the first few blocks so that the Americans, who had followed him, would have time to catch up.

"Are they following me?" he asked into the microphone of the helmet.

"Yes, they are a hundred meters behind you," the voice answered.

"Let me know when they've gone."

"Yes, Con Ma."

The last four hours had irrevocably changed him. He needed to know more about this woman. He knew the name Alex. That was the name that Lucchese had used—Alex Polonia. The name meant nothing to him, and now she was his aunt, or half aunt, if there were such a thing. Alex—a strange name for a woman. She apparently worked for the same security company that guarded—poorly—Lucchese's technology facility. Would she turn on her own people for money?

Lin spent the next hour randomly driving around the city trying to lull them into complacency, into making a mistake. He asked the AI in his helmet to find anything it could about the CIA agent and a cop named Alex Polonia from Cleveland. He also asked about information on Roger Polonia. More than once he looked at the shadow of the motorbike following him silhouetted in the confusion of headlights and taillights. The motorbike the man was driving was at least twenty years old and could barely go fifty kilometers an hour. Tired of the game, and after crossing over the Sai Gon Bridge, Lin accelerated at three times the speed of the man's ancient machine. He made three dramatic turns and disappeared into the sticky night of Saigon's District 2.

"They are gone," the voice said.

CHAPTER 35

Phan had not mentioned to his wife any of what had happened. Nothing about Alex or Roger Polonia, nothing about a sister or a family in Cleveland, Ohio, and sadly nothing about their son Lin. He'd slept maybe an hour. Much of the previous night he'd spent sitting in the small patio outside their home, smoking cigarettes and finishing a bottle of scotch.

When Jessica had come out last evening, she'd brought a tray with tea and cookies. She asked what was bothering him. Never one to lie, he'd simply said, "A case I'm working on." He would tell her more, soon. After twenty-six years of marriage, she understood. They'd married young, both at twenty. A boy came soon after, a boy they learned was damaged. They'd protected him as much as possible, but that protection could only reach so far. Lin had had a juvenile record by the time he was fourteen. Phan had bailed him out of jail more than once, and his fellow officers had helped to keep it quiet. Three days after Lin's seventeenth birthday, he'd disappeared. Phan tried to trace the boy but had found nothing except for one spark of hope, a report of someone who may have looked like Lin crossing into China a few weeks after the boy went missing. He had used a different name. That was eight years ago. Phan had heard reports since then of people who had died after crossing paths with his son before he disappeared, but he had refused to believe them—until now.

After Jessica left, he'd turned over the photo, the one that Alex had passed to him. The hair was all wrong—why would he do that? The boy's face was sparer, the blue eyes darker, angrier, but there was no denying that the face was that of his son.

Where had he been? Why hadn't he let his mother know where he was? There were too many questions, questions that had no answers—yet. He would wait to tell his wife when he had answers.

Phan had traced his finger over Lin's face. His son was a murderer, a criminal, and from what was said, a spy working for the Chinese government. How much damage had he done? Who else had he killed?

My son's become an animal. He is the evil that I'm fighting—feral, wild, and now a pariah—someone who contributes to the world's problems. Where did we go wrong?

The note with his supposed half sister's phone number sat next to the photo. He'd thought for a long moment, sipped his tea, then dialed and set up a meeting with Alex Polonia. They needed to talk.

That was last night. Now dawn was coming. He took a quick shower and dressed. By the time he reached his office, he was damp with sweat. A tap on his door, and Phan looked up.

"There's a man here to see you, Detective Phan," his assistant said. "His card."

Phan looked at the business card: "Agent Javier Castillo, Central Intelligence Agency."

It only gets better.

"Show him in, Sergeant."

When the man walked into his office, Phan extended his hand, and the man took it. Phan then pointed to a chair to the right of his desk.

Phan lit a cigarette. "She failed to mention you, Agent Castillo. Alex never said anything about the CIA or you. Your being here is, of course, no coincidence. Can I assume she's why you're here?"

"God, you are so like your sister. She does the same thing—direct, in your face. At times, it's infuriating."

"More's the pity."

"Detective Phan, that is not the primary reason I'm here. My government is troubled that your son may be involved in the theft of critical software and proprietary designs that affect the safety and security of governments around the world. And because he is your son, we are also concerned about the integrity of the Ho Chi Minh City and Vietnamese police departments."

"That's a lot of concerns, Agent Castillo. In fact, almost too many for this conversation. It is well above, what you call, my pay grade. And since I'm paid shit, that's pretty much my attitude about your government and those that work for it. Please, go play your games elsewhere. Two Americans are dead, and my superiors don't give a damn. Some are still fighting that war. What are two more dead Americans?"

"And you, Detective? Are you still fighting that war?"

"No. I simply think murder destroys order. I like order. I like simplicity and respect. Since yesterday, much of that order in my life has been thrown into the air like rice chaff. I'm still trying to catch the bits. I'm a simple cop. That said, I may lose my job over the actions of a delinquent son and an American family I never knew existed."

"Do you know where your son is?"

"No. I haven't seen my son for eight years. He's broken his mother's heart, and his brother and sister barely remember him—and now this. I'm going on what that woman has told me as the truth. Since my DNA is not on file, I'm having my people do their own tests. They've already run the test on the blood at the scene of the crime. I will know after the tests are concluded. I want a sample of Ms. Polonia's DNA to confirm her story."

"I'll have copies of the tests delivered to you."

Phan waved his cigarette in the air like a pointer. "And that will prove what? No, I'll take the sample personally, and we will process it. Then I'll see."

"I can't make her do it."

"Don't bother. I'm seeing her in a half hour." He studied the man. "I assume that you're sleeping with this woman, my alleged sister?"

"That is none of your business."

"Soon it might be."

"Do you know a noodle shop called Yvette's? On Mac Dinh Chi in District 1?"

Phan carefully ground the cigarette in the large ashtray on his desk, his eyes never leaving the CIA man. "Why?"

"I followed Lin, Con Ma as we call him, last night. He went to this noodle shop, parked his motorbike, and talked to an older woman. She fed him. He acted as though he knew her. Any idea who she is?"

Phan lit another cigarette, then lied. "No, I have no idea."

"Had to ask. She seemed happy to see him. Alex said that her father once knew a woman called Yvette . . . Coincidence? He stayed less than an hour, then went north over the river and disappeared."

Phan smiled. "I assume that you were following him and he shook you."

"It happens, sometimes."

"Even to the best of us. I will contact you if something comes up." He waved the agent's card. "Good day, Agent Castillo. You know your way out."

CHAPTER 36

Alex and Phan walked together along the waterfront in front of the Luccheses' apartment building. Phan found an open table and sat and motioned to Alex. She sat across from him.

She spoke first, even though Phan had called her. "I apologize for the way I presented the photo yesterday," Alex said. "It was insensitive."

"I'm not sure there was a better way," he replied. "We're both police officers. Direct is best, no matter how it hurts. I need to know for sure who you are, and who we are to each other. I'd like to believe you, but I need more." He removed a tube from his jacket. "Just a normal cheek swab. My people will do the test. Then we'll see."

"That may take too much time."

"I'm already rechecking the crime-scene blood samples to match my DNA with Con Ma's. I want to be sure he's Lin Van. I will also compare the sample to yours. May I?"

"Sure, why not," Alex said.

Phan opened the tube and removed the long cotton swab. Five seconds later he returned it to the tube and sealed it. "To be honest, I hope that this *is* a match. For years I've fought with myself over my father and who he may be. Was he alive? What had his life been like? Why hadn't he ever looked for me?"

"I haven't talked to him yet. I was waiting to hear from you. He knows about Lin—I have told him that much. May I tell him about you?"

Phan lit a cigarette. "I'm not sure that I can stop you—yes. The man, like me, needs to know."

"I will be as direct as possible," she continued. "But there has to be a confirmation. He'll understand. I just hope my brothers, when they find out, realize what this means."

"Thank you. But I warn you, if this is all a trick, you and your company will be escorted to the airport and never allowed back in. I will make it my purpose in life to see that—"

"This is all true. My initial reaction was the same—that you're using us to find a way to your son."

"The cynical cops in us—it puts us on guard."

"Truth sounds different to the listener."

"My mother's family was respected and honored in our village for hundreds of years. The war changed all that. The village was destroyed, hundreds killed. Mother says that was where they were going when they were ambushed."

"The same story my father tells."

Phan looked out over the skyline of Ho Chi Minh City, then to the Saigon River. "There are photos my mother has of this river, full of ships." He pointed. "Massive merchant ships were tied to these same piers. Many were American military ships, even a small aircraft carrier. All here to kill Vietnamese. This riverfront has never been as busy as it was then. The Americans came, then left, leaving nothing but tears."

"That was a long time ago," Alex said.

"You still argue in your country about Civil War monuments," Phan said. "No war is ever forgotten, no matter how much we try to rewrite history. Much has happened to this city during the last twenty years. It belongs to the youth now. Sometimes, I don't recognize it."

"My father—I mean our father—wondered what had changed since he lived in that apartment building, the one where he met your mother."

Phan looked back through the park to the concrete edge of the old wharf. "A few blocks that way"—he pointed—"is where the apartment building stood. It's been gone a long time. It's now part of a new waterfront redevelopment. My mother showed me the burnt-out building when I was a child. She said the Viet Cong blew it up."

"How is your mother? I'm sure that will be one of the first things my father will ask."

"She's well. In fact, she still opens her noodle shop every day. It keeps her busy."

"That's good."

"Your friend, CIA agent Castillo, stopped by my office less than an hour ago."

"I didn't know."

"He's pressuring me to go after my son. I am not one to be pressured."

"Me neither—it runs in the family."

"Unfortunately, he also told me something that's breaking my heart: my mother has known about Lin, and they've remained in contact. She has kept the truth from me. There must be something else, a reason for her silence."

"Families are complicated. I'm sure her intentions are good." Alex kept her knowledge about Lin's late-night dinner to herself. She was certain Yvette was her father's Yvette, but she needed confirmation this woman was the same person. She'd wait.

"I'm sure she's afraid if I catch him, I'll throw him in prison."

"Will you?"

"That will be up to him. First, I need to better understand him, and most importantly, I need to know for sure Lin is this Con Ma. Please be cautious. No matter who he is, he is extremely dangerous—a cornered snake will strike at anything."

CHAPTER 37

"Mr. Lucchese is at the plant," Maria said. "He left with Mr. Karns. Mrs. Lucchese saw you from the terrace talking with someone in the park below. She told me to tell you that she was taking the children to their school. You were supposed to go with them."

"That was supposed to be this afternoon," Alex said. "Why did they leave early?"

"I'm not sure. Someone called, and she gathered up the children. She said she would take a taxi since Mr. Karns, or that Mr. Quan, wasn't available."

"Did she say when they'd be back?"

"No, the school is just a short trip. Do you want me to call her?"

"I will. Thank you, Maria."

She looked at her phone: two messages, one from Ilaria, the other from her father. She went to the terrace and clicked on the speaker.

"Ilaria, I'm sorry I wasn't here. I thought we were going this afternoon."

"The headmaster called and had an opening this morning," Ilaria said.

"I'll be right there," Alex answered.

"I'm almost done. Just some paperwork. He also gave me a list of clothes and supplies."

"How are the children?"

"They're getting a tour. We'll be home soon. Alex, Mr. Lucchese is not happy. You're spending too much time away from the children. Who was that man you were talking to in the park? I saw you."

"A policeman. Mr. Campbell asked me to talk with him."

There was a pause in their call while Ilaria talked to someone else. "Yes, Mr. Smythe, I will have my husband look at the paperwork. We'll return it to you tomorrow." Then, "Alex, we'll be home soon. We can talk about this matter when I return."

"Yes, Ilaria." Alex clicked off.

Alex then called her father. It would be late at night, but it couldn't wait—he had to learn about Phan and Yvette.

He answered before she could say hello. "Are you okay? Is everything all right?"

"I'm fine, Dad. It's late. Is Mom there?"

"Yes, upstairs asleep. We talked about what you discovered. She said she thought this day might come. Sweetie, I adore your mother. She's more than I could ever want or need. Hard to believe that we've been married almost forty-five years. Vietnam was so long ago. For years I've tried to ignore it, but now it's all a strange and even miraculous thing."

"I found them."

"You found Yvette?"

"Yes. You and Yvette have a son. His name is Tran Phan."

"Yes, that was her last name, Phan. I couldn't remember it. How did you find them?"

She told her dad again about the DNA match to Lin and her meeting with the Ho Chi Minh City police detective.

"He's a detective? Like you and your uncles and grandfather."

"Yes, it seems to run in the family. He's married and has three children. You have three more grandchildren, Dad: a girl and two boys. He's married to another Amerasian, Jessica. Their children are in college and high school. They sound wonderful." She could hear her father sniffling. "Are *you* all right?"

"Better than I've been in years. Your mother was so pleased that I found out. Good Lord, it was so long ago. I wish I could have helped, been there to—"

"Dad, they're fine. Tran is heading the investigation about the men in my company who were killed. It's complicated. I'll talk to my boss later today. I don't know what will happen. Hell, he may even fire me."

The pause seemed endless. She heard her father breathing. "All this, and my son finds out that his son is a murderer? Good God."

"It hasn't been confirmed," Alex said.

"You're a detective, and he's a detective—what else could it be?"

"We're trying to find out."

"You had nothing to do with all this," he said. "It must be tearing at my son."

"He is shattered—nothing is fair in this world. You know that more than anyone. The two dead men were close to my boss."

"What's his name?"

"Christopher Campbell. He formed Teton Security and Defense. I'll tell you more about them later. He's the one who learned about the man and matched the DNA to me. It's all such confusion, but he's fair—or I hope he is."

Alex heard a voice in the background. "Is that Mom?"

"Yes, I'll tell her everything." Her father paused a moment. "She wants to talk to you."

"Alex?" her mother said. She sounded strong. "Are you okay, sweetie?"

"Yes, I'm fine. Dad will tell you the news."

"Good, I need some good news. Did you get an email from Annie? She said she was going to send you one."

"Mom, I haven't had a minute to look at my email. What happened?"

"She thinks the real estate company has found a few potential buyers for your house. When did you put in a security system?"

220

"About the time Ralph was arrested. I wanted to make sure that nobody broke in to sneak around. There was nothing of value other than my Harley. I put everything else in storage. Why?"

"Did you install the smoke detectors?"

"No, those were done a few years ago. We did them when we had work done on the house. Mom, why are you asking?"

"You didn't install security cameras in the smoke detectors?"

"Cameras? What cameras?"

"The home inspector found three: one in the garage, one in the hall-way, and one in the kitchen. They were hidden inside the smoke detectors. The inspector says he also found a server, whatever that is, behind the fuse box. It was connected to the phone lines. He guesses that the images from the cameras were sent via something called Bluetooth to the server and stored there. Someone could then remotely access the server and download anything the camera saw. I'm not sure what all this means."

"It wasn't me, Mom. Someone else put those cameras there. Does the inspector have any idea when they were installed?"

"No, but the dust on the server says it was a while ago. Maybe more than a year."

She thought for a long moment. "The smoke detectors were installed by the contractor when we replaced the porch. They were required for final approval of the building permit. The old ones were the battery types. We took them out, and they wired the new ones through the house power. They're smoke and heat detectors. When I put in the security system, the installer said the smoke alarms were good to go, one more layer of safety and security. Who the hell would have installed the cameras?" She stopped. She flashed on what Javier had said about surveillance on her family.

"You said there was dust on the server?"

"That's what the inspector said. He guessed maybe a couple of years' worth . . . Alex, you still there?"

"It had to be Ralph. He installed those cameras before he was arrested. I can't believe the gall of that asshole."

"You mean—"

"Yes, Mom. Ralph's been spying on me."

◆ ◆ ◆

"Why is Javier talking to Detective Phan?" Alex asked on her next phone call. "Did you send him?"

"I did not," Chris said. "He's doing this under orders from the government. They're panicked that this whole operation may be compromised due to your connections with the police and the Chinese agent."

"Did he tell you about our conversation, and about Detective Phan?" Alex asked.

"Yes, I know about that."

"What are you going to do? Am I out on the street? Honest to God, Chris, I had no idea about any of this."

"I believe you. It's all too coincidental to be a setup," Chris admitted.

"Thanks, I think. But the target right now is the Ghost, this Lin Van Phan. He must be found."

"We'll get him. *You* will get him. I've no other assets that I can rely on. Jake had to go back to Hong Kong this morning. I've only got you."

"Are you still in Saigon?" Alex said.

"Yes, same hotel. I'll be here until this is resolved. My company is hanging in the balance. Are you doing all right?"

"Why is everyone asking if I'm all right? I'm great. Peachy. All I want to do is shoot a few people, and it will all get better."

"Who else is asking?"

"Let's see, the Luccheses are pissed that I'm not watching the kids. My nephew is an international assassin and spy. And my mother just told me that my ex-husband has been spying on me."

"What do you mean Ralph is spying on you?" Chris asked.

She told him everything her mother said.

"This is not good. He may have seen me at your house."

"You think! I don't know what he knows about TSD, and where I am. But the man was a good detective. He can follow a trail, especially if he has an idea where to look. I have no idea what this means."

"It means we play this very close now. Just you, me, and Javier can know what's happening. Nothing more gets to Detective Phan or anyone else. Nothing is more important."

"Yes, there is," Alex said. "Ilaria is a big girl and can take care of herself. But the kids must not be caught up in this. They must be protected. That is my contract, and I intend to make sure nothing happens to them when all this goes to hell."

CHAPTER 38

"School starts soon," Ilaria said as she placed a bundle of documents on the kitchen table. "The headmaster gave me a list of things we need."

"I had to follow up on something to do with Teton Security," Alex said. "That's why I was meeting with the police."

"Nevio said you would fix it," Ilaria said, "and I know you will. The headmaster called and had an earlier opening available, and I took it. He also told me there's a shopping mall across town that carries Western-style clothes and school supplies. One shop also carries uniforms for the school. Gianna has done the investigating, and Paolo has discovered that there's a video arcade. The mall is called Vivo City. I called Nevio, and he suggested the car service. He said Mr. Karns will contact them."

Ilaria's phone pinged. She read the text to Alex. "The car will be there at one. Driver's name is Bobo. He's the cousin of Tommy Quan."

An hour later the young driver smiled and reintroduced himself. He was driving a new Honda minivan, which Ilaria, Maria, Alex, and the kids climbed into. Thirty minutes later they were crossing through Ho Chi Minh City.

The mall was in District 7, a neighborhood mixed with new high-rises and older homes. The shopping center was modern and bright, and not what Alex had expected. The driver asked, in English, if they wanted him to wait. Alex said yes, they would be finished at four.

For the next hour, the five of them wandered through the modern shopping complex. Alex thought she could be in any mall in the United States—many of the shops were the same. Gianna found jeans and tops, and Paolo a few T-shirts. They also found the shop that carried the school uniforms. Paolo bought notebooks and other supplies.

"Lucky for us they will wear uniforms," Ilaria said. "Polo shirts and shorts and skirts. Makes it a lot easier."

They passed a video game arcade near the Starbucks. Weeks had passed since Alex had even thought about an iced coffee. "Can I buy anyone a tea or coffee?" she asked.

"If you don't mind, there's a Topshop that direction," Maria said. "I'll be back in a few minutes."

"Be back by three forty-five," Alex said, looking at her phone.

After asking permission, the kids crossed the hall and entered the video arcade. After Alex ordered two iced coffees, the two women found a nearby table and placed their bags next to a chair.

"Are you okay?" Ilaria asked. "Nevio told me that you were dealing with some TSD issues. He also mentioned an ex-husband and a divorce. Then I saw you talking to that policeman in the park this morning. Should I worry?"

"No, or at least I hope not. But there has been quite a change in my life." Alex told her about her father having a child in Saigon and about Javier, an American helping her find the child. She avoided telling Ilaria about Phan and Lin in any great detail. Hers were unresolved issues, and to mention the police again was unnecessary. She didn't want to alarm the woman; her job was to keep Ilaria and the children safe.

"I've known Javier awhile. He works for the American government. My father told me there was a chance that his child might be here in Ho Chi Minh City. That's what I've been doing during the hours I've been away. I'm sorry if I've made you worry and not told you the entire truth."

"A half sibling, here?" She looked away a moment, as if calculating something. "He or she would have to be in their late forties."

"Yes, but we're not certain about the ancestry yet. I didn't want Mr. Lucchese to be worried. We hope to find out soon. Some Vietnamese agencies are investigating."

"How is your father taking this?"

"It's difficult. I just told him. It was through some DNA profiles that I've been shown. That's why my friend is helping. He tells me that there have been scams, especially here in Vietnam."

"I can imagine," Ilaria said.

"I apologize for this," Alex said. "My company knows about it, and they're keeping it quiet. No need to worry you or the family. It's just one of those things—life gets in the way."

Gianna came running out of the arcade, crying. Both women jumped to their feet. Gianna ran to her mother.

"What's the matter?" Ilaria asked as she went to the child.

"It's Paolo—I can't find him." She took short breaths, and tears ran down her face. "I looked and looked, but I couldn't—"

"What do you mean you can't find him?" Alex asked gently.

"I was playing a game. Paolo was across the arcade playing a game with explosions and shooting. I didn't like it, so I went to play this horse game. When I finished, I went to look for him. I couldn't find him. I looked everywhere. I got scared. Is Paolo here?"

"No, he's not," Alex said, trying to control her voice. "Can you show me where you last saw him? Maybe he went to get a Coke or something."

The three walked quickly across the hallway into the dark arcade, where the sounds of guns and bells filled the air. There were more than a hundred kids—teenage boys mostly—playing video games.

"Where was he?"

"There," she said, pointing at an empty console halfway down the wall. Alex looked around and walked to the back, then through the aisles of other machines. Nothing. She went to the concession stand.

"English, anyone speak English?"

A young woman turned when Alex asked. "Yes, can I help?"

"Did a boy—he wasn't Vietnamese—come and get a drink or a candy bar here in the last ten minutes?"

"European? Spoke English with an accent. Yes, he was here. Asked for a large Coca-Cola."

"Did you see him leave?"

"Yes. He went that way with the older man."

"Older man?" Ilaria yelled. "What older man?"

The counter girl turned to Ilaria. "An American, I'm sure by the accent. He was standing behind the kid. After the boy got his Coke, the man said something to him. The boy looked surprised, said something back, and then they left through the rear door."

"What did this man look like?" Alex asked.

"White guy, tall, black hair, and had gray here, had a mustache and a . . ." She stroked her chin.

"A goatee?"

"Yes."

"Where's the door?"

She pointed. "That way. I'd take you there, but I can't leave the counter."

"You go out into the mall and wait for Maria," Alex said to Ilaria. "I'll be right back."

Alex ran to the rear door and pushed it open. A long service corridor ran to the left and right, and a sign in both Vietnamese and English read "EXIT." It pointed right. She followed the signs until one last pair of double doors was left. She pushed the panic bars and opened them. Outside was a broad concrete plaza that faced what looked like a service dock. She shielded her eyes from the intense sun. The air was thick. A few cars passed by on an adjacent ring road. Beyond that was a sea of motorbikes parked row after row in a massive parking lot. A brown panel van with "UPS" on its side was parked in the loading zone. Three men were pushing carts filled with boxes toward another pair of doors.

She ran up to them. "Did you see a man and a teenager come out that door?" She pointed.

The man shrugged his shoulders and raised his hands, the universal "I don't understand."

"English, do any of you speak English?"

"Không nói tiếng Anh!"

"What?"

"No English, sorry!"

Behind her a man in a uniform burst through the same doors she'd used. He looked like mall security.

"You speak English?" Alex asked.

"Some," he answered.

"Ask them if they saw a man and boy come out that door."

For the next few minutes, a furious discussion took place. Fingers pointed, arms were swung in great arcs. Then the three UPS men said what Alex understood to mean, "We have to get back to work."

"What did they say?"

"Two people came out that door, an older man and a boy. Both were American or European. The boy was asking questions in a language they didn't understand. One thought some of it was English. Waiting for them at the curb was a man and a van—a Vietnamese man. He talked with the white man. Then two more men came out of the van and pulled the boy in. Then they all climbed into the van and drove away in that direction."

"Why didn't they stop them?"

"Stop them for what?" the guard said.

"They were kidnapping the boy."

He turned back to the men and said more in Vietnamese. The men responded in a furious chatter.

"They didn't know. To them, it was two Americans having a disagreement, a father and son. Then they were gone."

She looked at the three men, then turned to the guard. "Please get their names and phone numbers. I may want to talk with them again."

The double doors opened again, and out came Ilaria, Gianna, and Maria, her arms full with their bags. They ran to Alex.

"Did you find him?" Ilaria asked. "Did you find Paolo?"

"No, they took him."

CHAPTER 39

Alex made two phone calls, and within minutes four HCMC police cruisers pulled up to the plaza. Chris Campbell arrived in his rented blue Hyundai, and Javier Castillo in a nondescript Toyota. Soon Detective Tran Phan and another detective showed up too.

Ilaria was a wreck. She was crying and holding on to Gianna. Gianna asked questions, but Alex told her to be patient. Maria stood next to the Luccheses, trying to help, to calm them. Then Ilaria phoned Nevio and left a message. She turned to Alex once she was through.

"I told him to meet us at the apartment," she said. "I need to go to him. The kidnappers will try and contact us." Ilaria pointed at Javier and the detective. "Who are those men?"

"The American is Javier Castillo," Alex said. "He's the man helping me with my father's issues, and he's a friend of Mr. Campbell. The other is Detective Tran Phan, the policeman I was talking with this morning."

Ilaria gave Alex a strange and troubled look.

Javier must have seen Ilaria pointing.

"Alex told me about you," Ilaria said as Javier reached them. "Can you help?"

"I'll do what I can," Javier said, now quizzically looking at Alex.

"Mrs. Lucchese, do you need a ride home?" a voice asked.

Alex turned back to the road. Their driver, Bobo, stood next to his minivan, intently watching them.

"No, we have other transportation, but thanks," Campbell answered for her, and slipped the man a twenty-dollar bill.

Bobo shrugged and returned to his van. He pulled a hundred feet up the road.

No one was pleased to be in the heat and humidity, least of all Alex. They moved inside the mall to a corner of the air-conditioned entry. The UPS guys gave their statements to the police and then went back to work.

She reintroduced Chris to Phan; she knew she didn't have to introduce Javier. She told the three men everything she knew up to that point. They asked Ilaria if they could ask Gianna a few questions.

"Only if Alex asks them," Ilaria answered. "Gianna is afraid, very afraid."

"Did you see who talked to Paolo?" Alex said, making sure she didn't frighten the child into thinking it was her fault.

"No. The place was full, all Vietnamese boys. I didn't see anything. Where is he, Alex? Why did he leave?"

"I don't know, sweetie." She hated to lie, even though she had no idea why the boy was taken.

Javier and a detective went into the mall to talk to the girl at the counter of the video arcade. When Javier returned, he said she had nothing new to add. The detective remained to take the counter girl's statement.

"You, a pistol?" Phan said, leaning in to Alex. "That is not acceptable."

She guessed that he had noticed its shape under her shirt. "I have a license."

"They are very difficult to obtain." He turned to Chris and Javier. "I assume one of you is behind this?"

"It is all proper."

"You Americans think you own the world," the detective said.

Alex looked up at the corner of the entry lobby. A CCTV was secured high and out of reach. "Detective, where's the mall security office? They may have something from the cameras."

Ilaria pulled Gianna close to her. "Alex, we must get home. Someone may call. Nevio is waiting."

Alex looked at Chris. "Can you take them home? I can do more good here with Detective Phan than I can waiting at the apartment. And you can talk to Nevio."

"Not a problem," Chris answered.

"I'm going to stay with Alex," Javier said. "There's something strange about all this."

"Strange?" Alex said. "More like scary as hell."

Phan sent the mall guard to give the security office a heads-up.

Chris left with Ilaria, Gianna, and Maria. Alex, Detective Phan, and Javier walked through the mall to the security office. Two of Phan's uniformed cops followed. Phan showed the security guard his badge and spoke rapidly in Vietnamese; the conversation went on for at least two minutes. Then the detective slammed his hand on the counter and pointed to his men, and one of the officers began to remove handcuffs from his belt. The security guard threw his hands up in the universal sign of "What the hell?" and pointed to a door down the hall.

Minutes later, the three of them were looking through a mosaic of high-definition camera views on two large-screen TVs. Alex told the security guard operating the machine to rewind the playback to when the crying Gianna ran across the mall to Alex and Ilaria. The guard located the camera near the Starbucks and found the scene. At this point Gianna was under the arm of Ilaria, who was pointing back toward the arcade. The guard noted the time stamp, then synchronized the other feeds to the time. He moved the image of the arcade to the center of the monitor and then turned back the time. Paolo came into view, walking toward the arcade counter and the girl Alex had talked to.

"That's Paolo," Alex said. "He doesn't look anxious here." She scanned the dark images behind him. One figure was obscured, but his shadow was larger than the Vietnamese that passed between the boy and him. "Another view?"

Phan said something to the operator, and the screen changed. Now Paolo was seen in profile somewhere deep in the arcade.

"He says this camera is mounted over the exit to the service hallway."

"I went out that door. Have him advance the footage from this point."

They watched Paolo leave the counter and walk back toward the machines. The shadow walked up to the boy, and Paolo stopped. A conversation began. Paolo looked around as the shadow pointed at the camera or the door below it. Paolo turned away to walk back into the mall. The shadow took Paolo's arm and turned him toward the camera. Paolo went with him. About ten feet from the camera and the door, the face of the shadow appeared.

"Freeze it!" Alex yelled. The image stopped. She looked hard at the crisp, colored image on the screen. Her stomach flipped—she almost lost it. "Goddamn that asshole. I'm going to kill him."

"You know that man?" Javier asked.

"That is my goddamned ex-husband, Ralph Cierzinski."

CHAPTER 40

They watched the video from six other cameras, following Ralph and the boy down the corridor and then out into the service area. There, a Vietnamese man climbed out of a van and talked to Ralph. Then the Vietnamese made a signal to the van. Two men jumped out of the side door and pulled the boy inside. Ralph climbed in the front seat, and the van left.

Phan told the operator to refreeze the image. "License." They all looked. Where the plate should have been there was nothing.

"No help," Javier said.

"Unlike the rich United States," Phan said, "we have far fewer blue Mercedes vans in this city. We'll cross-reference and see if anything shows up. My guess, it's stolen."

Alex scanned the last image frozen on the screen, taken just after the van had turned the corner. "Can you make this image full screen?"

The operator did. The resolution was sharp, the view panoramic: the facade of the mall, across the service area, and to the parking lot beyond, where thousands of motorbikes were parked in neat rows, their chrome handlebars sparkling in the sunlight. In the center of the image, among the first row of motorbikes, one lone figure stood. His head was turned toward the disappearing blue van.

Alex tapped her finger on the monitor. "Zoom in there." The image enlarged. "More." The man now filled half the screen, but the image was becoming grainy.

"Do you have another camera that covers this area of the parking lot?" The detective translated for her, and a few seconds later an overhead view of the parking lot appeared. The operator zoomed in again.

He was thin and tall, his face full on to the sun. He was obviously not Vietnamese; a hoody covered the back of his head.

Phan gasped. "Move it forward in time," the detective said. "Slowly."

The image advanced. The man turned, and his head tracked the departing van. Then he picked up a helmet sitting on the seat of the motorbike. He dropped the hoody, and his spiky white hair grabbed the sunlight. The man secured the helmet, slid up the visor, and climbed on the bike. He turned his head toward the mall exit. In the peripheral edge of the camera's view, Alex ran out into the service court.

"Your son!" Alex said. "Why is your son here?"

"No idea," Phan said. He continued to watch the display. "How is he connected to all this?"

They fast-forwarded the action through the arrival of the police, Campbell, and Castillo, and the dismissal of Bobo, the minivan driver. The entire time, Lin remained in the parking lot on his bike, watching. They continued to watch until Bobo's minivan left the premises and Lin seemed, strangely, to follow after him.

In the quiet of the control room, Alex's phone pinged, a text message:

Hi Sandy Girl,

I miss you a lot. I want two hundred thousand dollars, or the kid will permanently disappear. More info later . . . BTW, this Saigon weather sucks! How can you stand to live here?

Danny Z.

"What?" Javier asked, seeing the stunned expression on Alex's face.

"A fucking ransom demand from Ralph. I cannot believe this is happening."

She showed the message to Phan and Javier. The detective still seemed in shock over the appearance of his son. Alex, like her brother, also did not understand what the connections were in all of this.

"Those are the same silly names he used in Venice, aren't they?" Javier asked.

"Yes, the guy just loves to rattle my cage—I don't get it. He's seriously psychotic."

She explained to Phan that years earlier, during one of the few periods of bliss she and her ex-husband had shared, they started calling each other the names of the characters from the play *Grease*. Phan said he'd never heard of the play.

Now, Ralph was in Saigon and had kidnapped Paolo. This was not the first time she wanted to shoot him. Her phone pinged again:

Sandy,

By now, you've called out the cavalry, watched me on the mall videos (damn they have a lot of cameras, wish I'd put that many in the house, especially the bedroom—just joking). I've always liked that about you, you're reliable and predictable. My demand remains the same. Between your boss, Campbell, and Como Motors, I'm sure you can dig up the money. You have twenty-four hours. I'll text you the details. Just send me a short and sweet confirming note.

Danny Z.

She showed the second message to the others. Alex's head spun. He'd obviously seen Chris visit the house in Cleveland through the cameras in the smoke alarms and had somehow found out about her involvement with Como Motors. The son of a bitch.

Alex looked again at Cierzinski's message, then replied:

You asshole—fuck you!! If anything happens to Paolo, I will hunt you down and kill you.

She didn't sign it.

Chapter 41

Beyond the enclosing ring road of the mall, Lin stood in the vast parking lot filled with thousands of motorbikes, his helmet on the seat. He'd watched everything that had happened during the last hour. His greatest shock was seeing his father. He'd not expected that—it had to be the woman, Alex. She must have called him.

He looked at the Honda minivan. It was the same one he'd followed earlier from the Luccheses' apartment building. The driver stopped the minivan near the women and the group talking with his father. Then the driver, having not picked anyone up, moved his van farther up the road and parked. Lin watched as some of the people and police climbed into their respective vehicles and drove away, while the others, including his father, went back inside the mall. A minute later he was alone in the sea of chrome and plastic motorbikes.

He made the decision not to follow the blue Mercedes van when it left. His target was the woman, the one claiming to be his aunt. She was the key to Lucchese and the continued feed of the last pieces of the information he needed. Lucchese's boy, the Anglo man, the Vietnamese helping him—too many variables. Now he was pleased he'd waited to see what developed. His father, the woman, and the head of Teton Security, all in one spot. Yes, waiting was the right decision.

Now that everyone was gone, he looked back at the minivan. The driver climbed out and lit a cigarette, then casually looked at his phone. Lin put his helmet back on.

"Enlarge view three times," he said. The image on the visor expanded, and the man next to the minivan filled the screen. Lin smiled.

"Bobo Bao, you son of a bitch," Lin said. "You haven't changed at all, and I assume that Tommy Quan is still holding your leash?"

Before Lin had left HCMC, he'd had a run-in with Bobo and his brother, Bing, both of whom ran with a drug gang under the control of the cousin, Tommy Quan. He guessed that the van service was one of their more legal enterprises. He was more than a little shocked to see the connection to the Luccheses. Then again, considering their common associate, he wasn't that surprised.

Bobo climbed back into the minivan, then pulled out onto the perimeter road. Lin snapped the strap to his helmet and followed closely behind the Honda.

Thirty minutes later, Bobo stopped at a street-side restaurant. Lin parked his motorbike and walked to the side of the minivan, found it unlocked, slid open the door, climbed inside, and waited.

It was getting dark when Bobo returned and climbed back into the Honda. Lin calmly placed a small pistol against the side of the man's head.

"Who told you to pick up the Luccheses at the Pearl, Bobo?" he demanded in Vietnamese. "And who was the white guy at the shopping center?"

"What family? What guy?" Bobo pleaded. "Who the fuck are you?"

"Your past comes back to fuck you—however, that is not your concern. The group that you took to the mall—the one with the three women and two children. Who sent you? Who is the *tây* that took the boy?"

"I don't know. An American. Before I picked them up, he gave me a hundred dollars—told me to wait."

"No. *First* I asked, Who got you the fare?"

Gregory C. Randall

"My cousin. He called me. This is his Honda. I drive it sometimes. He said to pick up this family at the Pearl Apartments. I did—then we went to the mall."

"Write down the name of your cousin and his address." Lin passed him a card and a pencil. "And your phone's passcode."

"My phone, why? You from the government, the police?"

"Something like that. Do it now." He pushed the muzzle of the pistol tight against the head of the driver. "Write." He then took the paper from him. He looked at the name on the card, and smiled. "Now, the man who came to your van, gave you the hundred dollars, who was he?"

"I don't know. I've never seen him until today. My cousin told me to stop at a specific location before picking up the people at the Pearl. I did that. As I waited, a man walked up to my door and gave me a hundred American dollars and a phone number and said when I get to wherever I'm taking them, to call him. I called when we got to the mall. I don't know who he is."

"Give me your phone."

"I need my phone."

"No, you don't." No one outside of the van heard the pop of the suppressed pistol.

Lin left Bobo slumped in the front seat and walked back to his motorbike. After crossing the canal and driving back into District 1, he pulled to the side of one of the busy streets and read the information the driver had scrawled. He recognized the address. It was in a neighborhood known for three things: drugs, prostitutes, and a gang he knew too well. As a kid, he and his friends—once they stopped harassing him and welcomed him as one of their own—were constantly at war with these crosstown gangsters. He knew they had connections to Laotian and Cambodian heroin dealers. He assumed that they now had international, cross-Pacific connections. How did this American know these people? How did he know Tommy Quan?

240

Lin drove the streets until almost midnight. Twice he'd passed the address, and each time a different pair of guards sat in front trying to be inconspicuous but failing miserably.

He turned down the alley behind the house and found an iron door with a grille over a small window. He studied the side of the building and saw, two floors up, an open window with a light on. A shadow passed by.

He drove a few blocks away and ordered chicken from a street vendor. The food in China was okay, but nothing like the street food he grew up with. He sipped his tea. Whoever this kidnapper was, he needed to be stopped. All the arrangements had been finalized with Lucchese. The Chairwoman was expecting the remaining pieces of software this week. Lucchese had been directed to bring the last two plug-ins and the helmet to a remote location. Lin would fly in, land, get the items from Lucchese, and leave. No one would see him. Now this American may have seriously screwed it all up. While Lucchese had questionable ethics, he would do anything to get his kid back. If the boy were hurt by this kidnapper, the deal would collapse. He was sure of it. Maybe Tommy Quan had answers to his questions. If not, too fucking bad.

He drove back to the gang house, and after a few minutes of climbing and quietly scrambling along corrugated roofs, he made it to the open window. The lights were off. He put on his night-vision helmet, removed the pistol, and climbed in—the room glowed green. A woman lay on the bed, a man next to her. Both were naked.

The woman, her mouth open, snored. Lin took a vial from his pocket and dripped a few drops of liquid on a cloth. He placed it gently over the woman's mouth. In seconds the snoring stopped. She still breathed. Her breasts slowly rose and fell. He took another piece of cloth and a small flashlight from his pocket and walked around the bed to the man. He placed the pistol against the man's skull. He then jammed the cloth into the man's open mouth. The man jerked upright. Lin aimed the flashlight into the man's eyes, blinding him.

"Do not say a word or scream, or I will splatter your brains all over your girlfriend. Do you understand me?"

Confused and disoriented, the man managed to nod and tried to speak through the cloth crammed into his mouth.

"Hands, behind you."

Lin zip-tied them together. Then he tied the man's bare legs.

"You're Tommy Quan, right?"

The man stared into the white light where Lin's voice came from. The light never wavered.

"Look, I know you're Tommy Quan." The man nodded and mumbled something.

"No, I'm not removing the gag, yet. I can learn all I need to know by you shaking your head. Let's begin. First, your cousin Bobo is dead. He gave me your address. I also have his phone. Let me try your number."

Lin opened the driver's phone and punched in the passcode. He went to the *Recents* list and pushed the second number. Immediately Quan's phone on the nightstand lit up and vibrated. The phone was on mute, as he'd hoped—the last thing he needed to do was draw more attention. "Well, that's confirmed. Now, did you send your cousin to pick up the fares at the Pearl Apartments?"

Quan shook his head yes.

"An American guy needed your help. Was it because of the American woman?"

Quan confirmed the question.

"Good. I will need the name of that guy."

Quan began to mumble through the cloth again.

"Be patient—I'll ask for it in a moment. There's big money in this arrangement, yes?"

Quan again nodded his head, yes.

"Good. Did you ever do business before with this man?"

He nodded yes again.

"Excellent, here in Vietnam? No? America? Yes? Was it drugs? Outstanding, we're almost done."

Lin looked at the girl. His night-vision visor had adjusted to the light of the flashlight. "She's very pretty; I would hate to have anything happen to her. So, I'm going to remove the gag. If you do anything, move anything, or even start to pray, I will shoot her. Do you understand?"

He nodded.

"Good. So, not to waste time, I'm going to ask you again to tell me how you know the man. I want his name, and where I can find him. Got it? One mistake, she will be first, then you."

Lin jerked the gag from Quan's mouth but kept the flashlight in his eyes.

Quan took a deep breath. "My hands?"

"No fucking way. So, who is the man?"

"He's from a place called Cleveland. I don't know where it is. Over the years through go-betweens, we sent black tar heroin to him. He paid top dollar, a good client. Then the orders stopped. I hadn't heard from him for more than a year. A few weeks ago, I get a call from him. He asks a lot of questions about a group called Teton Security. I tell him he's crazy—how does he know I work with these guys? He tells me to get some new IDs together, mail them to this place in Canada. Tells me there's big dollars. I tell myself, what the fuck, why not? So, I get him all new IDs. Then he calls again, two days ago. Says he's here in Ho Chi Minh City and needs help in a personal matter, something about a woman. I know her from TSD—good looking, Alex something. He wants to know everything she does. Earlier today the family she's looking out for called, said they wanted to go to the mall. I tell the American, then call my cousin to drive them. You killed my cousin?"

"Who knows, maybe yes, maybe no. This white guy got a name?"

"Ralph Cierzinski."

243

"Where's he staying? You must have found him somewhere safe, someplace to hide and stash the kid he took."

"He take some kid?"

Lin pushed the muzzle harder against the man's head. The girl started to moan and move. "Address!"

"On the docks, in Tan Thuan Dong, District 7. I have a warehouse; it's on Third Street, number thirteen. Now get the fuck out of here."

Lin picked up the pillow next to Quan and in one move placed the muzzle against the fabric and fired. Quan jerked, then collapsed.

Lin was out the window and crossing the roof of the house next door when the screaming began.

CHAPTER 42

After leaving the mall in the late afternoon, Alex walked down the hallway to the Luccheses' apartment from the elevator with Javier. On the drive over, Javier had talked to Langley and the embassy in Vietnam. Alex had talked to Chris and tried to sort through the chaos and bring him up to speed. Alex knew that Javier wanted to talk about Ralph, but that was the last thing she wanted to do.

Alex used her key and entered the apartment. The sun was low, and a strange, gauzy gray sky with a burnt sienna horizon cast its light into the apartment. Javier went to Chris, who was standing alone on the terrace. Alex went down the hallway to find Ilaria and the child.

Two minutes later she walked onto the terrace and said, "They're as good as can be expected. Did you find Nevio?"

"Yes," Chris said. "He and Karns were in a meeting with no cell access. They'll be here shortly."

Alex placed her back against the top rail, and Javier took the opposite corner. Chris closed the sliding doors, crossed his arms over his chest, and said, "So, now what? We wait?"

"Yes, it won't take long," Alex said. "Javier called his people. They're doing what they can to find out how Ralph got into the country. He had to have left a trail: fake passport, papers, something. They could try facial recognition. My bigger concern is why Lin was at the mall waiting in the parking lot. I assume he was following the Luccheses and me. Detective Phan will be here later, along with a team to set up monitoring the ransom drop, assuming there is one." She saw Chris's glare. "There is no way that Ralph and Lin could possibly be connected. Ralph's doing this to get to me, screw me over—somehow. I know we'll hear from him. He loves to play games."

"Asshole," Chris added, then turned to Javier. "Why did you come to the mall? It could have blown your cover. We're handling it."

"There's too much at stake, and Phan knows who I am," Javier said. "I need to make sure that everything stays on track and goes as planned."

"What goes as planned?" Alex said, standing straight. "I get the distinct impression that there's a lot of shit going on that I'm not read into. And it's putting this family and me in a very difficult position. I'm not happy about it. Chris, what gives?"

Alex looked through the slider and watched the front door fly open. Nevio stormed into the room. Karns followed in his wake. Nevio looked straight at Alex, went to the sliding door, and yanked it open.

His voice quivering, Nevio said, "It's all your fault. They took him from right under your nose. Campbell, I don't want that woman anywhere near my wife and children. Get her out of here."

Behind Nevio, Ilaria, Maria, and Gianna appeared. It was obvious that the child had been crying.

"Nevio," Chris said, walking between the two. "We'll deal with that later; right now we need to get Paolo back. And Alex is good at that, and besides, she's our best way to get to the kidnapper."

"Why, for God's sake?" Ilaria said.

"I know who did it," Alex said. "I will get Paolo back."

The phone in her pocket began to vibrate, so she removed it and looked. "It's him, a text message." She read it, then showed it to Chris.

Sandy Girl,

Tomorrow morning, at ten, be at the ferry boat pier at Me Linh Square. Walk to the south end. The ferry will arrive at 10:15. Do not be late. You'll be sent instructions when you arrive. The two hundred thousand dollars can be in euros and American money—old bills only, your choice, and only fifties and hundreds. Place the money in a clear, waterproof bag. Make sure it's well secured with clear tape. No transmitters or other devices—I will see them. The money must be visible. You are to be the only one on the pier. If I see another person connected to you, the boy will suffer. If you fail to follow any of these instructions, the boy will suffer. Attached is his picture. The same news broadcast, on channel HTV4, is on in the background of the photo.

Danny Z.

"Turn the TV to channel HTV4," Alex said.

Maria picked up the remote and clicked it to channel four. The TV's image matched the photo that Ralph had posted; the same news anchor, a pretty, young Vietnamese woman, was on the screen. The phone picture showed Paolo in front of the TV, duct tape across his mouth and a wide, scared look in his eyes, and a newspaper sat on his lap, the time "7:30 p.m." written in marker on its front.

"Is that Paolo?" Nevio demanded. "Show it to me."

Alex looked at Chris—he nodded. She handed Nevio her phone.

"Oh my God. What have they done to him?"

"Right now, he's okay," Alex said. "We need to talk, Nevio, and you too, Ilaria. Let's go into your office."

"My office?"

"Now! Chris, Javier?"

"Coming." Chris turned and looked at Karns. "You, stay."

"What the hell's going on, Chris?" Karns asked.

"Watch the family."

The five walked through the apartment to Nevio's office. Nevio led the way. Javier closed the door behind them after they entered.

"I want to know everything," Nevio said.

"I'm not sure you do," Alex said. "This game you're playing just got out of hand."

"Game? What game?" Ilaria shouted. "What do you mean?"

"Your husband has been dealing with some very unsavory people, people who want information he has, high-tech information. And I assume that you know all about it?"

Alex looked at Chris and Javier; they both nodded.

Ilaria turned to Nevio. "How did they find out?"

Nevio, stunned, just glared at Ilaria.

"Now, to add to this mess," Alex said, "my ex-husband has decided to screw with me. He took Paolo. He has no idea what's going on here between you two, Karns, this assassin, and the Chinese. But this Con Ma, this killer you've been dealing with"—she pointed at Nevio and Ilaria—"is afraid that it will upset everything he's been negotiating with you. And I believe he knows now who took your son."

"How would this ex-husband of yours be involved in any of this?" Ilaria demanded.

"He's a resourceful man. I don't know, but I'm going to find out. Unfortunately, Con Ma—whose real name is Lin Van Phan—knows about the kidnapping. He was there, at the mall. He saw everything. How do you think he'll react, Nevio? I'm sure he thinks he's been duped, by you."

"My God, Campbell," Nevio said. "How can you let an employee talk to me like this?"

"I think she's doing just great." Chris smiled and looked at Alex. "Go on."

"You've been passing top-secret software and plans to this Con Ma, an agent working for a dangerous and murderous syndicate out of China. And before you object, I have pictures of you in Dubai with him, and I saw you at the market a few days ago handing over a thumb drive to this man. Is there more? When is the next transfer?"

"My son was kidnapped because of you!" Nevio yelled. "These are all fabrications. I've done nothing wrong." He turned to Ilaria. "None of this should have happened—I had your promise. You said they would never find out." Alex suddenly realized the truth behind the whole sordid mess. It was Ilaria and her family who had involved the Chinese and masterminded the exchanges.

"You and your damn father," Nevio continued. "You said if I passed on the information, all our problems would go away. Now, you've made them worse."

"Shut up, you fool," Ilaria said. "It was what had to be done. Without the Chinese paying the Mafia for our debts, we would all be dead by now."

Alex looked at Javier. He nodded.

"It's her fault," Ilaria said, pointing at Alex, grasping at a straw. "Paolo is our concern right now, nothing else. She knows the kidnapper. She must be involved."

"We will do everything—" Alex started to say.

"Campbell, if anything happens to my boy, I will destroy you!" Nevio yelled. "And I'll make sure the world will know about it. I will have you dead!"

"It's a little late for you to be making threats," Javier said. "You're right, Alex; there is more to all of this."

"Ilaria and Nevio, I get that you have financial problems," Alex said as she glanced at Javier. "Your difficulties led to stupid decisions, and those decisions have led you to where you are now."

"How do you know?" Ilaria said, her eyes sharply focused on Alex.

"Little things, like the missing automobiles and tapestries in Milan. These are the easy things to liquidate for money. And I'm sure Mr. Castillo can add to this list as well."

"And who is this man?" Nevio asked Chris while pointing to Javier.

"I'm with the Central Intelligence Agency," Javier said. "And yes, Alex, you are correct. Ilaria's father, Enzo Giordano, is broke. The family's fortune has disappeared during the last twenty years: bad investments, high living, and some very questionable loans from the Mafia to both their family and their business. These came to light during the vetting process of his company and the contracts with NATO. And I'm the man behind this charade."

"Those are all lies," Nevio said. "Where is your proof?" He looked at his wife.

Ignoring her husband, Ilaria turned to Javier. "It's all a game to you, isn't it? Now my family is in danger, my son kidnapped. The money— it's always about the money."

"What did you do, Ilaria?" Alex asked.

"This American agent is right, but it was my father," Ilaria continued. "He told me that some Chinese men, 'investors' they called themselves, came to his office. Somehow, they knew about Como's prototypes and the software. They said they would pay off our debts to the Mafia—all we had to do was get them what they wanted. Father talked with Nevio and me, told us what needed to be done. Harry Karns would be our contact. In a previous trip, Nevio met with Karns, things were done. I don't know what. In Dubai they met again."

"Shut up, Ilaria," Nevio said. "You've said too much."

She glared at her husband. "Father had already given them one of the five pieces before involving us. That was what was in the technology facility here in Saigon. Those men weren't supposed to die, Chris. Karns told Enzo that no one would be there."

"You put your family in the middle of all this?" Chris asked, his anger growing. "I can't believe you would do that."

"We had to look normal. They said everything had to look normal," Nevio said, finally admitting that he knew more than he was protesting about. "No one would find out. That's why that woman is here"—he pointed at Alex—"to protect the children."

"But they did find out," Alex said. She turned to Chris. "You suspected Karns, didn't you?"

Chris stared at the Luccheses. Alex could see rage.

"Because of you two, good men have died, friends," Chris said. "And your father? Damn it, Ilaria, did you honestly think you could get away with all this?"

Nevio pulled open a drawer and yanked out a pistol. When he raised it, all he saw was Chris's pistol pointing at him.

"Don't even think it, Nevio," Chris said. "This has gone too far; there's no need to make your kids orphans. Set it down, and take a few steps back."

Nevio, his hand shaking, looked at Ilaria.

"Please, Nevio," Ilaria pleaded. "The children."

He set the pistol on the table.

"Back away," Chris said.

Nevio took two steps back. Alex saw the man was dying inside, crushed by what his family had been going through.

Chris never lowered the pistol.

"Karns wanted to hand over the software part by part," Nevio said. "He appreciated how our development team said the software needed to be in five segments. So, we worked out a plan, the first part would be left at the tech facility—Karns said they would then realize the value of the software. After that, we would hand over each of the additional pieces, one at a time. Money would be transferred each time. Ilaria's father would be told when the Mafia got the money, and we would prepare the next part. I gave the Chinese the next part in Dubai, then passed on the third part of the software at the market."

"You're committing treason," Alex said. "And you, Ilaria. You put the children in the middle of this!"

"If we didn't do this," Ilaria said, "our family would lose everything, and we would be destroyed."

Alex looked at Chris, her eyes wide. She was shocked and astonished. She started to say something.

Chris shook his head no, then said, "Right now, we need to get the boy back."

"I knew it was bad," Nevio said, ignoring Chris. He was talking to Ilaria. "Enzo told us no one would find out."

"We're bankrupt," Ilaria said. "There is no money. The house and everything else is gone—mortgaged against loans we needed to live. Alex was right. Father sold the cars and the tapestries. We spend money we don't have, the children's schools are a fortune, and the house costs millions to keep up. All the family money is gone. Father speculated, hoped for a turnaround—he lost it all. It was the Mafia that made the contact with the Chinese, arranging for the Chinese to pay them. Now, it's all blown up." She looked at Chris. "These people will pay us ten million euros and take care of the Mafia after we pass on the last of the data and the prototype. Don't you see this is the only way? Nevio, we had to do this. We did this for our family."

"Me? You did this for us?" Nevio said. "Now our boy is gone. Is that the price? And that woman says that she knows who did this. I don't believe her. I don't believe any of them."

The door crashed open. Karns stood in the doorway with a pistol. He saw Chris and his weapon. He turned his pistol toward Ilaria. "Drop it, Campbell. Now, or she's dead."

Chris took a deep breath and pitched the pistol to the couch behind him.

"Smart." Karns looked at Nevio, his weapon never moving. "Nevio, I told you to keep your mouth shut. You're a weak little shit and have sold your family for money. I told them I would handle it—I told *you*

I would handle it." He turned his weapon toward Chris and Alex. "You move over next to them," he said to Javier. "Now this is a situation, isn't it, Campbell? My Chinese associates want the rest of the data and the prototype. I know it was sent here. It's on Nevio's computer." He reached into his pocket and extracted a small black device. Alex guessed what it was. It looked like an unmelted version of the drive and transmitter she saw in Texas.

"You won't get away with this," Chris said.

"So trite, so buttoned up. Can't you see that I've already gotten away with it? I've been working on this deal for two years. I'm the one who suggested to Beijing the opportunity. They made the contact with the Mafia. The bonus was the financial problems that the Luccheses have. Sometimes you just get lucky. My cut is a nice, what you might call, finder's fee. And you, boss, couldn't see what was going on right under your nose." His eyes never left the three of them. "Ilaria, slowly walk to me. Give this device to Nevio; he knows what to do with it. Nevio, you will download the last two plug-ins. If you don't, I will first shoot your wife, then everyone in this apartment. You will watch them die; then you will still download the data. So, dammit, put in the device—it knows what to do."

Ilaria took the device from Karns and gave it to Nevio. Without saying anything, Nevio walked to his computer and inserted the device. A minute later after the lights turned solid green, he removed it.

"Good boy, now press the red button, please," Karns said. "And give it to Ilaria."

He did as ordered. The lights on the device began to blink. He handed it to his wife.

"Mama," a voice yelled from behind Karns. Gianna ran into the room.

"No, Gianna, stay there," Ilaria yelled.

Karns grabbed the child by the shoulder, stopping her. He gripped her tight. Gianna screamed.

"No," Ilaria shouted. She threw the device at Karns; it hit him in the face. He let go of the girl and tried to catch the falling transmitter. He fumbled it, and it flew up into the air.

Alex bolted to the child and gently tackled her. She rolled her over and protected Gianna from Karns. At the same instant, Ilaria grabbed the pistol on the desk and swung the weapon up at Karns.

"What the hell?" Karns roared.

Ilaria's first shot hit Karns midchest, knocking him back into the door; the second shot spun him around. Karns stared at the woman for a moment, not understanding what happened. The pistol fell from his hand. He then ripped at the blood on his shirt, tearing away the buttons, and collapsed to the floor. The device skidded across the hardwood floor. Ilaria aimed the pistol at the man on the floor and fired again.

Chris rushed to Ilaria, put his hand on the gun, and pulled it from her hand. "Enough, the child," he said.

Ilaria looked at Karns on the floor, her daughter wrapped in Alex's arms, then Nevio. "We have destroyed everything," she said.

"We're nothing," Nevio said.

The device, lying on the floor, began to smolder. The smell of burning plastic began to fill the room. It ignited. Alex grabbed the corner of the device and dropped it in the metal wastebasket. She took a bottle of water from the small refrigerator and poured it on the device. It continued to sizzle and smoke.

Javier went to the computer and opened some files. He looked closely at the screen, then at Nevio.

"You didn't send everything, did you?" Javier asked.

"No."

CHAPTER 43

Phan and one of his detectives strolled through the open door of the apartment. A policeman remained just outside.

Alex met him halfway down the apartment's hallway.

"Nice, very nice, and you live here?" Phan said to Alex as they entered the living quarters. Another policeman moved toward the closed door of Nevio's office. The three Luccheses sat on the couch, Ilaria and Gianna at one end, Nevio at the other. Neither parent looked at each other. Maria was in the kitchen; the smell of coffee was in the humid air. Chris and Javier stood in the open doorway to the terrace.

"The body is in there," Alex said, pointing toward the office.

"American?"

"Yes."

"That makes it easier. Less paperwork. Who shot him?"

Alex looked at the couch. "He was found in the office when Mr. Campbell returned with Mrs. Lucchese and the child. We don't know who shot him."

He looked at Alex. "I knew you having a gun was going to be a problem." Phan pointed to the policeman and said something in Vietnamese, and the officer opened the office door. "You stay here. My associate will take all your statements," he said to Alex, and disappeared into the office.

After five minutes, they realized that Phan's fellow detective spoke little English, and other than Maria, no one spoke Vietnamese. Alex,

Javier, and Chris spun a tale in English for Maria to tell the officer, as did the Luccheses in Italian, but the confused detective eventually threw up his hands.

Phan had heard some of what was said through the open door. He signaled to Chris to join him. "I know that man. He was your employee. Is this correct, Mr. Campbell?"

"Yes," Chris answered. "Harry Karns."

"You lose a lot of your employees this way?" the detective asked. "By my count that's three dead in just a few months. Must be hard during recruitment when you tell prospective employees about the dangers of working for you."

Chris didn't reply.

"The man was a traitor to his country," Alex said.

Phan looked at Javier. "Is this so?"

"Maybe," Javier answered.

Phan looked at Alex. "How so? And is that why one of you shot him?"

For the next half hour, they told Phan almost everything that happened. Chris and Javier conveniently left out the meat of the story—parts about the data, NATO, the Chinese, and Nevio's role in the transfer of the files. When Phan asked again about the shooter, no one stepped up.

"I want all your pistols," the detective said. "One, or all of you, is lying." He pointed to a policeman. "Collect any weapons you can find. Make sure you assign a name to each of them."

"You can't do that," Chris said.

"Of course I can, Mr. Campbell. I can do anything. Would you like to learn Vietnamese while waiting for trial here in Ho Chi Minh City? I can and will arrange it."

Chris put his hands up and removed his weapon from behind his back.

"And you too, Ms. Polonia," the detective continued. "I believe this has something to do with the kidnapping of the young Lucchese boy?"

Ilaria again broke down when Phan mentioned her son. "What are you doing to find him?" she asked. "What do you know?"

Chris looked at Alex and shook his head.

The detective looked at his half sister and said, "There's more, isn't there? I can hold you all for murder, manslaughter, justifiable homicide, accidental death, or being material witnesses in that guy's suicide—I have many options. However, and rightly so, Mrs. Lucchese is more concerned about her son. Mr. Lucchese, I'm not sure—he seems to have a lot on his mind. I believe that Ms. Polonia has a role in this escapade. So, Mr. Campbell, Mr. CIA, and my whatever you are will join me outside and talk. It's a little stuffy in here. I expect the coroner anytime, and he will remove the body." He looked at Chris. "I also saw a burnt piece of electronics in the wastebasket. It looked remarkably like the one I found in a vase at your client's facility a few months ago. Can I guess this might be the same type of device?"

"Yes, I believe that it's similar," Chris answered. "What its use is, I don't know."

Phan smiled. "I believe that you do. The terrace—I need a smoke, and the view should be nice."

As they walked to the terrace doorway, a commotion began in the hallway. Two Vietnamese men in white paper hazmat suits walked into the living room, and Phan approached one of them.

Alex watched what she assumed to be pleasantries between the two officials, one of whom she believed was the assistant coroner. Phan pointed to the office door, and the two men disappeared inside. She thought something was off about them. One kept glancing at Javier.

Phan walked onto the terrace, lit his cigarette, and blew a thick haze out into the evening. "The whole night is a mess. I can't even get my guys to remove the body. They sent another crew from another district. Ms. Polonia, please start from the beginning, and leave nothing out. I will know. You and I are detectives. We can tell, can't we?"

CHAPTER 44

Lin Phan flew low, almost silently, over the warehouse rooftops. Only the whirring of his cycle-drone's blades filled the air immediately around him.

"Have you found the address?" he asked.

"Yes, Con Ma, I have it," the voice in the helmet responded. "It is the middle building in a complex two-point-five kilometers from here, bearing zero eight five."

"Pick a suitable nearby building rooftop, and land the vehicle. I'll walk in from there."

"Understood."

The drone flew just a meter above the surface of the Saigon River. In the darkness, he was almost invisible. The night-vision screen, displayed on the helmet's faceplate, provided a wide-angle view of his surroundings. So much better than the limited equipment used by militaries around the world.

He slipped between a large freighter and a long row of houseboats. Through the frequency-canceling speaker of the helmet, he heard a dog bark as he passed. Maybe the noise of the blades had caused the pooch to react. No matter—in seconds, he was hundreds of meters past.

The cycle-drone was addicting. Before going to Vietnam, he'd spent a month training with the vehicle in the research laboratories of Dark Star in a western Chinese province. He'd reassembled it in HCMC from the parts shipped in from Guangdong. Only a dozen prototypes of this two-seat cycle-drone existed, he'd been told. One of the Chairwoman's partners was looking to produce the vehicle commercially, which would be a success; he could only imagine what a battalion of soldiers could do with tactical vehicles such as these. A "game changer," the Americans would call it. A force multiplier.

The illuminated facilities of the port were ahead. Massive stacks of shipping containers covered more than three kilometers of the water-front. Beyond it, and disappearing into the darkness, were the rooftops of hundreds of buildings.

"Are we near?"

"Yes, Con Ma. On your screen."

To the right side of the visor, a green rooftop was highlighted with an address floating over it.

"Thank you, and a suitable landing zone?"

"Immediately to the north. Would you like for me to take control?"

"Yes."

Lin released the grip on the handlebars and allowed the AI to take over. The cycle-drone slowed, then rose high over the stacks of shipping containers. Three streets beyond the last containers, the drone slowed to a hover.

"It is immediately below us, Con Ma. Do you wish to land?"

"Yes."

The drone dropped until it was three feet above the flat roof of the warehouse.

"Landing."

The drone settled on the roof.

"Drone stop," Lin said. Immediately the six double blades stopped. "Lockout."

"I am locked. Was the landing satisfactory?"

"You are never satisfied, always looking for compliments."

"I aim to please. The target warehouse is one building to the south. Satellite sensors identify three heat signatures in the building, two of which have moved during the last ten minutes. Do you wish continued updates?"

"Yes, continue updates. When asked, display on my screen."

He climbed off the cycle-drone, checked his weapons and gear. He removed a coil of rope and grappling hook from the storage compartment. In seconds he was in the alley that separated the landing roof and the target warehouse. Halfway along the passageway, he saw the blue Mercedes van that he'd last seen at the mall. Near the van's rear was a door to the warehouse. He checked the door. Locked. He clicked off his weapon's safety, attached a small box over the lock, and stepped back.

"Ignite charge one," he said. A half second later the lock exploded and the door flew open from the recoil. He stepped into the warehouse.

"Target, fifteen meters to the right," the helmet said.

He swung his weapon to a door that was opening. A small man appeared, a pistol in his hand. Lin fired, and the man collapsed. "Next?"

"Second target, behind you."

Lin spun on his heels and dropped to one knee. A man appeared on a catwalk above. Lin fired again, and the explosive round sheared off part of the iron walkway and knocked the man to the steel grating. Lin fired again just as the man raised his weapon. The man, cut in half, did not get the shot off.

He checked both bodies—neither was the American male from Cleveland.

"Are there any other heat signatures?" Lin asked his helmet.

"Only one, twenty meters to the right."

He scanned the open warehouse floor. A shipping container sat in the middle of the room. He walked to the double doors, threw open the latch assembly, and pulled one of the doors open. Inside, duct-taped to a steel chair, sat a boy shaking with fear, his mouth taped shut.

Lin holstered his weapon. He'd seen the same child climb into the minivan that afternoon at the apartment building, along with the Alex woman and the Lucchese family.

"Are you okay?" he asked in English. "Just nod your head."

The boy nodded.

"Good, I'm going to remove the tape. We are alone, and no one can hear you. We are then going to leave this building. You will say nothing. If you do, I will bring you back here and tie you up in this chair. Do you understand?"

The boy nodded again. Lin removed the tape.

"Who are—"

"Say nothing—do you understand?"

The boy nodded.

They walked past the body of the first man he shot. The boy covered his mouth and gasped.

In the alley, Lin spoke into his microphone. "Please bring the drone to me. I'm below you in the alley."

"Coming, Con Ma."

From above, he heard the drone's blades begin to whir, and in seconds it had lowered itself into the alley and had landed behind the blue van.

The boy looked at the machine, turned to Lin, and began to say something, but seemed to think better of it.

"Speak," Lin said.

"What is that?" the boy asked.

"Your ride."

CHAPTER 45

Detective Phan leaned back against the plaster wall of the interview room in the district's police station. Sitting opposite, at the center of the steel table, were Nevio and Ilaria Lucchese. Nevio's wallet and phone were on the table; Ilaria's phone was next to her husband's. Nevio's head rested despondently on his arms next to the phone. Ilaria glared at the detective. To the Luccheses' right sat Chris Campbell, and to their left, Javier Castillo. At the far end of the room, resting her butt on the edge of the windowsill, sat Alex. The window was dark.

"Why do you Americans drag your shit into my country?" Phan asked as he lit a cigarette and looked directly at Javier. He then noticed Alex's disapproving look; he smiled and took another drag. "My house, my rules," he said, waving the cigarette. "Let me get this straight. Mr. Lucchese is the manager of the new Como Motors plant that employs more than two thousand Vietnamese citizens. Agent Castillo, you tell me that Mr. Lucchese may have provided top-secret information to a foreign power, most probably China. And you cannot, or will not, tell me why he's doing that or what that information is. Correct?"

"I'm as shocked by this as you are," Javier said.

"I really doubt that," Phan said, inhaling again. "These are games that all you big boys play, and for more than one hundred years Vietnam has been your playground. And my people have died in this proxy war.

If there is one good thing about this current little adventure of yours, it's that no Vietnamese have died. I intend to keep it this way."

"Detective Phan—" Chris started to say.

"Stop. You will wait until I'm done asking my questions. Now, Mr. Lucchese appears to have completely fallen apart, and I cannot verify the CIA's accusations. Mrs. Lucchese looks upset, and it seems she's pissed at all of you. For argument's sake, let's assume you're telling me the truth. Agent Castillo, I'm not going to involve my country's security forces in this situation. However, there is a child at risk. Does the kidnapping of the boy have something to do with this? I'm not sure. However, Ms. Polonia—my alleged half sister—" At that Ilaria looked up at Alex with a death stare that a Medici would have approved of. She started to say something.

"Mrs. Lucchese, there will be time for that later." He looked back at Alex. "She tells me that the kidnapping of the boy may have something to do with her ex-husband, a man called Ralph Cierzinski. I've checked customs and border control, and they have no record of a Ralph Cierzinski entering Vietnam." He looked at Alex, who started to say something. "Hold that thought—I completely understand this can easily be circumvented with false documents. Nonetheless, why would a man come thousands of kilometers, risking arrest, just to kidnap a boy that he has no connection to? Do you have an answer to that, Ms. Polonia?"

"To piss me off," Alex replied.

"You must have *really* pissed *him* off. I've just met you, and from what I've found—it's entirely possible. We shall see."

"You don't know my ex."

"Yes, I'm doubtless glad I don't. Ms. Polonia, you have been given directions to deliver a package of money later this morning to this Cierzinski fellow. He says that he will then return the boy, Paolo. Is this correct?"

At the mention of his son's name, Nevio looked up.

"Yes," Alex answered. "Ten o'clock at Me Linh Square. Two hundred thousand dollars or euros."

"You Americans certainly throw your money about, don't you?"

"Detective Phan, I'm insulted that you would say that," Chris said, and started to stand.

"Sit. You and your government will get over it." He turned to Javier. "And you, Mr. Castillo, as an agent of the Central Intelligence Agency, you're on board with this, I assume? Is it *your* money that's being used?"

Ilaria jerked her head around and looked at Javier, then again at Alex.

"No, I'm just an observer. My interest in this is over. I'm here as a friend to Alex and Chris."

"You two are so lucky to have such friends." He looked at the Italians. "Mr. and Mrs. Lucchese are witnesses to a homicide, a homicide that no one will admit to." Phan continued, "They're here for no other reason. If they've performed other illegal activities, I'm not aware of them. I am solely concerned about what happens in Vietnam."

"I want to make sure that our good relations with the Ho Chi Minh City Police are maintained," Javier said.

Phan crushed his cigarette and immediately lit another. "Phooey, my guess is you're the containment guy to make sure everything stays in the box. It will be interesting to see how the late Mr. Harry Karns fits into that box." Phan looked at Campbell. "The killing was executed well. I have three people in this room who obviously know their way around a firearm, so my assumption is one of you fired the shots. Care to volunteer?"

Chris glared at the detective.

Nevio's phone began to vibrate. Phan looked at the screen; it read *Anonymous*.

"Now who would be calling you at five o'clock in the morning, Mr. Lucchese? Please answer the phone and put it on speaker, and I want the rest of you to be quiet."

"Lucchese here."

"It took you long enough to answer, Nevio. Where are you?"

The detective cocked his head; the voice was familiar.

"I'm at home, in my office. My son was kidnapped; we're trying to find him. If you had anything to do with—"

"Calm down, old man, your son is safe. I took him from the man who kidnapped him at the mall. I saw it all. My employer says that you sent files earlier this evening to the secured server. They were sent using the transmitter Mr. Karns had. I haven't been able to reach Mr. Karns to confirm this. They want to know why it was just one file and not the remaining two. Mr. Lucchese, they are not amused. We have an agreement. I would hate to take out my displeasure on your son."

"It was all a mistake," Nevio lied. "It was Karns who sent the files. Why he didn't send the complete set, I have no idea. I gave him the right ones. Maybe Karns is trying to trick you. I want to talk with my son."

"Nice boy, handsome. I bet the girls like his face. It's a pretty face. It would be tragic if it were damaged."

"You bastard," Nevio said.

"Not to worry. He'll be fine."

"What do you want me to do?"

"I want the files, the complete ones. I also want the prototype of the helmet. I know you have it at the factory—Karns told me. I'll send you a text later this morning with specific directions that you will follow—exactly. Be careful, or your handsome son will not be so handsome anymore." The connection went dead.

Nevio dropped his face into his hands. "What the hell have you gotten us into, you and your father. Our boy is out there, alone. You see, this is what happens—"

"Shut up, Nevio," Ilaria said. "We have to do what we have to. I had to do what I had—"

"Interesting," Phan said, interrupting. The voice of his son still in his head. "Seems we have a family argument brewing. I may have to expand my list of murder suspects."

"This is all screwed up," Alex said. "How important is all this, Javier?"

Javier looked at Detective Phan. "All I can tell you is that the systems that the Luccheses have compromised have set back a NATO program by a couple of years. We'll get past this, but the real issue is the continued thefts that this Chinese group conducts. How much is under investigation. We arrested two men in Bonn a week ago; one was a Chinese national. He killed himself in jail before he could be questioned. These people are very serious."

"My, my! You Americans have been busy," Phan added.

Alex's phone pinged. Phan looked annoyed. She took it from her pocket.

Sandy Girl,

Just a reminder, don't forget 10:00, Me Linh Square. And yes, I'm a fucking asshole. You be there and do exactly as I said.

Danny Z.

"Who is that?" Phan asked. "Show me the phone."

"My ex-husband."

"This is getting to be fun, in a weird Western superpower's sort of way," Phan said.

"You're a bastard," Chris said to the detective.

"To quote an old American movie: 'In my case, an accident of birth. But you, sir, you're a self-made man.'"

"There's something strange about this last text," Alex said. "It's as if Ralph doesn't know that Paolo is no longer under his control. Maybe we have a chance to catch him when he comes to get the money."

"There's no extradition treaty between Vietnam and the United States," Phan said.

"There may be other ways," Chris said, looking at Javier.

"You Americans can be so creative when it suits your purpose. Personally, once all this gets out about Ms. Polonia and me, the whole pile of shit will hit the fan. I suggest that the less that's publicly thrown about, the better."

"There's no reason the Luccheses have to remain here," Alex said to Phan. "They have enough to deal with. Chris, this is what you'll do: I want two thousand pieces of paper the size of an American dollar bill, and eight color copies of an American one-hundred-dollar bill, both sides. Bring them to the Lucchese apartment by nine o'clock this morning. Also, find clear plastic wrap and packing tape. I'll leave for Me Linh Square at nine forty-five. Javier, you can drive me to the apartment. Chris, when this is all over, there is much to talk about."

Chris looked at Detective Phan. "Are the Luccheses free to go?"

"I've no reason to hold them," Phan said. "However, I'll keep their passports for now."

"After I drop the Luccheses at the apartment, I'll get the things you asked for," Chris said, looking at Alex. "And yes, there is much to talk about."

CHAPTER 46

Twenty minutes after Alex arrived at the apartment, the Luccheses entered. Ilaria immediately went to Gianna's room. Nevio, ignoring his wife, went to his office. Maria was sitting on the couch. Alex could see that she'd been crying.

"How is Gianna?" Alex asked.

"Tired and frightened. She is confused and upset. She fell asleep an hour ago," Maria answered. "When will you get Paolo?"

"This should all be over this evening," Alex said. "I'm exhausted, so I'm going to get a little sleep."

Alex went to her room, set the alarm on her phone for seven. It seemed like she'd just closed her eyes when it went off. She took a shower and dressed, then went to the kitchen. Javier sat at the counter drinking coffee. Maria was making him eggs.

"Don't you ever sleep?" she asked.

"I got a little, but this helps." He held up the cup to Maria. *"Grazie."*

Alex poured herself a cup and sat next to Javier. "Strange road we walk, isn't it, pardner. Do I know how to throw a rodeo or what?"

"Never a dull moment, pardner! Do you think this will work?"

"Ralph's biggest problem is his greed. He'll do anything for a buck. The bigger the bucks, the bigger the anything. By now he's probably found out that he doesn't have Paolo. He's confident, or at least hopeful, that we don't know. He's also freaked out about how he lost the boy.

Since we didn't blow him off, I hope he believes that we don't know anything about what happened to Paolo. I don't know what that sociopathic nephew of mine has done, but I'm sure he's left no witnesses. And since Ralph texted me after we talked to Lin, he doesn't know where Paolo is either. If Ralph had been wherever he was hiding the boy when Lin showed up, he'd be dead. He's a lucky SOB. Most likely, Phan will get a notice in a few days about some bodies being found in some forgotten part of the city." She took a long sip of the coffee. "I'll make the drop—at least I can stiff him—and show him that two can play his stupid games."

Chris arrived, and they bundled the two thousand dollar-sized pieces of paper and wrapped them in clear plastic. The color copies of the hundred-dollar bills neatly covered the blank papers wrapped underneath. Alex had used this trick a few times on drug busts; she hoped that Ralph would buy what he saw. When they were done, even she believed she was carrying two hundred thousand dollars.

"I don't understand why you're doing this," Chris said. "The guy's an asshole, and he doesn't have Paolo. He believes he's pulling one over on you. I don't get it. Send him an email—tell him to fuck himself."

"In due time—two can play his charade. And why am I doing this? Ralph is completely nuts. Maybe this will throw him over the edge, maybe he'll do something stupid, or maybe Phan and his people can grab him and throw him in a Vietnamese prison."

At nearly ten o'clock, Javier parked at the curb across the roundabout from Me Linh Square.

Alex got out and entered the square with its massive bronze sculpture of some important-looking general wearing military clothing from eons ago. She crossed the boulevard and walked down the ramp to the T-shaped pier that extended out into the Saigon River. She checked her phone—no new messages. The posted ferry schedule read the boat was due in twenty minutes. She wasn't sure if she was to get on board, wait, or meet someone. She hoped that the men Phan had put on the ferry a few stops earlier would spot anyone suspicious before they reached her. Looking around, she thought that would cover half the people she saw milling about waiting for the ferry.

She looked up and down the river. A thin wet fog covered the low-lying island across the waterway. Fronting the far side were collapsed buildings, advertising signs, and rank vegetation. Dozens of moored houseboats and a rusty freighter were also anchored. Behind her and dominating the city skyline was the Bitexco Financial Tower, with its weird duck-bill-shaped helicopter pad sticking out of its upper stories. It looked as if the iconic Rolling Stones' rude tongue logo was giving a vulgar rebuke to the city.

The midmorning heat and humidity had returned. Downriver, through the haze, she saw the bow of the ferry as it plowed toward her. She glanced at her phone: ten minutes. She jumped as it pinged in her hand.

Walk to the south end of the pier.

She saw no one that even remotely looked like a six-foot-one American of Polish ancestry. She did as ordered.

Ping.

Stand ten feet back from the edge—wait.

She stepped back a few feet. From below, a buzz filled the air like a hundred bees were swarming. She took another step back. Slowly, a four-prop drone rose from the surface of the river, hovered for a moment, then moved toward her and stopped. It then lowered itself to the concrete surface of the pier.

Ping.

Take the envelope taped to the drone's deck, then secure to the drone's deck the package with the bungee cords. Open the envelope after the drone leaves. I can see you with the onboard camera—don't screw up.

Pissed, she did as directed. The drone rose off the pavement and headed out over the river, just passing in front of the bow of the ferry as it turned toward the pier. She lost the drone behind the boat.

Goddamn it.

"Did you see where it went?" Javier said as he ran up to her. The ferry slowed and began the process of docking. "Here, take these." He handed her a pair of binoculars.

She scanned the river and spotted a flash as the drone turned and headed toward a low stone pier on the far side, where a man stood on the end, holding something.

"That has got to be him," she said.

She pointed and looked again. The drone flashed again in the sunlight and disappeared near the pier. The man walked to the spot where the drone disappeared. He bent down, moving out of sight, then stood up. She saw what looked like binoculars rise to his face.

Ping.

You bitch. Now you won't see the kid.

She furiously typed, then sent: *Screw you, we have the kid.*

Seeing the message, Javier said, "But we don't."

"He doesn't know that."

She looked back at Ralph standing on the pier. He raised his hand in some gesture. She raised her right hand and gave him the finger.

"What's in the envelope?"

She ripped it open. A folded note was inside.

Sandy Girl,

I'm sorry about all this. I needed traveling money, not too much but just enough to get your attention, thanks. By the way, someone took the kid. I don't know who. If it had been you or that Campbell guy, my guess is that you would have just blown me off, so I'm thinking you don't have him. Whoever took the boy killed some of the guys my Saigon contact provided. He will not be happy. I need to boogie before he finds out.

Good luck,
Ralph

She handed Javier the note to read for himself.

"What, no funny Danny Zuko, or some other cute remark?" he said.

"I guess he's trying to be serious. He's still an asshole."

CHAPTER 47

At precisely three thirty that afternoon, Nevio's phone received a text message. In English it read:

> *Deliver the final plug-in and the prototype helmet to me this evening. When the data is handed over, it will be checked to see if it's correct. After verification, I will release your son. He seems like a good kid. Don't mess it up. I will meet you on the helicopter platform of the Bitexco Financial Tower at precisely 9:00. I fully expect the police to be there or nearby. However, the result of any interference by the police or the Americans is the boy's death. If there is any attempt to stop me from leaving, he will die.*
>
> *Reply by just sending the words: "I understand."*

Detective Phan was standing outside on the terrace of the Lucchese apartment when the message arrived. He was holding Nevio's phone. He walked back inside and looked across the room to Nevio, who sat next to Ilaria. On the other chairs were Chris and Javier. Gianna was with Maria in Paolo's room. He read the message to them and then responded as Lin requested. Alex took the phone and reread the message.

"Why is he doing this?" Alex asked.

"Why is my son doing this, you mean? I don't know. Until the other day, we thought he might be dead. Something in Lin snapped when he was fourteen. He got into a fight with some boys at school. He was badly beaten, suffered head trauma and almost didn't make it. I was the first cop on the scene—it broke my heart."

"He was just a teenager?" Alex asked.

"When he got out of the hospital, he was different. Always an active, almost hyper child, he became manic. Bad days followed good days. His studies declined. Then he started spending nights outside the house. I had my men watch him; he always found ways to lose them. I received reports that he'd become involved with a gang. Then, one day, three of the boys that were suspected of beating him were found brutally murdered. I could not believe that it was my son. When I confronted him, he walked out of the house. The next time I saw him was the photo you showed me."

"You have no idea where he's been?"

"None. It's obvious he has access to significant assets. You now tell me that he may be involved in murder and espionage all over the world."

"Yes, Dubai," Alex said. "That's where he met with Lucchese and Karns. There're reports from other governments that describe someone just like your son. He may be responsible for more than twenty deaths and the theft of billions in technology. Chris tells me that he's on a shoot-to-kill order in many countries. My guess, there are businesses and governments that would like to interrogate your son as well."

"There's something broken in him," Phan said.

"Probably," Alex said, and put her hand on his. "Can you get us access to the helicopter pad on the tower?"

"That should not be a problem. I'll get Mr. Lucchese there. Lin is expecting him."

"Good," Alex said. "We need to play his game. Is this location difficult to get to?"

"Other than the elevator or by helicopter, it's impossible to reach. It's on the fifty-second floor of the tower. It's a large dish shape attached to the side of the building. Everyone in the city can see it. I've been told it doesn't function properly as a helicopter pad; the winds are too chaotic to safely land. It's higher than any adjacent building; that makes a sniper useless too. For someplace in the middle of the city and fully exposed, it's also isolated. Lin knows that. My guess is that he will arrive in that cycle-drone vehicle and demand the data. After that, I have no idea what he will do."

Thick clouds rolled in from the South China Sea sixty kilometers to the south and now blanketed Ho Chi Minh City. Their undersides were illuminated by the millions of lights that stretched across the landscape of the city. The air was fresh, damp, and breezy on the open landing deck of the Bitexco Financial Tower. Alex, Chris, Javier, and Phan stood just outside the glass doors of the deck's lobby. Inside, Nevio and Ilaria remained with two uniformed officers and one of Phan's plainclothes detectives. The deck was floodlit by dozens of powerful lights that washed across the concrete. A yellow target with a white *H* was painted on the center of the deck. The Vietnamese national flag, a red banner with a yellow star, flapped in the wind at the farthest point. It was nine fifteen.

"He's late," Javier said.

"He told us to be here at nine," Detective Phan said.

"This is the most bizarre payoff I've ever been on," Alex said, looking across the city skyline. "Are your men up?"

Phan held a two-way radio. "Yes, they're holding about a kilometer away. If needed, they can be here in seconds."

"Not sure what they can do," Chris said.

"They're there to follow," Phan said. "That's all."

An intense, high-pitched whirring filled the canyon of buildings that spread out below the tower. Beyond the edge of the landing deck and its stainless-steel railing, as if an apparition were rising from the grave, two seated figures riding the cycle-drone rose into the wash of lights. The front passenger had his hands on the handlebars. The person behind him was smaller, and his hands were secured with duct tape, his legs taped to supports under his seat. Both wore black helmets and black clothing. The vehicle itself was flat black. The only visible lights were flashes from the dials and gauges on the dashboard. The sound the four people on the landing pad heard was a buzzing that reminded them of a thousand motorbikes racing through the streets of Saigon, fifty-two floors below.

Ping.

Phan looked at Nevio's phone.

I'm glad that you haven't disappointed me, Father. I expected you to be here. Do nothing or the boy will disappear and you'll never see him again.

Phan watched as the cycle-drone passed over the railing and then drifted just above the deck. It constantly adjusted itself to the cross breezes. Six meters past the railing it stopped, hovered for a few seconds, and gently dropped to the deck. The rotor blades continued to spin. The rider dismounted and unhurriedly strolled toward the four people. He removed his gloves and secured them to his belt. He wore a backpack and a black web belt with several devices and two weapons attached to it. He removed his helmet.

"What a fine party we have here," Lin said as he scanned the four. He then looked through the glass. "And my pathetic associate, Nevio Lucchese, is waiting inside. Father, it's good to see you again. It's been too long, but Grandmother always kept me informed. How such a good woman could have such a fool for a son, I just don't know. I've been telling her that I'm a secret agent working for the Vietnamese government. You might keep my current employment from her. I don't want to break her heart."

"Listen, you punk," Chris started to say.

Lin glared at Chris. "Shut up, old man. Do not interrupt. If anything happens to me, that machine will take off with the boy and explode. That will give the Luccheses something to remember for the rest of their lives. I want the data and the helmet. Whoever has it, give it to Mr. Lucchese to bring it out." Lin scanned the people on the deck. "Where's Harry Karns?"

"He's dead," Alex said.

"Really, that's too bad. He had a bright future, but never trust someone who isn't loyal. I will release the boy as soon as the data is verified. However, if anything or anyone interferes, I will explode the vehicle." They heard an audible squawk; Lin put his hand to his ear and listened. "Thank you, I understand." He turned to the detective. "Father, tell the helicopter pilot to return to his station. He's too close. If he ventures any closer, I'll shoot him out of the sky."

Phan raised the radio and said something that was lost in the winds and whirring. "He's backing off."

"Excellent," Lin said. "Now, I know about you, Mr. Campbell, and your organization. Someday you should hire me. I can help you better understand all the screwups you've accomplished these past six months. And you, Mr. CIA agent Javier Castillo of Waco, Texas; Washington, DC; and Milan—my, such a world traveler. And yet you don't have a clue as to who my employer is. So typically American." He looked at Alex. "But you, I do know what you are to me, but little about *who* you are. Reports relayed to me say a disgraced Cleveland cop, yet here you stand in the middle of an international trade negotiation that will change the course of militaries and transportation for a century. Someday, I would like to see this Cleveland."

"Cleveland is where *your* grandfather lives," Alex said. "I'll bet that little voice in your head didn't know that." She paused when Lin smiled.

"You do know—how the hell? Did you know that I'm also your father's sister?"

Lin laughed. "You, my aunt? Yes, I listened to your conversation with that man." He pointed to Javier. "It was all a fabrication, lies to entrap me. And I knew you would follow me. So, I think you are the fool. This is a joke, something to distract me."

"Lin, there is more to all this than your self-indulgent and childish problems with your father. Can't you see that you're just a tool being used by that crazy woman in China?"

"Possibly, but a well-paid tool." He turned to his father. "Tell Mr. Lucchese to bring out the data and the helmet, now."

"And if we don't?" Chris said.

Lin said something into his headset, and the drone slowly rose a meter and rotated 360 degrees.

"As you can see," Lin said, "the machine will do what it does. It's aware of everything that's happening. If anything happens to me, it will explode, taking the boy with it. So, Father—and I'm losing my patience—have Mr. Lucchese bring me what I want."

Phan signaled to the lobby. Nevio pushed the door open and walked to the group. He carried a nylon bag. He kept looking at his son sitting on the machine. Paolo jerked and pulled against his restraints. The drone returned to the deck and remained stationary, its blades still spinning.

"Good to see you again, Nevio," Lin said. "Nice kid. The thumb drive, please."

Nevio handed him the small device. Lin removed a box from his belt, like the one Karns had used the previous night. Lin inserted the thumb drive. "Until the data is confirmed, none of you move." Lin looked at Nevio. "He seems like a great kid; we had some good conversations. He has a future in technology. Nevio, he's a far better man than you ever were." After a seemingly endless minute, the device buzzed, and Lin's earpiece squawked. "Excellent, the data transfer is confirmed. Now the helmet."

Nevio handed the bag to Lin. He removed the helmet and studied it.

"I can't let you go with my son," Nevio said. "He's my boy. Why are you doing this? Leave him here, then go."

"Sorry, I can't. I need insurance."

"I said leave my son here."

"The traitor has a backbone. Excellent." Lin began to back away.

Nevio lunged and tried to tackle him. Lin smashed him across his head with the helmet, knocking him to the concrete platform. "And gutsy, as well. Anyone else care to take a swing?" Lin continued stepping backward toward the machine. Halfway, he secured the bag with the helmet to a clip on his belt. He put on his own helmet and looked across the platform to the drone and the boy; there was an audible squawk from inside Lin's helmet. "Understood." He turned to the five people on the deck. "Change in plans. Listen carefully. There is a device built into the drone. I have no control over it; it's completely out of my hands. It will explode in two minutes. So, for now, goodbye. Father, I will see you in hell."

Lin spun around. Alex pulled her pistol and, with both hands, aimed it at Lin.

"No!" screamed Phan, and knocked her arm away. "Don't kill my son."

Lin ran to the handrail, took one look back at his father, slammed closed the visor, and vaulted over.

"Your knife, Jave!" Alex shouted.

Javier tossed her his pocketknife. Phan watched as she ran to the drone and severed the tape binding Paolo's hands and ankles, freeing the boy. Chris then came in from behind, just avoiding the blades, and pulled Paolo from the cycle and handed him to Phan. The detective looked at the dashboard. A series of numbers was counting backward. There were only fifteen seconds left.

"Everyone inside!" Phan yelled. Chris took the boy and threw him over his shoulder and ran toward the doors. One of the officers pushed them open—Chris was the first in. The others followed and pulled the doors tight. Ilaria was all over her son, pulling the remaining tape from his hands, removing his helmet, and making sure he was all right. Almost everyone looked back at the amazing piece of technology. It continued to whir and vibrate, almost like a live animal. Then it rose off the deck about three feet, hovered and adjusted to the gusts of wind, and exploded. Pieces of the drone spun out over the city, and chunks of plastic and steel flew at the doors and the building. Everyone in the lobby dropped to the floor just as parts slammed against the unbreakable glass windows. There was no fire, at least not like the kind you'd expect from a gasoline-powered machine, just the burning battery pack skidding across the pad.

"I can't believe he jumped," Javier said. "He could have easily escaped."

"I'm sure he did," Chris said. "That backpack was like those worn by BASE jumpers. I've seen them jump—he's gone. He could be anywhere in the city."

Phan ignored the comments. He just stood at the glass and looked out over the city. His son was gone, again.

CHAPTER 48

Three hours later, Alex sat in one of the wicker chairs on the small outside terrace of Campbell's hotel room. Javier and Chris sat in the other two. Chris was smoking one of his maduros. She nursed a vodka on the rocks, the others, bourbon.

An hour earlier, when Alex had left the apartment, all the Luccheses had gone to bed. Ilaria had stayed with her son. Paolo, outside of a few bruises, was shaken but well. Gianna had been elated to see her brother again. Paolo had told her he would tell her everything the next day. He'd been exhausted and quickly fell asleep, his head in his mother's lap, her hand holding his. Alex knew Ilaria was strong; she would have to be to deal with all the repercussions that would be coming. Detective Phan would want to pin Karns's death on someone, regardless of the attitude of his superiors. Alex knew he was wired a lot like her; she hated unfinished business.

She thought that the Luccheses would be under a microscope. Javier would probably see to that. She looked at Javier; he seemed oddly pleased.

"Do you know who this Chairwoman is?" Alex asked Chris and Javier. "She's the catalyst for everything. Was the information important enough to kill people over?"

Chris took a sip of his drink, then looked at Javier, who nodded.

"Alex," Chris began, "America wants a balance of peace and security throughout the world, but more than that, they want to control that security and balance. It's a burden we've assumed since World War II. My company and a few others help carry that burden. It's like a chess game: pieces move forward and back, and each move is an attempt at blocking or advancing an agenda. But often a move can be a feint, a ruse. This group in China—we've learned it's called Dark Star Security—steals as much technology as they can, and spins off these thefts to the highest bidder. It is a quasigovernmental organization based in Beijing that has its fingers in almost every country worth stealing from. They've kidnapped scientists, engineers, and creative thinkers, who we assume now work for this organization or are squeezed for their expertise, then liquidated. We believe the head of this syndicate—the Chairwoman as she is known—is also a high-ranking bureaucrat in the Chinese government, which of course denies that she exists. One of our informants said that she's the third chairman to hold this position in the last thirty years. Our informant died from polonium poisoning soon after he got us this information. Obviously, Lin Van Phan, the Ghost—your nephew—is one of her agents. They're well trained and as ruthless as she is. Why she chose him, I don't know."

"And this technology, was it worth all this?" Alex asked. "Was it worth the deaths, and the trauma to a family?" She was still trying to figure Chris out.

"This technology is good," Javier said. "Very good, so good that even the engineers at Como Motors believe it will work. It will; however, not nearly at the capacity they think it does."

She looked at him. "You went fishing."

Both men smiled. "Yes," Javier said. "I've been cleared to tell you this. It was bait, bait with an expiration date. This is something that Nevio Lucchese didn't know. In fact, we knew from informants in the Mafia that Ilaria's father was involved. That was what I wanted to tell you in Milan, but couldn't. Desperate people will do desperate things."

"You sons of bitches," Alex said. "You were using them."

"All we did was use their fear and greed. The software is a Trojan horse. In fact, when they plug this last piece of data into the others, it will perform as expected. Then, in a few weeks, it will secretly transmit its own location through the nearest available router. After that it will slowly begin to disassemble itself. Our hope is to use this piece of data to find Dark Star's servers and through them, their base."

"This was a trick?" Alex asked, stunned.

"Yes and no," Javier said. "We needed Nevio, and Ilaria's father, to believe that what they had was the real thing; in fact, ninety-eight percent of it is real and functional. We needed Dark Star to believe that this was critical information, military software and hardware that could be a game changer. We contracted, through NATO, Como Motors to develop and advance these technologies based on some of their own designs for artificial intelligence as well as a few ideas of ours. The story we let slip implied that the technology would do more than it could actually accomplish. We were surprised to discover, after leaking this fake story, that Dark Star had advanced well beyond many of our own technologies. Their prototypes were built on our platforms, like the stolen plans for the drone. It looks like Con Ma received the plans from an engineer under Nevio's control, who handed them off to Con Ma. For some reason, Con Ma then killed the man. Your brother is still trying to find the engineer's killer."

"I can't believe this, a Trojan horse?" Alex said.

"Yes. The drone was the first part, the software the second. This was a way for us to draw them out as well. Every drone part from the explosion that could be found is on its way to our lab in Silicon Valley. We'll put it back together. The Pentagon and Langley want more information. We now have identified this Ghost, thanks to you. What we didn't count on were the anomalies that stuck their noses under the tent of this operation."

"Thank you; now my family is a camel with its nose under the tent."

"Your connections to Phan and Lin were way outside anything we could have anticipated. And to make matters even more bizarre is your ex-husband," Javier said. "Again, anomalies."

"You put the Lucchese family up as targets, including the children," Alex said. "You are heartless bastards."

"We did nothing; we only provided the props," Chris said. "They were the ones who were passing on the information. It was Karns who helped make it happen. Nevio and Ilaria, as naive as they are, knew what they were getting into. And her father seems to be the promoter. His Mafia connections led to the Chinese and Dark Star. This is one more piece of information about this Chinese syndicate, and their connections throughout the criminal world. All I could do was help protect their children, that was your job. Here I failed."

"The children are fine now," Alex said. "And Detective Phan, once his coroner autopsies Karns's body, will know it was one of the guns in the apartment. The pressure will fall on all of us, and most especially the Luccheses."

Javier looked at Chris. Then he looked at Alex. "That will not be a problem."

"What do you mean not a . . ." Alex stopped as a scene ran through her head. "The coroner's people, the ones that Phan didn't recognize." She paused again. "Goddamn you, you sons of bitches."

"His body will not be found," Javier said.

"And the dead men . . . their deaths will haunt me forever," Chris added. "They weren't supposed to be at the warehouse. They had just come in from Japan; Jake and I sent them here. I guess Karns tried to keep them out of the facility, but they reacted too quickly to the alarm. Damn that man. Then Lin fought his way out, and my people died."

"My God, this is all senseless," she said.

"This is a war. A cyber war of ideas and technologies, but it's also more than that."

"More than what? Like Phan said, a murderous game played on his 'playground'? Who picks the battlefields?"

"I don't," Chris said. "They can be anywhere. Afghanistan, the Sudan, Central Africa, Vietnam. That was why you were assigned to the family. To protect them."

"It seems I needed to protect them from *you* guys too," Alex said. "Yes, you are all cold-hearted bastards."

"Wait just a minute," Chris said. "It was your ex-husband that threw the grenade in the room. No one could have seen that coming, no one. Did you? Until a few months ago, you hoped he was dead."

"Obviously, hope and reality are two very different things," Alex said. "I have no idea why he was here. Someday, when I get the chance, I'll ask him. I'm beginning to see why Professor Moriarty drove Sherlock Holmes crazy—simply because he could." She turned to Javier. "Who built the virus for the software?"

"We did. Dark Star must believe in what they got," Javier said. "Very visible emergency changes will be made to various systems and programs to make it appear to Dark Star that we're trying to counteract the effects of this theft—add reality to the fiction. In time, they may come to see the weakness of the tech, and they'll either write it off as Western incompetence or understand they were snookered. Either way, we come closer to identifying their players."

"I can't believe this—people died."

"Ilaria was protecting her daughter; none of that was foreseen," Chris said. "She did what I was about two seconds from doing myself."

"When this goes public," Alex said, "it will be a disaster for the Luccheses and their family. The repercussions will roll though his company. Is that what you want?"

"None of that will happen," Javier said. "All of this will be kept quiet. No one will ever know. It can't and won't get out. Dark Star must believe that what they have is real. It's just that simple. If the Chinese think that there's a chance that the data is bad, they'll dump it. So, nothing will happen to the Luccheses. Actually, they're returning home next week, a surprise promotion for Nevio. They'll stay in Milan. Don't worry about what Ilaria said about her family; the raise is substantial. The kids will be fine. How the Luccheses deal with this good fortune is up to them."

"You *all* are bastards," Alex said.

"The world is not like Cleveland," Javier answered. "The games are bigger and more dangerous. We know that some members of Dark Star's infrastructure are highly placed military personnel from North Korea, Iran, and even eastern Russia. However, most of them are Chinese. All quite businesslike."

"And people die."

"Yes, and sadly people die," Chris said. "In this case, they were friends and associates. I will not let that go unavenged. I don't care that this Con Ma, Lin Van Phan, is your nephew. There will be a day of reckoning—that I can assure you."

"Do you know what happened to Ralph?" Alex asked, looking at Javier.

"No," Javier said. "Your ex is an incredibly resourceful man. We don't know how he got into Vietnam, and we don't know if he got out. Our informants in the Cambodian and Vietnamese drug cartels hint at a possible connection to a local gang here run by Tommy Quan. He was one of our local service providers; they provided the limos and the Honda minivan to TSD. He and his cousin were murdered the other night. We have found that they were connected to this same drug cartel. It slipped under our vetting. Our guess is that your ex used them when he was in business—it cost them their lives. Right now, we assume he got out. He likes to play games, and you seem to be his focus. Why? First guess: he still cares for you. Anyway, he's just a text message away. Send him a note; ask him. With his ego, he'll probably tell you."

"If I find him, I will resolve this one way or the other. So, Christopher Campbell, now you and I have a problem. Do I buy into this whole international quasi-military chest puffing and cock strutting going on? Stay with you and Teton, or walk away?" She looked at her boss; he smiled, a Cheshire cat type of smile. "Then again, you could just fire me and make it simpler. Maybe I can get unemployment."

"Outside of the strange revelations about your family," Chris said, "you've handled yourself exceptionally well. That was a nice touch with

Ralph, the fake money, the in-your-face attitude—I liked it." Chris blew a smoke ring in the air. "To be blunt, I need you."

"Well, I don't know whether I need you. I need some time to think about all of this," Alex said. "To go from babysitter, to pawn and shill, to savior of the world is a little too much to consider in an hour. I have a half brother and his wife to get to know. I want to meet my new nieces and nephews, and most of all help my father and my family understand all of this. I'll let you know. And you, cowboy: we need to talk, and not here."

She tossed her pistol onto the tabletop and left.

Alex moved out of the apartment the next morning. Maria was disappointed, the kids heartbroken. Gianna said there were so many other things they wanted to see and do. Alex understood. A resigned Ilaria hadn't yet told the children they would be going home in a week. Alex said she was sorry that it came to this. Ilaria gave Alex a hug as she walked down the hallway. Her bags would be sent to the hotel. Nevio stood at the end of the hallway, his stare blank. He didn't say anything.

Javier called and invited Alex to dinner that night. She wanted to say no, but realized that now was as good a time as any to resolve this mess. She wore an outfit that Ilaria had bought her in Milan. The thin threads of gold woven into the blouse's fabric shimmered in the lights.

Javier was waiting in the bar. She watched him from just outside the entry and mentally figured that this was the sixth or seventh time this same scenario had played out: hotel, bar, drinks, dinner, brandy, and a tumble. It sure as hell would not end like that tonight. She slid up into the seat next to him.

"I wasn't sure if you would show up," Javier said. He pushed a tumbler filled with ice and vodka across the bar to a spot directly in front of her.

"I wasn't sure I'd come either," Alex answered.

"You look nice."

"For what this blouse cost, I'm a lot better looking than nice, cowboy."

"I've never been one with words."

"Not even close to a good excuse. It seems you can plot the future courses of nations, but can't even offer a simple compliment."

"I'm sorry."

"That's a woman's way out, apologizing. Not going to happen. You hurt me bad, real bad. Potentially fatally. Do you understand that?"

Javier used his finger to stir his drink.

"Look at me, you son of a bitch," Alex said. Javier did. "This hurt, but I'll get over it. I see the big story, but can you? This game you and Campbell played put a lot of people in danger. And don't give me that excuse about national security, military secrets, world peace. I signed on, I knew what to expect, or I thought I did. But this was way over-the-top. And for some reason, somehow I have the feeling I was used. And between us—that's not good."

"We all have reasons for doing what we do," Javier said. "Mine is to protect the United States."

"That doesn't change anything between us," Alex said.

"Don't you think it's time for you to grasp what's happening out in the real world?"

"Damn, you still manage to step in your own horseshit. Give me some credit. I've seen a lot more depravity than you, bucko. Children left abandoned in tenements full of rats by cranked-up moms, drunks dying in their own filth, a bodega owner gunned down for a handful of dollars, kids shot for a pair of sneakers. On your level, it seems to be some type of worldly us versus them. On the level I've been working, it's about hearts and souls, and stopping innocents and children from being killed."

She thought she saw a tear.

"Are we done?" he asked.

"I don't know—I really do not know. I need time to think. We never had expectations; our future was day to day. We had opportunities, and

Lord knows, we've had adventures—more in the last six months than most have in a lifetime. So, I honestly don't know. I like you, cowboy, and some days it verges on love; but right now, it's all way too complicated. Time may lessen the pain; then again, time may make me see reality."

Javier looked at Alex's empty glass. "Another?"

Alex looked at Javier, stood, and kissed him on the cheek. "I think I've had enough."

Later that evening, as she sat in her hotel room, she tried to understand everything that had happened during the last week. It was impossible; the revelations were piled thickly on top of each other. Her phone pinged. Her first thought was Javier.

Sandy,

Nicely done, well played. Until next time.

Danny

One week later, Alex stood at gate fifteen at Tan Son Nhat International Airport with Detective Tran Phan. No one questioned them when he showed his detective badge to airport security. Two days earlier she'd been in the same terminal, just a couple of gates down, helping Ilaria and the children board a plane back to Italy. Gianna was crying and said she would miss her. Paolo, still a little confused, smiled and gave her a hug. Maria had elected to stay in Vietnam and go north to see relatives that her parents had told her about.

Alex wasn't sure what would happen long term to the Luccheses, even with Nevio's promotion. Chris had said that he would stay in Vietnam for at least two weeks until a replacement manager could be found. Alex hoped that Dark Star would just leave the family alone. It would take a lot for Ilaria to make them whole. They would never know the extent of the charade. Alex knew that, at some point, what Ilaria did to Harry Karns would come back and begin to haunt her, no matter what the justification was. *That's the way we are wired,* Alex thought. *Unless you're truly psychotic, killing someone stays with you.* She hoped that Ilaria would find help.

Alex had significant issues with Chris: personal, moral, and maybe even governmental. Just how much she could adjust her view of the world to fit into the universe of Teton Security and Defense was undetermined. Time would tell. Chris hadn't fired her—yet. She had a six-month contract, and she would honor it. But she knew that the parameters would be a lot different from now on.

Alex and Phan watched the massive airplane maneuver up to the gate. Alex's bag was over her shoulder.

"I was never sure if this day would ever come," Phan said. "I've believed, for most of my life, that a piece of me was missing, and now you drop into my life and my family's. It's strange on the one hand and on the other, healing. My mother raised me as a Catholic, but Buddhism pervades our culture and has influenced much of Vietnam's soul. Buddha said that we need 'to support mother and father, to cherish wife and children, and to be engaged in peaceful occupation—this is the greatest blessing.' And now, Alexandra Polonia, I have come to understand what Lord Buddha meant."

The exiting passengers began to file past them. European, Australian, and American tourists; Vietnamese returning to their homes carrying babies and herding children; and the fresh face of Vietnam, businessmen and women, with their ears to their cell phones. Outside the glass windows of the gate rose the new skyline of Southeast Asia's most exciting city.

Alex pointed; Phan looked to see where. In among the arriving passengers were Roger and Alice Polonia.

VIETNAM

NOTES AND A BRIEF HISTORY

Vietnam has been a battlefield of cultures and politics for more than two millennia. First the Chinese invaded, then the Mongols, then various tribal factions and warlords warred among themselves, then again the Chinese, and eventually, more internecine battles coalesced into a less than unified national government. In time, Buddhism, brought by the Chinese, became the accepted state religion. The arrival of French Catholic missionaries, who entered the country in the seventeenth and eighteenth centuries, led to France's eventual nineteenth-century colonization and exploitation of the country. France was the dominant foreign culture for the next one hundred years.

After World War II and the defeat of the Japanese, the United States continued to support the French in Vietnam with advisors, materials, and funds to help retain their tenuous hold on one of the last remaining colonies in their vast, but collapsing, post–World War II colonial empire. This empire, at one time, extended from Africa, across the Caribbean, through northern South America and the islands in the southern Pacific, to Vietnam. In 1954, nine years after the Japanese were defeated in Vietnam, the French were themselves defeated by the communist Viet Minh at the Battle of Dien Bien Phu.

As the French withdrew, the country was partitioned near its narrowest portion along the seventeenth parallel. As a result of the peace settlement in Geneva, Switzerland, the countries of Vietnam, Laos, and Cambodia were granted independence. The consequences of this accord left the northern portion of Vietnam controlled by the communist Viet Minh, and the south by the predominantly Catholic government of the facile Emperor Bao Dai. For a year following the peace agreement, members of the Catholic minority in the north flooded south fearing persecution, while at the same time many of the supporters of the victorious in the south, the Viet Minh, headed north.

During the next eight years, a civil war developed between the northern Viet Minh and the corrupt southern regime of the Catholic Ngo Dinh Diem who had replaced the emperor. But then, no civil war is simple or civil. During this decade, the United States government supported the South Vietnamese government, and as international sides were chosen and the expansion of the Soviet and American Cold War was now manifest worldwide, political positions in Vietnam became entrenched. Thousands died at the hands of the state executioners and assassins in both the north and south of Vietnam. Most Vietnamese, at the time, supported the northern communists. In the south, Diem offered elections to support his regime. In Saigon, he won elections by majorities that were greater than the number of voters. Corruption was rampant.

The "domino theory" was proposed as the reason for American support of the Diem regime. This theory held that if the southern portion—called the State of Vietnam—fell to the communists, then, as John F. Kennedy said in a speech, "Burma, Thailand, India, Japan, the Philippines, and obviously Laos and Cambodia [would be] among those whose security would be threatened if the Red Tide of Communism overflowed into Vietnam."

As president, Kennedy steadily expanded the financial, logistical, and military support of Diem's government. More pressure was also exerted from the north and from outside the country. Then, in the weeks before his own death, Kennedy turned on the South Vietnamese government, and Diem and his brother were executed by his own generals. Subsequently, at the time of Kennedy's assassination, American support expanded until there were more than 16,000 American advisors in South Vietnam. The new president, Lyndon Johnson, sustained this support until all-out war raged the length of both countries. The cities and harbors of the north were bombed; whole regions of the countryside were defoliated and poisoned. By the end of 1965, over two hundred thousand American military personnel were in South Vietnam.

Tens of thousands of Vietnamese, both in the south and the north, were killed, maimed, and displaced during the late 1960s. In America, sentiment turned against the American government and its military actions in a country that many Americans considered irrelevant to their personal and political beliefs. Johnson and his government realized that the war could not be won, and they also began to recognize that their own generals were not telling the truth. After the Tet Offensive in February 1968, the United States was desperately trying to find a way out of the quagmire.

By 1970, the American military had been in South Vietnam for almost twenty years. After Johnson chose not to run for reelection, the new president, Richard Nixon, began to substantially reduce the number of American troops. Within two years, hundreds of thousands of American troops, their weapons, and logistical support had been withdrawn. Vicious, yet indecisive, battles would continue to rage in Cambodia, Laos, and across North and South Vietnam for the next three years. This burning region of the world would be the focus of intense partisan politics in the United States and across the globe. Eventually, by 1975, the war would take down a president, bring blood to the streets of America, and lead to the eventual collapse and fall of South Vietnam.

ACKNOWLEDGMENTS

While the primary foci of *Saigon Red* are the characters and how the past sometimes will catch up with the present, the hazy background is the Vietnam War. For my generation, Vietnam was the seminal moment in our young lives. The war protests, the treatment of the returning soldiers (most the same age as the protestors themselves), and of course the war's effect on American politics all defined this age. On one hand, it was all a strange and evil stew of deceit, lies, death, and cover-ups; on the other, battlefield heroics, the search for the truth, and the belief in the Constitution and human rights. To enumerate the references I used—books, television shows, memorials, and friends (soldiers and protestors)—would fill the rest of this page. I will spare you. However, to all these sources, I say thank you.

I am also reminded how DNA testing has changed our perceptions of ourselves and where we come from. It is so common now to use one of the testing services; it has almost become a parlor game. The day I wrote this, a woman (after a test of her DNA) found a father she never knew, and a father found a daughter he knew nothing about. This is not unusual; stories abound about family discoveries and even family tragedies becoming known, all due to a simple swab of the cheek. When it involves criminal actions and convictions, we are no longer surprised. We live in an era of instant communication and strange coincidences—a novelist takes a simple idea and stretches it out into an international thriller. The story of Alex Polonia and Detective Tran Phan, while peculiar, is not at all impossible. I want to acknowledge fellow thriller writer and crime analyst Spencer Kope for his help in understanding the arcane art of DNA analysis.

I also want to thank the editors and marketing staff of Thomas & Mercer for backing *Saigon Red*, the second in the Alex Polonia series. A special thank-you to Matthew Patin, developmental editor and copyeditor; his efforts made this a stronger story. And most especially a huge thank-you to my editor, Jessica Tribble, for believing in Alexandra Polonia, and Sarah Shaw and Gabrielle Guarnero, for handling the marketing. When it comes to author relations, they are a special team in the publishing universe.

I am pleased to call my literary agent, Kimberley Cameron, both friend and mentor. It is exciting to be a client of her agency, Kimberley Cameron & Associates, and among amazing writers whose careers are enhanced due to the efforts of this incredible person.

And a special hug to my wife and love of my life for forty-eight years, Bonnie, who is involved in every book I write. Her sharp insight, ideas, critiques, edits, and most especially friendship and patience make these stories happen. To be honest, they are as much her work as mine.

ABOUT THE AUTHOR

Photo © 2010 Penelope Lippincort

Gregory C. Randall is the author of *Venice Black*, the first novel in the Alex Polonia series; the Sharon O'Mara Chronicles; and the noir Tony Alfano Thrillers, *Chicago Swing* and *Chicago Jazz*. His young adult novel, *The Cherry Pickers*, won critical acclaim and awards and a five-star rating from Readers' Favorite. Gregory was born in Michigan and raised in Chicago, and he currently lives in the San Francisco Bay Area. For more information, visit www.gregorycrandall.info.